"Ge[...]"

"My lord!" S[...] Hugh's touch—the [...] tendrils of heat through her chilled body. "This is unseemly! You cannot—"

"I most certainly can," Hugh said. "I've already saved your foolish life once today. I'll not see you take ill and die of fever and let my efforts of this morn go to waste. Now be still. These wet laces are the devil to open and I have little time."

"I object, my lord!" she cried, his strong hands on her back making her tingle in agony. What kind of magic did the man possess to cause such feelings? Why had she never felt these sensations…this odd yearning before?

"Your objection has been duly noted, my lady," Hugh said, as he released the final loop of the lace….

Dear Reader,

For all our Medieval readers, *Dryden's Bride* by Margo Maguire features a lively noblewoman en route to a convent who defies her family and takes a detour when she falls in love with a noble knight. This stirring tale is Maguire's second book, a follow-up story to *The Bride of Windermere,* which was one of our featured titles in the March Madness promotion for 1999.

If you're a Western reader, Liz Ireland's *Trouble in Paradise,* with a pregnant heroine and a bachelor hero, is a heartwarming story you won't want to miss. In keeping with the season, look for *Halloween Knight,* complete with a bewitching heroine, a haunted castle and an inspired cat, by Maggie Award-winning author Tori Phillips. It's a delightful tale of rescue that culminates with a Halloween banquet full of surprises! And *USA Today* bestselling author Margaret Moore returns with her new Regency, *The Duke's Desire*—a story of reunited lovers who must suppress the flames of passion that threaten to destroy both their reputations.

Whatever your taste in historicals, look for all four Harlequin Historicals at your nearby book outlet.

Sincerely,

Tracy Farrell
Senior Editor

Dryden's BRIDE

Margo Maguire

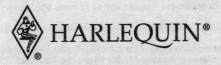

HARLEQUIN®

TORONTO • NEW YORK • LONDON
AMSTERDAM • PARIS • SYDNEY • HAMBURG
STOCKHOLM • ATHENS • TOKYO • MILAN • MADRID
PRAGUE • WARSAW • BUDAPEST • AUCKLAND

ISBN 0-373-29129-9

DRYDEN'S BRIDE

This edition published by arrangement with Harlequin Books S.A.

® and TM are trademarks of the publisher. Trademarks indicated with ® are registered in the United States Patent and Trademark Office, the Canadian Trade Marks Office and in other countries.

Visit us at www.eHarlequin.com

Printed in U.S.A.

As always, this book is for Mike and our gang.

It is also fondly dedicated to the women in my life—
for Julia, Justine and Fran; for my mother-in-law,
sisters-in-law and nieces; and for my remarkable friends,
in cyberspace and in person.
Heroines, every one!

Chapter One

Northern England
Autumn 1423

Casting a grudging glance up at Castle Clairmont with his one good eye, Hugh Dryden stalked toward the huge stone fortress and again cursed the day he was born. He reviled the fates that intervened in his life, still refusing to let him be.

His depth perception had never improved after losing the eye, so he had difficulty judging how far away the castle was, though his companion, Nicholas Becker, said they were a mere mile from Clairmont's portcullis. They'd stayed one last night in the woods, planning to broach the castle at a civilized time of day—in the morning, after they'd had the opportunity to bathe and ready themselves.

For Hugh's bride.

A pox on her, Hugh thought, muttering other more serious oaths under his breath. He had no interest in marrying. He cared not a whit about adding land to his estates, nor a woman to his life. He would never understand why his friend, Wolf Colston, the Duke of Carlisle, believed Hugh was the man to carry out the council's wishes. Wolf and his wife could not be unaware of Hugh's preference for solitude. It had taken many long months for him to recover from the injuries sustained during his imprisonment at Windermere, and in those months, Hugh had done nothing, said nothing, to indicate a need or an interest in a woman. If anything, he'd shown a decided *lack* of interest.

He was a solitary man now. The agony he'd suffered alone and in the dark caverns under Windermere Castle, helpless to defend himself, powerless against the pain of mutilation, of near death... He shuddered with the unwelcome memory. Nightmare images plagued his daylight hours and tortured him as he lay tossing and turning every night.

It was better to keep to himself now. He had nothing to offer the world of light. No strength or determination for his country. Certainly nothing left for a woman.

Besides, Lady Marguerite Bradley would likely turn tail and run for cover when she saw his shattered visage, as all others did, save his closest friends.

Hugh adjusted the patch that covered what was once his left eye, and walked on. It was a fool's errand, he thought again. To Hugh's recollection, widows were not usually overanxious to remarry...unless there was some good reason. He doubted *he* could provide reason enough for the widow of the Earl of Clairmont to remarry. In fact, if truth be told, the only one who benefited—

A woman's scream pierced the early morning silence. Acting on sheer reflex—reflex he hadn't known he still possessed—Hugh turned toward the sound and ran through the thick wood toward the source of the panicked voice. Covering territory quickly, he moved determinedly, with the agility of a trained knight, a formidable knight, in possession of all his considerable skills. Heart pounding, nerves on edge, Hugh's well-muscled legs ran swiftly but stealthily.

Simply dressed in hose and hauberk, he was without armor, but carried his longbow and a quiver of arrows, in earlier hopes of shooting a brace of hares to present to the Clairmont kitchens. Now, it seemed, his one-eyed skill might truly be tested in a matter of life and death. It was not something he cared to think about, having only practiced with the bow at Windermere, and *not once* shooting to his satisfaction.

Siân Tudor clutched the tree branch desperately, swinging her legs up in an attempt to gain purchase on the branch—away from the charging pig. The huge boar had surprised her only moments before as she'd ambled carelessly through Clairmont's forest. Unskilled in the wielding of weaponry, Siân was forced to flee the fearsome boar, and flee she did, though the great beast's tusks had nearly been upon her as she'd jumped for her life onto the low oaken branch.

Terror made Siân's hands strong as she held on for dear life, but her cumbersome woolen kirtle prevented her from throwing a leg over the saving branch. She glanced down at the enraged boar snorting fiercely under her, his sharp and gleaming tusks in the air, his snout flaring. She knew it would be certain death to let go, but her hands were weakening, her nails tearing! She began to slip.

By the Holy Cross, the lass was falling!
Hugh notched his arrow and let one fly, then another

one followed in rapid succession, all the while, his stomach churned with the agony of self-doubt. How could he be certain his arrow would meet its mark and not kill the woman? How could he know the arrow would reach anywhere *near* its mark?

The sudden screech of the huge creature was testament to the wound.

Hugh didn't stop to relish his victory. He scrambled down the ridge as the beast squealed in fury and pain. Dry leaves and dust flew, and Hugh could feel the heaving of the boar against the earth itself. Bright yellow wool fluttered and fell. Blood, dark and red, flowed. Then all at once, all movement ceased.

Hugh approached cautiously through the hazy rays of morning sunlight, with silent steps, an arrow at the ready.

Then he thought he heard something. A groan. A slight, feminine groan. A rustle in the leaves. The bright yellow wool moved.

Siân looked up at the man who'd rescued her, and squinted against the bright morning sunlight. Though she'd banged her head and was more than a little dazed, she could see that he was tall, and well made. His physique was strong and wiry, 'twas that of a knight-at-arms, well-honed and able. As Siân pushed herself awkwardly away from the monstrous boar, the knight shot another arrow directly between the eyes of his prey.

Apparently satisfied now that it was dead, the soldier turned to Siân, showing his entire face for the first time.

She was surprised by the black patch over his eye, but not by the strength of his other features. Strong bones, jutting jaw and high cheekbones suited him. Full lips and straight nose; forehead scarred, but high and bright; brows thick and dark. His uncovered eye was an uncommon, light blue color, strangely remote and guarded. His dark hair was overlong and untamed, with a few silver strands shining in the morning sunlight like the steel of a lethal blade.

A dangerous-looking man, Siân thought hazily. Different from anyone she'd ever encountered before. His powerful presence sent a chill of awareness through her and she was unable to call forth the caution required of her situation. She should not be alone with any man, especially a lone knight who might be a rogue. But her head ached and her vision was oddly blurred. Under the circumstances, the ability to muster the necessary wariness was beyond her.

Hugh knelt beside the young woman in the deep pile of leaves. She was moving again now, and he wanted to be sure she was uninjured before she attempted to stand.

"Hold, woman," he commanded.

She ignored him and sat up. He could see the pulse pounding in her throat, above the tear in her gown where the boar's tusk had gone through. An ugly bruise had already begun to darken near the joining of her shoulder and arm, and the flesh was torn by an ugly diagonal rent in her perfect ivory skin.

She should have been killed.

Hugh could not tear his one-eyed gaze away from her as she swept her red-gold hair back from her face. Saucy eyes, the deep blue of the evening sky, were thickly framed by gold-tipped lashes. Delicate bones, cleft chin, impish mouth... Even now, she had the look of a mischievous child about her, although it was clear that she was no child. She was lovely. Hugh forced his gaze away from her beguiling face and looked back at her injury.

The wound was not a deep one, would not even leave a scar above her perfectly formed breasts, he thought. He looked away from her barely concealed attributes, then silently took one of her injured hands in his own and raised it, palm up, examining it. The act was a strangely sensuous one, with her pulsating heat flowing through to his own hand from hers.

The woman drew her hand back quickly, as if burned. Hugh furrowed his brow, unsettled by the strange effect this slight physical contact had on him. Not since before his captivity had he been so stirred by a woman's touch.

It was not a welcome sensation.

"*Diolch*," she said in her native Welsh. "I th-thank you, sir knight," she stammered, returning to English, "for your assistance this morn. Without your intervention—"

"You could have been killed," the knight said gravely, his rich voice somehow wending its way into a secret place deep within her being. She couldn't be sure whether her sudden tremor was due to her misadventure or the knight's proximity. "Why do you wander these woods alone?" he asked. "Where is your escort?"

Siân swallowed and glanced away from his penetrating gaze. She knew she'd been foolish to go so far beyond Clairmont's walls alone, but could not resist the lure of freedom. In one short week she would be banished to the convent of St. Ann, and all such small freedoms would end. In truth, she would become little more than a slave to the abbess when she arrived at St.

Ann's, for the dowry her brother Owen had been able to raise was a poor one, indeed.

"I walked here from Clairmont, sir," Siân said. "It is not far, nor—"

"What lunacy..." he muttered harshly. Contrary to his tone, with his scarred brow furrowed with concern rather than anger, he ran his hands with the utmost gentility across her ankles and feet, assessing, she supposed, for an injury that would prevent her from walking.

Ignoring the unsettling feelings caused by those competent, Saxon hands, Siân pulled away and raised a hand to her breast, only to wince with discomfort when she touched the long scrape. "I am no lunatic, sir," she said with indignation, "merely unfamiliar with the terrain and the—"

"Spare me such lame explanations," the knight said curtly. "Can you stand?"

"No. Yes! I think so..." she said, confused by his sudden hostility, though she should never have expected less of one of these Saxons.

Before she could protest, the knight gave an exasperated look, scooped her up as if she weighed nothing, then turned to glance quickly at the dead hog. Without another word, he began to make his way through the forest whence he came.

"Put me down, sir!" she cried, confused by this contradictory man. His tone was gruff, yet he handled her as if she were precious goods. "You cannot intend to carry me all the way to Clairmont!"

"True enough," he answered sourly as he continued on.

Siân was caught between her gratitude and her prejudice. For several weeks she had been in the company of her brother's Saxon friends and found most of them to be arrogant, heartless snobs. They were rude, and perhaps a bit cruel to the little Welsh bumpkin in their midst.

Yet this Saxon man had come to her rescue without question. It was puzzling. "What is your name, sir knight?" she asked in spite of herself, "that I might thank you properly for helping me."

"Hugh Dryden..." he said, and after a pause he added, "Earl of Alldale."

He'd received the title and lands from Henry V, for his long and faithful service in France. But Henry had been dead over a year, his son now less than two years of age. Queen Catherine currently resided in London with little King Henry, by the grace of the council, while Bishop Henry Beaufort and the dukes of Gloucester and Bedford waged a silent but deadly war against one another. It was a battle Hugh Dryden had every intention of avoiding. Perhaps that was why Wolf Colston had managed to convince him to come to distant Clairmont and woo the widow. Clairmont was far in the north country, safely removed from London.

"Then I thank you again, Lord Alldale," Siân said. She leaned toward him and lightly kissed his cheek. Hugh nearly dropped her. Her lips were soft and cool on his skin. The scent of wildflowers invaded his senses. Though her kiss was innocent and guileless, Hugh found himself responding in a manner that was not altogether respectable. He could not determine whether the sudden pounding of his heart was due to the exertion of carrying her, or her kiss.

"I am Siân *verch* Marudedd," she said, slowing Hugh's runaway reaction.

"Far from Wales, are you not?" he forced himself

to ask as they went on through the thick woods. He recognized her softly accented "Shahn" as a Welsh name, as well as the reference to her father, Marudedd. Well dressed in her finely woven, brightly colored kirtle, Siân *verch* Marudedd was clearly a Welsh noblewoman.

She was as dignified as the situation would allow, yet there was a fascinating vulnerability about her. Lady Siân raised his interest as no one else had in many a month, though Hugh did not particularly welcome it.

"London is where I've been of late, My Lord..." Siân said quietly, careful not to offend the nobleman, whose manner was unfathomable. "I've just recently come to Clairmont with my brother."

Hugh let her statement drop in silence while he tramped back in the direction where his horse was hobbled and Nicholas was likely still sleeping. The sooner he returned her to Clairmont and got her out of his hands, the better.

"You may put me down, my lord," Siân said. "I'm certain I can walk."

By now more than willing to put distance between them, Hugh let her down.

Apparently still slightly dizzy from her fall, Lady Siân took one step, then staggered a little. Hugh quickly wound an arm around her waist and, with an impatient sigh, guided her carefully along the rugged terrain.

Siân was unaccustomed to this kind of gallant, masculine attention, and her reaction startled her. She'd never thought herself capable of the emotions churning through her now. To think that one strong, male— *Saxon*—arm around her could cause such an upheaval! It was ridiculous.

She may as well have spent the last few years in St. Ann's cloister for all she knew of men and their habits; how hard and powerful a male body could feel against her own. After all, no man had ever shown the least interest in her before, and Siân had had little use for them in all her nineteen years.

At least until now.

"Satan's heels, Hugh," a voice called out as they moved through the woods, "where have you been?"

"On a fool's errand," he muttered.

"I resent that!" Siân whispered back.

In the small clearing, Hugh and Siân came upon a man saddling his horse. With a thick mane of light blond hair and pleasing features, Hugh Dryden's companion was easily the most comely man Siân had ever seen. And she had seen many, in Wales as well as in England, though none of the preening, conceited louts had roused her interest in the least.

Nor had she particularly roused theirs, unless she counted a few unsuitable advances made by some of her brother's highborn Saxon friends.

"Nicholas Becker at your service, my lady," the man said, smiling, showing his perfect white teeth. He bowed courteously.

Hugh grunted and introduced her grudgingly. "Lady Siân *verch* Marudedd." He didn't miss Siân's open and guileless appreciation of Nick's pleasing countenance. Nor did he begrudge Nicholas his golden good looks. Hugh had never been able to compete with Nick's success with the ladies, even before he'd been scarred and maimed. And they'd been friends too long to let a mere woman come between them. "From Castle Clairmont."

Nicholas turned a wry expression on Siân. "Conditions are a trifle rough at Clairmont?'' he asked with humor, indicating the condition of Siân's clothes and hair.

''Surely not,'' she said, a little breathlessly. For a Saxon, Nicholas Becker was well endowed with charm. ''This did not happen at Clairmont. A boar chased me through the woods and his lordship rescued me.''

Nick raised an eyebrow. ''Oh?''

''He shot the beast through the heart,'' Siân said, ''and again betwixt the eyes.''

Nick turned to look at Hugh. ''I thought your sight was still damaged.''

'''Twas a lucky shot.''

''*Two* lucky shots?'' Nicholas queried.

''Aye, well…'' Hugh cleared his throat and bent to pick up his saddle. He lifted it and threw it over the broad back of his destrier. ''We'll break our fast on pork at Clairmont today.''

Two horses and three riders. 'Twas awkward, but Nicholas was able to convince the lady to take her seat ahead of him on his mount. Hugh found himself fuming quietly as Nicholas and Siân bantered easily with each other, but he did not speak out.

Lady Siân *verch* Marudedd was nothing to him.

Breaching the castle gate a short time later, they found Clairmont a hub of activity. The setting reminded Hugh of Windermere Castle, the now-prosperous family seat of his friend, Wolf Colston. Perhaps marriage and stewardship of Clairmont would not be such an onerous thing, Hugh told himself. After all, Wolf and his lady wife seemed content. With their lively little daughter, Eleanor, and another babe expected within the month, Wolf and Kit were more than content. They were *delighted* with life.

It was quite beyond Hugh.

Reaching the great hall, Hugh dismounted and watched as Nicholas assisted Lady Siân from his horse and guided her up the stone steps. As if *that* were necessary, Hugh thought as he regarded the lady's sprightly step. Any evidence of her prior mishap was absent now. Deliberately turning his back on his two companions, Hugh spoke to the page who had arrived to take charge of the horses and instructed the lad to have someone fetch the great boar in the woods.

Ignoring the familiar hollowness inside him, Hugh began his own climb up the steps to meet his intended bride.

Chapter Two

Fresh rushes coated the floor of Clairmont's great hall, and all the trestle tables were covered with clean cloths. No one lazed about, not even the dogs that were commonly seen in the great halls of the kingdom. Sunlight filtered in through lofty, narrow windows, and colorful banners hung from high oaken beams.

An elegantly dressed, efficient, silver-haired man approached them. "Lady Siân!" he exclaimed, noting her disheveled appearance. "Your brother—"

"—need not hear of my mishap, Sir George," she said, a little too brightly as she gathered her skirts in hand and moved away from the newcomers to the castle. "All is well... No need for concern... I shall see to my little scrapes and bruises...."

Then she turned and was off, flitting like a candle into the dark stone depths of Castle Clairmont.

And Hugh wondered why the analogy of the candle came to mind.

"Lord Thornton, Lord Alldale," the man said, still taken aback by Siân's disheveled appearance. "I—I greet you on behalf of the lady Marguerite, and her son, Lord John. I am Sir George Packley, steward of Clairmont.''

"Thank you," Nicholas replied, his German accent causing his speech to be distinctly different from that of his peers. An illegitimate grandson of the Margrave of Bremen, Nick had grown up in his grandfather's court, along with his cousin, Wolf Colston, and Wolf's young squire, Hugh Dryden. They'd gone to France together to serve King Henry in his pursuit of French possessions, and all three had been rewarded handsomely with English lands and titles.

Hugh, however, was the only one to never have laid claim to his estates. A trusted steward administered Alldale, but Hugh had not yet seen it. Two years before, he'd been ambushed and taken prisoner by the earl of Windermere, a cruel and perverse relative of Wolf Colston's. Hugh had been kept chained to a wall in one of the damp, dark caverns under the castle, and tortured by the corrupt and wicked earl. With him in that terrible donjon had been the earl's mad stepmother, whom Windermere had personally tortured and killed before Hugh's eyes.

Though he'd never spoken of his ordeal under the castle, the atrocities committed were etched all over his body. One eye gouged out...a finger dismembered. Burns and lacerations covered him. Dehydration, filth... It was a wonder he'd survived.

But that's all he'd done. *Survived.* Hugh had recovered to become a mere shell of his former self. He was a man alone, without purpose or intensity.

It was Wolf Colston's wife, Kit, who was especially determined to see Hugh's soul restored to him. A fair and compassionate woman, Kit wanted to see her husband's closest friend healed in every way. The start of negotiations for Hugh's marriage to Marguerite of Clairmont had been, in good measure, Kit's doing.

Not that Lady Kit believed marriage would be the answer to Hugh's indifference, but Clairmont was of strategic importance to the crown. Near the Scottish border, Clairmont lands provided the buffer between the northern warlords and England. A strong leader, a man with military experience, was essential to maintaining the integrity of the northern border.

Kit Colston hoped that if Hugh married Marguerite, he would take seriously his duty to defend the border for England, and protect Clairmont holdings for Marguerite's infant son, John. She was confident that this challenge would rouse Hugh as nothing else had in the last two years.

And if his marriage should become a happy, fruitful one, then all the better.

Sir George escorted Hugh and Nicholas to a pair of chambers where they were to spend the night, and were informed that Lady Marguerite would see them at midday meal, as she had other matters to attend at present. Though they were both somewhat taken aback that Lady Marguerite did not deign to greet her guests immediately, they were even more surprised by the steward's next words.

"The queen, however," Sir George said, "is most anxious to see you."

"The queen?" Nicholas asked. "Catherine is here?"

"She is," the steward replied as he pulled open the heavy curtains covering the windows. "The royal entourage is here at Clairmont for the remainder of the month... Lady Siân Tudor is part of the queen's party."

"*Tudor!*"

"Squire Owen's sister," Sir George explained.

Both men knew Owen Tudor from his presence in the court of Henry V. Neither of them had known, however, that he had a sister—a sister who'd chosen to identify herself in the old Welsh way rather than call herself Tudor. Hugh wondered if there was some reason she hadn't wanted to be associated with Owen.

Hugh and Nicholas remembered Tudor as a competent young man in King Henry's court, a man with winning ways. He was exceptionally handsome, ambitious yet careful, and absolutely loyal to the crown. Hugh could not imagine any reason for Siân's reticence to be associated with her brother's name, but he let the irrelevant matter drop from his mind, and went along with Nicholas and Sir George to a spacious solar high in the castle tower.

"Your Majesty!" Nick said as he and Hugh knelt before their queen. She was a young woman, as lovely and elegant as ever, tall and slender, with intelligent, light-brown eyes sparkling in welcome. Neither Hugh nor Nick had seen her in over two years. Their last meeting had, in fact, been at the marriage of Kathryn and Wolf Colston in London.

"Your Majesty, it is an unexpected pleasure to see you here," Nicholas said.

Catherine smiled sadly. "Ah, but London is tiresome this time of year," she said.

"London?" Nicholas asked.

"*Oui.* London." The queen's eyes sparkled. "*And*…my brother-in-law and his uncle."

"So, Gloucester and Beaufort are at it again?" Hugh asked.

Catherine bit her lip and looked away. "I will not become a pawn in their despicable power struggle."

"What is it this time?" Nicholas queried.

"A hideous little plot to get me wed."

"Wed? To whom?" Nicholas demanded. Only the council could approve the queen's marriage, and neither he nor Hugh had heard of any such consent. But the Duke of Gloucester and Bishop Beaufort wielded a great deal of power among the lords of parliament. If either one were to choose a suitable husband for Catherine, and a guardian for her small son, the lords could be persuaded to approve a marriage.

And the "winner" of the power struggle could then control the king through the boy's stepfather.

"It is of no matter, my lords," Catherine said with a sigh. "*Mon petit Henri* and I are *not* in London. We are beyond the sway of any of his uncles."

"For now, at least," Hugh muttered under his breath as he wandered to a far window seat while Nick and Catherine continued to speak quietly together. A little boy, dressed in rich clothing, toddled about the solar, throwing a leather ball at some standing pins, then running to retrieve it and replace the pins, only to throw it again. Before he knew it, Hugh was caught up in watching little King Henry, reluctantly admiring the two-year-old's patience and ability.

It was unfortunate that his father hadn't lived to see the boy grow up, hadn't lived to give him brothers, and to keep the predatory powermongers at bay.

But that was the way of things, Hugh thought. Death claimed them all. And sometimes it was better if death came sooner rather than later.

Outside the window, the sky was blue and a flock of common brown sparrows swooped together, enjoying the play. Mirthful noises drew Hugh's attention down to the bailey, where a game of camp-ball was in progress. Goals were set up on either end of the lawn, perhaps sixty yards apart. Several young boys with sticks were riding squealing pigs, and trying to hit a large ball into the opposing goal. This was a variation on the game that Hugh had never seen and he gazed down with curiosity. Crowds of people had gathered 'round to watch the play and were laughing at the antics of the players.

And in the midst of it all was Siân Tudor.

She had changed clothes since he'd last seen her, and was now wearing a gown of vibrant blue...the same shade as her eyes. Hugh willed himself to look away, but the sunlight caught the golden strands in her russet hair and he was struck by the radiance of her person. Had he seen any such brightness of color these last few years?

Hugh doubted it. He'd seen only the colors of war in France, then the dismal darkness of Windermere's torture chamber.

Shaking off the thought, he watched Siân Tudor as she moved among the players, her lucent voice occasionally floating to his open window, her lithe movements drawing his eye, her joyful enthusiasm bewildering him. What reason, he wondered, had she to be so jubilant?

Likely no reason at all. She was obviously an emptyheaded, frivolous child.

Siân clapped her hands and stopped the play, unaware of her audience up high in the tower above her. "Not legal!" she cried, trying to contain her laughter at the silliness of the game. It was unlike any form of camp-ball she'd ever played, but the pigs had been herded into the bailey, and the thought of riding them had been just too comical to resist. "You must guide your sows back to the line of pumpkins and begin again!"

"Aw, m'lady," one boy cried as his teammates clamored with him, "you are ever changing the rules! We were so close—"

"Nay, Jacob Johnson!" Siân yelled, laughing out loud now, "you may not argue with the judge, or you'll be further penalized!"

"But—"

"No exceptions," Siân interrupted his plea. "Now! Go on!"

The game resumed as Siân ran alongside the field of play, turning one wayward pig back into the fray and helping another boy back onto his "mount." She enjoyed sporting with the children, organizing games and outings. It was what she had done at Westminster to while away the dull days as her brother worked out plans for her future. Never had it occurred to her that he would buy her into a nunnery.

She was trapped. Without a proper dowry, with no property to speak of at all, and a somewhat tarnished family reputation, marriage into a reputable English family was highly unlikely, not that it was especially desirable to Siân. Though Owen had managed to insinuate himself into the king's house, and had even engendered a high degree of trust among the English elite, Siân knew that she, herself, was a lost cause. Because she got into trouble more often than not, there wasn't a man in the kingdom who was willing to take her to wife.

Even in Wales, she'd been something of a pariah. Living at the house of one uncle or the other, Siân never felt she really belonged *anywhere*. Even in Pwll.

That was all she ever really cared about—belonging somewhere. For years she'd dreamed of Owen coming to take her away from Pwll. But it was not to be, not now, not ever. She could only hope that at St. Ann's she would finally find her place. In the environment of the cloister, mayhap she would be alone no longer.

"Siân!"

She turned to look, only to see her brother's stormy face as he approached the playing field. She hardly knew him, but she was quite familiar with *this* face. Owen had left Wales years before, leaving Siân to be raised by their mother's brothers while he went to live with a noble family near London. How different things would have been, Siân thought, had he grown up with her in Wales. Perhaps he would not be the tiresome, humorless gentleman she now saw before her.

Owen grabbed her by the arm and hauled her off to a small enclosure near the kitchen. Then, in angry hushed tones, he lambasted her again for her indecorous behavior.

"Is it not possible for you to join the other ladies in their work?" Owen asked, frustrated with his sister's lack of womanly accomplishments.

So tall and handsome, Owen kept himself impeccably attired. He was very determined to overcome the sins of their father, who had taken a prominent part in a Welsh uprising against King Henry IV. Siân, with her unsophisticated ways and lack of feminine charms, could never further Owen's cause, as well they both knew it.

The ladies of court shunned her, not wishing to associate themselves with one so common, so unschooled in courtly ways. To make matters worse, various young courtiers had attempted to seduce Siân soon after her arrival at Westminster, thinking that because of her naive, ingenuous manner, she would willingly provide a convenient outlet for their lust. Her repeated refusals had not won her their admiration.

"I am sorry, Owen," Siân said contritely, her gaze flitting back toward the game. "I am a poor weaver, as you know, and my stitchery is cursed by the very—"

"Do not say it, Siân!" Owen admonished, slapping his thigh in fury, his fair complexion darkening. "Your language is appalling, as is your dress... Look at your hair...where is your veil? By the Holy Cross, sister, do not disgrace me here!"

"I shall try not to, Owen," Siân said, truly sorry to have caused him such distress. She would try harder. She surely would. If only he would care for her half as much as he cared for his position in the queen's court. Siân cast her eyes downward and noticed a smattering of dirt and dust across the hem of her bright blue silk kirtle.

And wondered how she would get it clean by mealtime.

"Nervous?" Nicholas asked. They were to meet Lady Marguerite in the castle garden just before the noon meal.

Hugh snorted with disdain.

"I merely asked," Nicholas said. "Were I meeting my intended bride, I'm certain I'd be..."

Seated on a wooden bench near some stone statuary, was the lady in question, along with an infant in her arms.

"...dumbfounded." Nicholas concluded his sentence as the two men laid eyes on Marguerite Bradley.

She was a beautiful woman, with shining black hair arranged intricately and becomingly around her head. Her violet eyes were sparkling and lovely, framed by thick, black lashes. The lady's demeanor was gracious and serene, her movements elegant and graceful as she received Hugh and Nicholas.

"Welcome to Castle Clairmont," she said, her voice a pleasing melody to the ear, laced with undertones of her native French. "I am Marguerite Bradley, and this is my son, John."

Servants brought chairs for the gentlemen, and a nurse took the infant from his mother. When they had completed their greetings and were seated, an awkward silence ensued. Even Nicholas, who seemed always to have something to say, was rendered speechless by the lady's poise and exceptional beauty.

"I trust your journey was a pleasant one?" Marguerite asked. Her gaze flitted uncomfortably from Hugh's scarred appearance to Nicholas's more comely one.

"Yes, quite," Nicholas said, and they spent a goodly portion of time discussing the best kind of weather for travel and the incident in the wood that morning with Lady Siân and the boar.

Hugh was quiet, his usual state, leaving most of the conversation to Nick. He'd become accustomed to ladies' reactions to his eye patch, and the scars that emanated from beneath it, and it had no effect on him anymore. Oddly enough, Lady Marguerite also had little effect on him.

He realized, of course, that she was breathtakingly beautiful, but he could not muster much enthusiasm for taking a wife. He tried to appreciate the delicate arch of her black brows, and her flashing violet eyes, the aristocratically straight nose, and voluptuously full lips.

But it was useless. Whether or not he wed this woman, Hugh knew he was destined to a life of lonely isolation. For no one would ever come to understand the blackness of his soul.

The music that Queen Catherine brought to Clairmont delighted Siân. Naturally, the queen had her own musicians and minstrels, and they provided an enchanting accompaniment to every evening meal.

As Siân sat in her assigned seat at supper, she wished for some of Lady Marguerite's elegance and competence. Not only did the countess's beautiful and saintly appearance do her credit, but as chatelaine of Clairmont, Marguerite kept everything in splendid order. All of Lady Marguerite's domain was neat and organized. Guests and servants alike were simply perfect.

Siân picked at the food in the trencher she shared with her tablemates as she watched all the noble gentlemen at the dais vie for Marguerite's attention.

All but Hugh Dryden, Earl of Alldale. He was different from the other Saxons. He alone seemed indifferent to Marguerite's abundant and obvious charms, and held himself apart from the excessive adulation. Though he kept his face carefully expressionless, Siân noted the familiar spark of intelligence in his eye.

Alldale was truly a man alone, Siân thought. She'd sensed that about him in the woods that morning and had been wondering about him ever since. He was not a handsome man, exactly.... Still, there was something about him: a depth of fortitude and endurance that had surely served him in the past. A man wouldn't survive the kind of injuries that had damaged and scarred Hugh Dryden without a well of inner strength from which to draw.

Of all the ladies on the dais, only Queen Catherine
seemed unaffected by Hugh Dryden's appearance. The
scars that were barely concealed by the leather
patch…the ravages to his hand… Siân knew Hugh
must be aware of the aversion he aroused, and her heart
went out to the quiet and solitary man. She, at least,
knew what it was to be alone in the world. Siân
doubted that anyone else on the dais knew what *that*
was like.

Alldale joined in the conversation only when addressed, and Siân considered that he might be ill at ease
among the highborn folk at his table. He was like one
of the hawks she'd seen out in the woods. With craggy
features and a taut, sleek power, hawks prized freedom
above all else. Flying high above the land, circling,
riding the wind, they were masters of their domain,
subject to no one.

Hugh Dryden was as well made as any hawk, Siân
thought, with powerful arms and chest, and strength
enough to carry her without effort through the forest
that morning. She doubted there was anything that
could ruffle the feathers of this man, outside of being
caged here in polite company, listening to the idle chatter of the queen's ladies and gentlemen.

Her Majesty eventually took her leave of the company, along with several of her ladies and gentlemen.
The minstrels stayed in the hall, continuing to entertain
those who remained. Siân forced herself to ignore the
thinly veiled, lewd remarks made by the young London
courtiers with whom she was seated, and cast several
furtive glances toward the main table, hoping to catch
a few more glimpses of Hugh Dryden. It did her heart
good to see that he remained indifferent to the glorious

Marguerite. It was gratifying to know that at least one man in England was unaffected by her perfection.

Soon after the queen's departure, Hugh excused himself and Siân watched as the earl made his way through the hall and out the main doors. She couldn't help but wonder how and where this solitary man would choose to spend his time.

And as she daydreamed girlishly about the way his powerful arms had lifted her and carried her so chivalrously through the woods, Siân knocked over her goblet and spilled ale all over her blue gown.

It was the only decent one she had left.

Stone walls began to close in as darkness approached and Hugh often sought solace outside, where the open sky was immense and he could breathe easily. He walked through the town of Clairmont and followed a path up a hill, then down into a clearing to a small lake with a rugged, rocky bank.

Hugh sat on a large, flat rock near the water's edge and threw a stone into the black depths, where it sank with a *plunk!* Then he threw another.

He breathed deeply.

It had been a strange day. He'd killed a boar with an arrow. Found his target and dispatched the arrow to its mark. Without hesitation, without fail. A quick, clean kill.

He nearly smiled.

Plunk!

The darkness that dwelled inside him day after day refused to be assuaged by that puny success. He was still half blind, still a maimed man. Tonight, as usual, he would be unable to sleep without images of red-hot tongs and sharp little knives plaguing him. He would see his enemy's leering face and feel the tongs burning his eye; the cruel mallet breaking fingers and toes....

Plunk!

In the two years since his ordeal, it had been the same. He'd been stripped of his honor, of his potency as a man. Held prisoner like a child, he'd suffered every depravity with as much dignity as he could rouse. Though his dignity had been sufficient, his faith and endurance had not. He'd reached a point where he'd closed himself off from consciousness intentionally, rather than suffer the agonies planned by the twisted earl of Windermere. He'd have bargained away his soul for his freedom.

He had given in to a knight's ultimate disgrace. Despair.

How could he possibly offer himself as husband to the chatelaine of Clairmont? How could he tie himself to that beautiful, accomplished lady? Hugh was a man with nothing more than a title, an estate...a past. There was nothing for him to offer Marguerite of Clairmont. There was no future for Hugh Dryden.

A light drizzle began to fall and a thin mist gathered across the surface of the lake. Hugh wondered if it would thicken much, for he'd lost his appreciation of the beauty of the mist. Where once it had leant an unearthly, magical appeal to his world, it now made him feel trapped, suffocated.

That was something he could not bear. He'd spent days—he could never be sure how many—chained in the darkness. Unsure what his fate was to be. Waiting...always waiting.

From nowhere came the sound of running feet along the packed earth of the path, disrupting his dismal thoughts. Partially hidden by the rocks where he sat,

Hugh turned to see if the intruder was visible in the near darkness. Dark clothing concealed the figure as it ran down toward the lake, but the sound of weeping was clearly a woman's.

Something about the voice was familiar. Untamed, bronzed hair and a dusty blue kirtle came to mind, along with flashing eyes and soft, delicate skin.

Hugh sat still, hoping she would go away. Instead he saw her drop to the ground near some large stone boulders a short distance away, and commence to weeping in earnest.

He did not care to have his peace shattered by this gauche display of emotion. But if he moved off his perch on the rock, he'd surely disturb the young woman, and have to deal with her—a choice he was not pleased to make.

He could end up waiting forever for her to be done with her foolish tantrum, and leave. He saw no choice but to approach her.

How could life be so cruel? Siân wondered as she stifled her sobs. She sat up with her back to a cold, standing stone, and wrapped her arms around her knees, wiping her eyes. She'd never been much of a one for tears, knowing they couldn't change anything, but the past few weeks had shown her how utterly useless she was—how entirely inept and clumsy. 'Twas no wonder she was to be consigned to a nunnery. What man in his right mind would have her?

Owen was lucky St. Ann's had taken her so cheaply.

She could not go home—for there *was* no home anymore, now that her uncles were dead; her aunts and cousins barely eking a living for themselves as it was. Not that Pwll had ever been any great haven for her, but at least she'd understood her place. She'd always known what was expected of her.

The unpretentious people of Pwll were accustomed to seeing her in mended and dusty kirtles. They had come to expect her to instigate frolicking games and pageants, and caroles, and rhyming contests. Siân didn't understand what was so wrong with merriment; of sharing mirth and joy with others.

She had firsthand knowledge that there was more than enough sorrow in the world, without having to look for it. Her life in Wales had not been an easy one, especially as the daughter of Marudedd Tudor, cohort of Owen Glendower, the Welsh rebel. The Saxon lords—one hateful earl in particular—had been especially severe with her people after the uprising, and Siân had suffered as much as any of the other villagers. Perhaps even more, because she'd been doomed to a life apart—tolerated, but kept separate from the people she considered her own.

Siân and the people of Pwll learned early that closeness to a Tudor only brought tragedy.

Oblivious to the mist in the air, Siân hugged her knees, resting one cheek against them. Sniffling once. Hiccuping.

She had been reluctant to leave Pwll along with everything and everyone familiar. In the weeks since being summoned by Owen to this foreign, *Saxon* land, Siân was constantly making mistakes. She didn't understand the ways of the courtiers in London—neither the men and their improper, unwanted advances, nor the women and their vicious taunts and gossip.

Without understanding what she did that was so wrong, Siân disgraced herself time and time again, invoking Owen's wrath with every mistake.

Owen had made a fine place for himself as Keeper of the King's Wardrobe. Now, with King Henry dead, Queen Catherine relied heavily upon Owen for his support and counsel. He could not have a stupid and clumsy sister about. Her incompetence would naturally cast aspersions on him.

Siân leaned back, pulled the sticky cloth of her ale-soaked bodice away from her breast and let the misty rain fall, cleansing her skin of the spilled drink, and her heart of the oppressive thoughts that plagued her. The air was chill, and Siân knew she should return to the castle, but she could not bring herself to confront the ridiculing faces of those who had witnessed yet another ignominious episode in the life of Siân *verch* Marudedd.

But then, why not?

She would hold her head proudly erect as she walked through the great hall, as she always did, and ignore the sly looks and rude whisperings behind finely manicured, aristocratic hands. She'd lived through enough true horrors in Wales that this, her most recent mishap and Owen's embarrassingly public censure, hardly rated her notice. So what if she'd spilled her cup of ale? Was everyone in England so infernally perfect, with nary a spill or a speck of dirt anywhere that they could not understand and accept a few small imperfections?

Wiping her tears, Siân got herself to her feet, only to be startled by the earl of Alldale, who'd come upon her without making a sound.

He said nothing, but stood formidably, with his arms crossed over his chest, as if awaiting her explanation for being there.

Siân, having already worked herself up into a defi-

ant, peevish mood, raised her chin. "If you've come
to laugh at my lack of grace, my lord—" she started
to push past him "—rest assured that I am well aware
of my shortcomings. I've—"

"Look!" Hugh grabbed her elbow and gently guided
her back against the rock where she'd sat moments ago,
crying. Their presence was concealed as he turned her
to look toward the movement he'd noticed in the distance behind her. "Men are gathering in the mist."

Siân peered down the shoreline, and forgot her own
small troubles instantly. Directly north of them, were
men leading their horses to the water. They did not
appear to be Clairmont people. "They're wearing
plaid," she said in hushed tones. "We've heard that
Scottish raiders have been attacking the town and stealing livestock!"

Hugh knew that Richard Bradley had met his death
leading Clairmont's defense against just such Scottish
marauders. "Would you estimate..." he asked
"...about thirty of them over there?"

Siân peered into the mist. "Yes," she said, realizing
that he didn't trust his own sight. "But there are more,
with wagons—still making way down the hillside."

Hugh shot his gaze abruptly to the northward hills
and realized Siân was correct about the others. He
hadn't noticed them before. She had a keen eye, even
with her sight obscured by tears. Looking down into
her guileless face, Hugh gave a fleeting thought as to
what had made her weep, and resisted the urge to touch
her face, to wipe the tears from her flushed skin.

His spine stiffened with the odd notion. She could
find her comfort from her brother, or from one of the
courtly ladies back at the castle. Siân Tudor certainly
had no need of *his* kind words, even if he knew any.

"We'll need to get back to Clairmont and alert the men," Hugh said as he took Siân's elbow and drew her back to the footpath.

"They seem very well equipped, My Lord," Siân said. "This will be devastating to Clairmont."

"Not if we're prepared," Hugh replied gravely.

They hurried through the light rain, running through the town and up to the castle. Both Siân and Hugh were soaked through when they reached Clairmont's outer bailey. "Go and get those wet clothes off," Hugh ordered her.

"I'm coming with you," she said defiantly.

Unwilling to waste time arguing, Hugh proceeded to the great hall, where Lady Marguerite and many of her noble guests were gathered around talking, laughing and watching a pair of jugglers, while the queen's musicians continued to play their festive music.

Hugh spotted Nicholas Becker, standing with Lady Marguerite, and he made his way toward the handsome pair, thinking that Nick was a much more suitable swain than *he* was.

"Hugh!" Nicholas exclaimed. He glanced at Siân, who stood a little behind Hugh. "You're soaked!"

Ignoring his friend's words, Hugh spoke urgently. "There are Scotsmen gathering at the lakeshore beneath the northern hills, preparing for attack," he said. "The knights need to ready themselves for battle."

Marguerite blanched white and started to sway. Nicholas was closest, and caught her before she fell, then swept her up off her feet, causing a stir among the guests in the hall. "Sir George will know the chain of command," he said, "best consult him." Then he turned and carried the lady out of the hall and up the main stairs.

Hugh's appearance with Siân in the hall had caused
more than a minor disturbance, so they did not have to
go looking for Lady Marguerite's steward. Sir George
quickly found Hugh amid the revelers who had stopped
their amusements and were already questioning him.
Hugh spoke of the developing threat near the lake, and
the crowd in the hall quickly dispersed—the noblewomen fled to areas of safety, the knights headed for
the barracks to arm themselves.

Hugh and Sir George went down to rouse the troops,
then headed for the armory where Hugh began issuing
orders as he put on his armor.

"Send runners into town to rouse the people," he
said as a young squire helped him to fit his jack over
his hauberk. Sleeves and pauncer were added, then
sword and dagger.

"But, my lord—"

"Have all able-bodied men remain in the town, but
send everyone else up here," Hugh ordered. "Have the
people round up their livestock and herd their animals
inside the castle walls. Stress the importance of speed
and stealth."

"But, my lord," Sir George protested, "we must
have a plan. We cannot just—"

"This *is* the plan, Sir George," Hugh said. "What
did Lord Richard do when faced with an enemy attack?"

"We were never forewarned before, so the earl always met the enemy face-to-face," the old squire said,
"head-to-head on the field of battle."

"It's time for a new tack," Hugh said with authority.
He had assumed leadership for lack of another to do
so. "We'll protect the townspeople as best we can by

removing them to the castle. Ah, Nicholas," he said, taking note of his friend's appearance in the barracks.

Nicholas was stunned by the sight that greeted him. Hugh had shown little interest in anything, his lengthy malaise certainly due to the tortures he'd withstood at Windermere Castle. Yet here he stood now, as formidable as he'd ever been, arming himself for battle and issuing orders as if he'd never lost an eye, a finger, a toe… Never been chained to a wall and forced to witness the atrocities committed against a defenseless old crone.

"Don't gape, Nick," Hugh said as he picked up his quiver of arrows. "Arm yourself."

And as Nicholas began putting on his armor, it crossed his mind that it was unfortunate they hadn't found a war in which to involve themselves before this.

"Is it possible the Scots know that Queen Catherine is here with young Henry?" Hugh asked Sir George, his astute mind quickly calculating all possibilities, and surprising Nicholas yet again.

"It is doubtful, my lord," the aging knight replied pensively. "Her Majesty has been here less than a week—not nearly enough time for the Scots to muster a force of fighters such as you have described."

Hugh let the matter rest, although he was far from satisfied that Sir George was correct. Whether or not the Scots knew Catherine was here, it was up to Clairmont to see that King Henry's heir and his mother were kept safe. "How many archers have you?"

"Twenty-two, my lord," George said, answering Hugh's question.

"And foot soldiers?"

"Thirty-five…give or take," George replied.

The attack would likely come at midnight, since that

had been the Scots' most common strategy, though Hugh learned that the Scottish raiders were an unpredictable lot. Nothing was certain, other than the fact that haste was essential.

As the men made ready for battle, activity within the castle walls increased. Siân had disappeared some time before, and Hugh assumed she'd gone to find dry clothes. Instead he found her standing in the rain in the inner bailey, amid wheelbarrows and small coops, wagons and livestock, directing the newly arriving townspeople to shelter, along with their children and animals.

Vexation possessed him as he observed her dripping, wet hair, the sopping blue gown that fit her like a second skin, the shivers she couldn't conceal. She looked small and vulnerable. "Fool woman," he muttered, coming up behind her, putting his hands on her shoulders. He turned her toward the stone steps of the castle and gently guided her up, ignoring her objections all the way.

"There is work to be done, my lord," Siân protested as they moved through the hall to the castle stairs. "The people do not know where to go. Children are frightened and—"

"You are going to catch your death," Hugh interrupted, escorting her down the gallery where his own sleeping room was located. "Which of these is your chamber?"

Siân stopped in her tracks, a single bleak wall sconce lighting her angry face. "You cannot bully me so, my lord."

"You need a keeper, my lady!" he said, raising his voice for the first time in recent memory.

Shocked by his insult, Siân's chin began to quiver. "I do *not!*"

"Then behave as if you do not!" Hugh bellowed with irritation. "Get out of those clothes!"

"No!" Siân crossed her arms and stood toe-to-toe with him.

"God's Cross, woman, you try my patience," Hugh said, exasperated. She'd also wrenched more emotion out of him than he'd allowed in the past two years. Annoyance, aggravation. An idiotic sense of protectiveness. "What could possibly be so difficult about changing into dry things?"

She dropped her hands to her sides and glanced away self-consciously. Then she spoke truthfully. "I...I have no others."

"Surely you..." He let his words fade as he saw the truth in her wary eyes. "Nothing presentable?" he asked gruffly.

She shook her head.

Owen had arranged for two acceptable gowns to be made for his sister when she'd arrived in London, but had seen no need for any more since she was to be pledged to St. Ann's. Siân would soon be wearing the rough, brown woolen tunic of the convent nuns, so any more fine gowns would be a waste of Owen's rare and precious coin.

Refusing to be thwarted, Hugh put his hand on Siân's back and ushered her into his own room, kicking the door shut behind him. Siân, taken by surprise at first, began sputtering protests, but Hugh disregarded her words as he threw a few sticks on the smoldering fire. Then he pulled her over to the hearth where he turned her roughly and began untying the wet laces that fastened up the back of her bodice.

"My lord!" Siân cried, trying to pull away from his touch—the very touch that sent strange and wild tendrils of heat through her chilled body. "This is unseemly! You cannot—"

"I most certainly can," Hugh said. "I've already saved your foolish life once today, I'll not see you take ill and die of fever and let my efforts of this morn go to waste."

"Then I'll find someone to help me," she snapped. "Someone more...*suitable!*"

"Be still, Siân," Hugh said, ignoring her. "These wet laces are the very devil to open and I have little time."

"I object, my lord!" she cried, his strong hands on her back making her tingle in agony. What kind of magic did the man possess to cause such feelings? Why had she never felt these strange sensations...this odd yearning before?

It was awful! She had to get away from here, from *him,* before she was rendered incapable of rational thought, of movement, of escape. His touch was nothing like the soft, unwelcome pawing of the London dandies. The earl of Alldale acted with the potent certainty of a man. His was a bold and commanding touch, with strong hands honed in battle, and Siân could not help but wonder if there was any softness in him at all.

"Your objection has been duly noted, my lady," Hugh said as he released the final loop of the lace. The stiff, blue gown fell away from Siân's skin, dropping in a steaming heap to the floor. She was left wearing her thin, linen under-kirtle, which was also soaked, and not nearly as concealing. With her russet hair curling in a wild tangle down her back, she looked especially fragile, like a piece of vividly colored glass reflecting moonlight.

Siân lowered her head, puzzled by the strange feelings coursing through her. Did he feel it, too? she wondered. Did he ever long to be touched with care and tenderness?

Presumably not, she thought, certainly not from her. He'd called her foolish. He'd said she tried his patience. She was naught more than a pest to him.

Hugh stood rooted to the ground for an eternal moment, transfixed by the vision of Siân's delicate back, her smooth buttocks nearly exposed through the thin material. Thoughts of her soft lips on his rough skin nearly made him tear off his battle gear.

Seeing her tremble suddenly, he gave himself a mental shake, then spun on his heel to reach for the thick woolen blanket from his bed. Quickly, he wrapped Siân in it, unable to avoid enclosing her in his arms momentarily.

With wonder in her deep blue eyes, Siân turned to look at Hugh, a crease of bewilderment marring the perfect skin between her brows. The moment grew thick and heavy as their bodies drew closer to each other. She felt his breath on her face, his heat warming her. Longing to touch him as he'd touched her, she stopped herself, remembering what he thought of her. Siân spoke quietly instead. "I thank you for seeing to my welfare again, my lord. I will try not to bother you again."

Then she pulled the blanket tightly around herself and fled the earl's chamber.

Chapter Three

The battle was long and fierce. Every able-bodied man joined in the fray, the untrained townsmen using whatever weapons came to hand: axes, hammers, poles and daggers. As the highest-ranking knight at Clairmont, Hugh decided the strategy of battle and commanded the troops, with archers in ambush on every rooftop. Still, they were outnumbered by the Scots, who were well-supplied, savage fighters.

It was the archers who finally won the day for Clairmont. A masterful strategy, keeping archers positioned on the rooftops, left the Scots unable to escape their deadly volleys. Arrows rained down whenever the Scots broached the town. Clairmont's foot soldiers finished the job.

When it was over, however, the damage to the town was extensive. As he walked through the aftermath, Hugh felt strangely detached from the chaos around him. The burning thatch and smoldering embers…the bodies of the fallen men being gathered for burial…women and children weeping. There were moans of pain that echoed some distant agony of his own, an agony he could not bear to relive.

He made his way back to the castle, oblivious to the salutes and hails he received from the people within the walls, who now considered him a hero. They gave him credit for discovering the Scots early, forming a plan of attack, leading the soldiers in defense of the town...and emerging victorious from it all.

After so many lost skirmishes, this victory was sweet to Clairmont.

Within the walls of the castle, Hugh dismounted and left his horse in the care of a groom, then proceeded to the keep, where he sought the chapel entrance. Finding it on the eastern side, he slipped in quietly and stood with his eyes downcast, shivering in his sweltering metal shell, even as the autumn sunlight shone through the stained glass above the altar.

And Hugh Dryden then prayed for the souls who'd been dispatched this day.

Siân distractedly helped two little girls wash their hands in a trough in the outer bailey as she searched the faces of the men returning from Clairmont town. Battle-weary and bruised, bleeding and bandaged, the men had victory in their eyes nonetheless. The women and children welcomed their men back amid hugs and endearments, tears and laughter.

Hugh's troubled visage eventually came into Siân's view, and she started toward him, anxious to see him at close range, to assure herself that he was unscathed. She'd worried about him throughout the night and all day long, even though she knew he would never appreciate such attention from her. Her heart overflowed with relief when she saw him, and with the need to touch him. To feel his solid body near hers again, as she had the night before—only to affirm that he was unharmed. He was covered with the grime of battle mixed with blood, and Siân could only hope it was not his own.

When he was within an arm's reach, Siân spoke his name, but he walked on numbly, ignoring her.

Irrationally hurt by his complete disregard, Siân looked down at herself, in the rough peasant's dress she'd thrown on in the previous night's confusion. It was ill-fitting and ugly, exactly the kind of dress a highborn man would abhor. The condition of her hair hadn't improved much since he'd seen her last night, either. 'Twas no wonder he'd ignored her, though his indifference gave her a peculiar ache in the vicinity of her heart.

"God's ears, Siân," a harsh male voice said. Owen took hold of her arm and roughly ushered her to the rear of the kitchen. "Must you disgrace yourself at every turn?"

"Owen, I—"

"You are pitiful!"

"You're hurting me, Owen," Siân cried, dismayed by the anger flashing in his dark gray eyes. What could she possibly have done wrong? It was nothing but her Christian duty to help these poor people in their time of need. How could Owen construe it otherwise? "Please!"

He let go of her arm and pushed her through the kitchen door. The cook fires were being tended by maids, and Owen surprised Siân by refraining from giving her the tongue-lashing he obviously felt she needed. He propelled her beyond the kitchen and down a dark passage, till they reached a small, isolated alcove.

"Is it too much to ask you to comport yourself as

becomes your station?'' he demanded. ''You are not some lowborn varlet, at liberty to dress as you please, to sully our already inglorious name.''

''Owen, I didn't mean—''

''I am doing everything I possibly can,'' he said, running a hand through his wavy, golden hair, ''to restore honor to our name. To see that our progeny is afforded the respect it deserves! But you!'' he cried in frustration.

Siân felt her heart would burst—not only in shame, but with sorrow. For this talk of progeny had nothing to do with her—not when she took the vows of St. Ann.

''*You* thwart my every effort,'' Owen continued, pacing in front of her now, in his anger. ''You lower yourself to the level of those villein, dressing like them, dirtying your hands with them. Why can you not observe and learn from your betters? Look at the queen, for example. Her Majesty is a woman above all others! She is kind and gracious, beautiful and refined. And Lady Marguerite…''

Siân bit her lower lip to keep it from trembling. She was powerless to stop the trail of tears coursing down her face, but she somehow managed to refrain from weeping openly. Owen was right, of course. Siân rarely ever thought of dire consequences before she acted, nor did she give much consideration to her clothes or the state of her hair.

As for dirtying her hands…Siân wasn't afraid of hard work, nor could she see any dishonor in it. At home in Pwll, there'd been no elegant house or servants to take care of her. There'd been no one to tutor her in the fancy ways of the gentry, though she'd learned more than enough about aristocratic harshness from Edmund Sandborn, the arrogant Earl of Wrexton, whose English estates bordered Welsh lands near Pwll.

Years ago, Siân had sworn on the graves of two youthful Welsh friends that if she ever met up with Wrexton again, she'd somehow contrive to run a blade through his cruel, black heart.

Siân wondered what her brother would make of *that*.

"The lady's hands were sullied in good cause, Tudor."

Siân whirled, mortified, to see Hugh Dryden approaching from the vicinity of the chapel. Had he heard Owen's scathing chastisement in its entirety?

"There is no shame in the help you've rendered today," he added, taking one of Siân's hands and raising the back of it to his lips. It was bad enough that he now knew what little regard her brother held for her...she could only hope the earl would not notice the quivering of her chin or the excessive moisture in her eyes.

"Get out of my sight," Owen growled after Hugh had walked away. "And don't return until you've made yourself presentable."

Hugh Dryden sank down into his tub of hot water and sighed. Cupping his hands, he lifted water up and over his shoulders, down his powerful swordsman's chest. As his tight, brown nipples beaded, droplets of water stuck in the thick dark hair that matted his chest.

"That's a nasty-looking slice on your arm," Nicholas said, making himself at home on Hugh's bed while Hugh soaked his aching muscles. "Bet it smarted when you got it."

"I was too well occupied at the time to notice," Hugh replied dryly, thinking of how his shoulder piece had become dislodged just before the Scot got in his lucky strike. It was a terrible wound—a deep slice through the muscle below his shoulder that had bled and crusted over, then bled again. He had some salve to put on it, but he wanted to get it clean first. When it healed, *if* it healed, the scar would be just one more to add to his already well-marked body.

"That's your bad shoulder," Nicholas said. "You should have it sewn."

Hugh made hardly more than a grunt in response. He'd had enough needles pass through his skin to last a lifetime. Still, it was a deep, ugly gash, and that shoulder had already undergone punishment enough during his imprisonment.

"All went exceptionally well today," Nick said. "You should press your suit to Lady Marguerite now, while your victory is fresh in her mind."

Hugh refrained from comment, other than a weary, noncommittal grunt. He'd hardly given Lady Marguerite a passing thought, yet he could not rid himself of the image of Siân Tudor being dressed-down by her brother for helping out in the courtyard. Hugh doubted that she'd slept at all this past night, and looked as if sheer willpower alone kept her from shattering under her brother's harsh and unnecessary words.

The man was an ass.

"There will be more suitors, Hugh," Nicholas said, forcing Hugh's thoughts back to the matter at hand. "You must make your proposal now."

Wearily, Hugh picked up a thick bar of soap and began to wash, wincing as he worked to cleanse the wound in his arm.

"The queen said that Marguerite has received missives from two other noblemen." Nicholas stood and began pacing irritably. "There was one from some southern earl, and another from a London dandy, Viscount Darly."

"So? Let one of *them* take her to wife," Hugh replied to Nick's warnings. "Either one would likely suit her better than me."

"Damn it, man!" Nicholas said as he stopped his pacing and put his hands on his hips, exasperated. He'd promised Wolf Colston he'd see that Hugh got settled with a wife. Not just any wife, but *this* one. Marguerite Bradley.

"Marguerite is perfect, Hugh! She is incomparable! Between Alldale and Clairmont, you could become one of the most powerful peers of the kingdom. You cannot just—"

Yes, he could, he thought as he slid under the water, submerging his head, blocking out all extraneous sound. Hugh hoped his little maneuver would take enough of the wind out of Nick's sails so that he could finish his bath in peace.

Hugh did not know if he could ever marry. He'd come to Clairmont with every intention of offering for the hand of Lady Marguerite, but he was not so certain of it now. Two years ago, something had been damaged inside him. Whether it was his heart or his soul, Hugh could not say. He only knew that he was no longer a whole man, and had not been for a long time.

He doubted he ever would be again.

Besides, he thought as he heard the door to his chamber slam shut, he was battle-weary. Time enough on the morrow to consider such things as marriage and estates.

Siân cuddled the precious infant to her breast as she paced the length of the castle parapet. She had truly planned to find something more suitable to wear, but when she'd come upon the infant's grieving young mother in the courtyard, she'd had no choice but to offer help.

Her heart had reached out to the woman, who was newly widowed and overwhelmed by the infant in her arms and the two older children who held on to her skirts, weeping. Siân could also see that she was with child.

The babe was irritable, cutting teeth, the mother told Siân dully, her voice empty of all emotion. Siân had expected to hear the pain of loss, but the woman was numb with grief, exhausted by her pregnancy. Without thinking, Siân had offered to take the babe, to walk her and care for her until the mother felt more capable.

As she paced the high parapet, Siân hummed absently to the child, a repetitive, rhythmical, comforting lullaby. If the babe stirred, Siân bounced her gently, lulling her back to sleep. She wrapped the blanket more securely around the child's head, protecting her from the brisk wind up high on the parapet. She paced aimlessly, relishing the feel of the babe in her arms, the smell of her perfect skin, the whisper of downy hair on her cheek.

The sky was laden with thick, low-hanging clouds, so the full moon was visible only intermittently as it appeared from behind the clouds. A guard nodded to her as she strolled by, and Siân was struck by the thought that these Saxons were just like her own people. Striving to make their way in the world. Honoring their parents and loving their children. Eating, drinking, sleeping, laughing.

Fighting to keep what was their own.

Isn't that what they'd done in Pwll? Lived, and laughed, and fought against the Saxon Earl of Wrexton, who was determined to take what was theirs?

Siân shuddered, thinking of her two young companions who, many years ago, had been victims of Wrexton's terrible cruelty. Beyond the loss of her childhood friends, the most painful part of the memory was knowing that the entire, horrible episode had been no more than a game to Wrexton, a simple exercise in "cat and mouse."

The contemptuous *bastard.*

Siân swallowed back the bitter tears that never failed to come when she thought of the two youthful friends, gap-toothed Idwal and freckled Dafydd. Never in her life, if she lived for a century or more, would she forget her pain, or her guilt in the deaths of those two young boys. For *she* had been the one Wrexton was after, not two innocent Welsh boys. She, Siân Tudor...the daughter of the rebel.

The babe in Siân's arms began to cry again, and she was diverted from further thoughts of the two boys as she rocked the child and increased the volume of her song. It was a simple little Welsh song, a lullaby, but it seemed to soothe the child nearly as much as it soothed Siân's own soul.

> *"Huna blentyn yn fy mynwes,*
> *Clyd a chynnes ydyw hon...*
>
> Sleep my baby, at my breast,
> 'Tis a mother's arms round you..."*

If only she *were* the little one's mother, Siân thought wistfully, motherhood being one of many simple pleasures she was to be denied. Owen had decided that marriage was beyond her. As her closest male relative, Owen would not allow Siân to marry any of the young men of Pwll, all of whom were below the high and mighty—but impoverished—Tudors. Which was just as well, as Siân would never again put another Welshman at risk of Saxon vengeance.

There certainly weren't any Saxon noblemen of Owen's acquaintance who would offer for her, even if she would deign to have one. She was too Welsh, too unsophisticated, and entirely too lacking in dowry.

Siân had considered running away from Owen and the life he'd chosen for her, but she did not know where she could go or how she would manage to live. A woman alone had little chance of survival. On more than one occasion, Owen had told Siân that she was not the kind of woman to attract a man for anything more than a lighthearted tryst. She was too headstrong, too impertinent, and just too unsuitable.

As a result, she was to be consigned to the nunnery.

And Siân was afraid that would prove a difficult burden for one who had never been particularly pious.

Hugh stretched his tired muscles and leaned back against the stone corner of the parapet. He heard the sweet tones of Lady Siân's singing as she paced the length of the stone walk, and he felt his own soul quiet within him. He did not understand her words, but the sounds of comfort were clear, and the infant in her arms was soothed by the song.

An unfamiliar contentment filled him as he listened to her. Siân was a fey child, not nearly as beautiful as Lady Marguerite, but she was interesting. Perhaps more than interesting, he decided, she was even compelling at times. He thought of the incident the previous night, when her saturated gown had dropped and she'd stood nearly naked before him. Hugh could not remember ever wanting a woman as powerfully as he had at that moment, and had she not run from his chamber, he was not sure what he'd have done.

Even now, hearing her pleasing voice in the distance, Hugh could envision her eyes, deep blue as they'd been with arousal; her lips, moist and full. Curling tendrils of her fiery hair had framed the pure white skin of her delicate cheeks and gently shaped chin. Her lush body against his own was a torture he could not have imagined, a torture he had wanted to continue at any cost.

His groin tightened even now with the thought of her, and he knew it was a mistake ever to have thought of her as a "fey child."

Hugh quickly turned his thoughts to the festivities presently going on in the great hall. He had declined to participate. Not only was he too weary, but he felt like no one's hero, and didn't care to be feted by anyone in any way. He had yet to make his proposal of marriage to Lady Marguerite and still wasn't convinced it was the right thing to do, in spite of Nicholas Becker's arguments.

Hugh had no stomach for warfare anymore. His entire life had been spent either in training for war, or in actual battle. Here at Clairmont, there were no signs of the Scots giving up. Hugh knew that if he wed Marguerite, he'd have to withstand ever more of these border skirmishes until the Scots were defeated once and for all.

Perhaps, though, with an able leader at Clairmont and more victories against them, the Scots could be induced to stop their raids all the sooner. It was something to consider. Clearly, this had been the goal of the Parliamentary Council when they'd suggested the marriage.

Hugh was dressed in a most unassuming manner, but the dark patch that covered one eye was not easily hidden. The parapet guards spotted him quickly and saluted him as their recognized leader—the man who'd led them to victory. Hugh acknowledged them, but turned away to find a dark and quiet perch near a turret, where he could watch the turbulent sky without being seen. He sat back against the stone wall and stretched his legs out before him.

Hugh had surprised himself by rising to the challenge of battle last night and all through the day. It had been gratifying to discover that he was still a fully capable soldier, archer, swordsman, commander; that men still followed his confident lead.

The question was whether or not Hugh cared to acquiesce to the council's wishes and provide Clairmont with the leader that was so desperately needed here. He had his own estate to the south, nearer to Windermere, and though he did not believe that Castle Alldale was as prestigious as Clairmont, Alldale's lands were prosperous. No reasonable man could be dissatisfied with the holding. And there was peace in Alldale. No borders to protect, no marauders to overcome.

No killing to carry out.

The clouds thickened and obscured the moonlight, and night intensified around Hugh. Deep in shadow, he sat still, preoccupied with his ruminations, hardly aware of the gathering storm or anything else going on around him.

When Siân inadvertently tripped over Hugh's feet, it

was only because of his quick reflexes that she did not
drop the babe she carried and fall on her face.

"*Och!*" she cried as the infant took up howling
again. "I am sorry, my lord! I did not see you there in
the dark." She felt like a fool. Always awkward, forever clumsy—especially around Alldale. He must think
her an absolute dolt. As did Owen. As did everyone
she met.

"It is nothing, Siân," he said darkly, holding her
arms to steady her, "do not fret so."

"You are kind, my lo—" But before Siân completed
her thought, the infant belched loudly and spit a goodly
amount of mother's milk onto the shoulder of her bodice and down one sleeve. Siân wanted to crawl into a
cave and hide.

Hugh's brows rose.

Siân stifled a groan. Truly he *did* think her an idiot,
and with good reason. She had plenty of experience
with babies, yet she had wandered away unprepared,
without so much as a cloth to clean the babe if necessary.

Siân shook her head in dismay just as fat droplets
of rain began to shower them. Hugh quickly pulled her
and the child into the shelter of the nearby turret and
watched as the clouds opened up. There was soon a
curtain of rain all around them, with ominous rumbles
of thunder and shimmering bolts of lightning in the
distance. The infant settled down, and drowsed on
Siân's shoulder.

Siân looked around the dark and empty turret. She
knew she should not be alone with the earl, for there
were proprieties to observe, her innocence to preserve.
She was pledged to St. Ann's, but looking at him
now…the breadth of his chest, the strength of his

hands, the power in his thighs… Siân suppressed a shiver that had nothing to do with the chill in the air, and everything to do with the way he'd touched her the night before, how he'd stood up for her to Owen, and kissed her hand.

"Perhaps, *genethig,*" Siân said to the babe, turning her attention from the kind and competent man standing next to her, "it was not a new tooth at all, but rather a sour stomach that caused your troubles."

Hugh Dryden wreaked havoc on her equilibrium. Working to regain her composure, she spoke softly to the babe in Welsh. Siân knew she looked awful, as Owen had told her so not long ago, and now she smelled like sour milk, too. Very impressive.

"I—I had no time to change…" she offered lamely. She knew she must look like a troll.

"Clearly, there was further need of your skills amongst the villagers," Hugh said offhandedly as he peered out the narrow window of the turret.

This Saxon earl cut an imposing figure, Siân thought wistfully. Wearing a light tunic and dark chausses, he stood tall and quiet in the faint light of the turret. He truly was the hero of Clairmont, Siân thought, just as the people were saying.

Lightning flashed again, and thunder rumbled in the distance, giving Siân a new reason to be uneasy. Her brow creased in concern. "Will we be safe up here?"

Hugh nodded in reply, and Siân realized that she could see him better now. The low rumbles and faraway flashes of light had become almost constant; their faces were illuminated often, as if by an unearthly, flickering fire. She tried to make herself relax, but the fierceness of the storm was beginning to frighten her.

"The worst of it is still in the distance," he said.

"Will it get worse here?" Siân asked, gazing worriedly through the narrow window at the driving rain outside. Violent storms always frightened her, and this one seemed to carry the wrath of God with it. "Lightning? Floods?"

"Could be," Hugh said absently. "But it could blow over. Or change direction."

Siân was not reassured. She shivered suddenly, violently, and backed away from the open window, holding the infant more closely. "We should go down," she said.

"Not yet," Hugh replied, just now realizing Siân's fear. "This will let up in a few minutes, then I'll escort you down," he said to reassure her.

Siân glanced out the doorway, and Hugh could see that the fool woman was considering whether to make a run for it through the rain to get to lower ground. Haste would likely make her slip on the wet stone and injure herself, perhaps even drop the child. He could not let her go.

"Lady Siân," he said, attempting to mask his exasperation, "the storm is in the distant hills. You need not be concerned for your safety."

Siân wasn't so sure. Lightning had struck the church tower in Pwll many years before, and that was a memory she would never lose. She did not care to be high up in the castle turret when the worst of this storm struck, although a run through the cold rain was not appealing, either. She knew the earl was right—that there was time before the storm worsened—but still, it was difficult to remain calm.

Stiffening her backbone, Siân strove to rein in her anxiety. She was a grown woman, not some child to be ruled by her fears. "I've seen storms," she said, "that— *Och!*"

A fierce arc of lightning lit up the near sky, then instantly a bone-rattling thunderclap sounded. Siân jumped. At the same time, Hugh turned to reassure her, but somehow drew her into his arms, surprising them both, and waking the babe Siân held. The wound in Hugh's upper arm began to bleed, which Siân noticed as they broke apart.

Over the infant's crying, Siân exclaimed, "You're hurt!"

"'Tis naught," he replied. "I'll tend it when we go down."

"But it's bleeding badly," she told him. Hugh's need momentarily surpassed Siân's fear. She looked around to see if there was a cloth to be used to stanch the flow of blood, but there was nothing. Her mind off the storm for the moment, Siân went to the doorway and looked for a guard.

They must all have taken cover from the rain.

"Here," she said, handing the infant to him to hold with his unhurt arm. "Take her for a moment."

Hugh felt an instant of shock when she shoved the child at him. He held the babe awkwardly with his uninjured arm, and watched as Siân turned around, then bent over and pulled up the hem of the ugly, dark over-kirtle she wore, to expose the fine, white linen gown underneath. A smooth, elegant length of leg was exposed, as well, and Hugh's mouth went dry as he turned quickly away from her inadvertent display.

He heard the tearing of cloth, then suddenly she was there, taking the babe from him, pressing the clean linen to the wound near his shoulder, stanching the flow of blood.

"You should have this attended to, my lord," Siân admonished severely. She could not see the wound through his light tunic, but by the volume of blood staining the cloth, she knew it was long and deep. "You might well lose your arm with a wound this severe."

"And what would *you* know of lost limbs?" Hugh answered with derision.

Siân froze. His tone of voice had changed. Now he sounded just like all the other haughty Saxons she'd recently met. For all she knew, he could have been one of the Saxon soldiers who'd repeatedly harassed Pwll and the other Welsh border villages in retribution after the Glendower revolt. She should have known better than to allow herself any warm feelings for a Saxon aristocrat.

They were all the same.

What did she know of lost limbs, this *earl* wanted to know? Siân didn't care to recount the terrible price of those bloody raids on her people—the lost *lives,* as well as lost limbs. Nor did she want to recall the atrocities committed by some of the Saxon pigs, when their victories had already been secured.

With lips pressed tightly together, Siân plopped the makeshift bandage into Hugh's free hand. She wrapped the child securely in her little wool blanket and ran from the turret, moving quickly down the open stone steps in the pouring rain.

Hugh slapped the bloody dressing back on his wound and cursed himself for a fool.

The lady had only tried to be kind, but he'd insulted her intelligence, speaking to her as if she were a simpleton. He hadn't really meant to offend her, but any talk of lost body parts always set him to boiling. How could anyone know how it was to lose a limb...an eye? Certainly not Siân Tudor, the softhearted, stormy young sister of Squire Owen.

She'd been angry with him—there was no doubt of it in Hugh's mind. Her mouth had been pressed so tight that her lips were nearly white in the unnatural light of the storm. Her eyes, too, Hugh thought...deep blue, and flashing with fury.

And as Hugh leaned back to watch nature's tumultuous display outside, he knew a moment's regret for the few sharp words he'd thoughtlessly thrown at her. She received enough harsh treatment from her own brother. She certainly did not need more from *him.*

Chapter Four

Hugh assisted Queen Catherine from her horse and walked through Clairmont town with her entourage as she surveyed the damage and bolstered the spirits of her son's people. Hugh gave Catherine a great deal of credit. Her *petit Henri* would become King Henry VI one day, and the queen had learned some valuable lessons from the boy's father during their short marriage. One of those lessons had been the importance of the people's good wishes toward their monarch.

Hugh Dryden and Owen Tudor walked with the queen as she progressed on foot through the town, speaking to everyone who crossed her path. As she passed, she gave small tokens of her presence—ribbons, a bit of silk, a small leather pouch—and questioned individuals on how they and their families had fared in the battle.

Lady Marguerite accompanied the party, following at a close distance with Nicholas Becker and Sir George, as well as the reeve of Clairmont. They discussed grain and food stores, survival of the livestock, and the death toll in the town. Hugh and Nick were asked about methods of securing Clairmont and how to protect themselves from further attack.

There were no easy solutions to the problems Clairmont faced, though Hugh knew they were not insurmountable. Between himself and Nicholas, they could call a hundred knights to battle. The only question was one of payment. Was Clairmont rich enough to support additional knights?

With careful portioning, there would be enough food to last the winter. Some goods could be imported—Hugh knew that Alldale, among other estates, had had very productive growing seasons. It was possible there were surpluses that could be purchased. Again, it was a matter of funds.

"Look, Owen," the queen said, pointing toward one of the distant fields. "It is Siân, *non?*"

Hugh looked up as Owen followed the queen's glance and everyone saw that Siân was indeed on the hillside with a large group of children. To Hugh, she was little more than a spot of bright blue on the hillside, topped by a cheerful crown of red-gold. She was too far away to see her features, although he didn't need to see her to know how her mouth quirked in laughter. Or the impudent tilt of her chin.

Her brother, Owen, sighed in frustration and said, "I'll go and get her, your Highness, and try to—"

"*Non*, Owen," Catherine interjected. "Leave her."

"But—"

"Do you not see, Owen?" the queen asked. "She has taken all of the smallest ones and gotten them out from underfoot. She has them playing at a…" She searched for the English word. "A pageant. See how some are sitting in a circle around the performers in the center?"

"You are right, Your Majesty," Lady Marguerite said. "How clever of her."

Hugh heard Siân's laugh carry over the distance, then the gleeful giggles of the children in her care. He supposed it *was* clever of her to have gotten the children out of the way as the adults cleaned up the town and tended the wounded. Tudor's sister seemed to have a way with the little ones, he thought, perhaps because she herself was so childlike.

She ought to get back to the castle, Hugh thought, or at least closer. No telling whether or not they'd been successful in routing every Scotsman from the area. He'd never met anyone so naive, so ingenuous. Hugh doubted she ever gave a thought to her own safety.

Hugh's attention was drawn back to Lady Marguerite. With a no-nonsense manner, Marguerite Bradley saw to her responsibilities with a deep sense of duty. Her assessment of the situation at Clairmont was astute. Action had to be taken to ensure the success and continuity of her town, and Hugh had no doubt that the lady would manage it. Everything about Marguerite indicated an efficiency of mind and deed.

Her manner in all things was serious and thoughtful. Hugh doubted there was a foolish or frivolous bone in her body.

Even Marguerite's clothing bespoke her elegant competence. Expensive silks and woolens were dyed to perfection and tailored into fashionable gowns. Shoes were made to match. Her sable hair was perfectly arranged—not a hair out of place under stylish headgear.

Hugh glanced back at Siân, just as she dropped to the ground amid the laughter of her small charges. Then he studied Marguerite's profile. The lady of Clairmont was certainly beautiful, he thought, as well as intelligent and competent: a prize any man would be proud to claim.

She would be a perfect wife, and Hugh decided to make his marriage proposal when they returned to the castle.

But not until after he'd seen to it that Lady Siân and the children moved themselves closer to town.

Siân desperately wished she had a few more weeks of freedom. To be allowed to sing and play with the children, to ride the horses lent her by the castle grooms, to swim in the cold waters of the lake... She lowered her eyes in resignation. All too soon, she would travel to St. Ann's, where she would be far removed from everything familiar, from all that was dear to her.

She knew little of nunneries, only the stories she'd gleaned from different people over the years, and Siân had no reason to doubt what she'd heard. She was certain, for example, that the abbess would lock her in a ''cell'' every night to sleep on a narrow bed of straw. She'd heard that nuns had their hair chopped off and their bald heads covered by tight, ugly wimples that firmly bound their chin and cheeks. Siân assumed she would be compelled to wear a hot, itchy under-kirtle that would chafe her sensitive skin, and she would be required to spend hours upon hours on her knees, praying for the salvation of souls all across Britain.

But the most dreadful thing was that she would have to put all thoughts of Hugh Dryden out of her mind. Siân wasn't sure if that was going to be possible. The man had plagued her thoughts ever since shooting the boar out from under her in the forest. He had saved her life, and she wasn't about to forget him…or the way her heart seemed to skitter when he was near.

She shivered slightly when she recalled the way Hugh had efficiently unlaced her soaking gown that first night, then wrapped her in his own blanket. Siân had never experienced such remarkable sensations before. It was as if he had somehow reached inside her and kindled a mysterious fire within. Parts of her body became exquisitely sensitive, and he had barely even touched her.

His hands were strong, but gentle. His words curt, but not unkind. At least, he'd been kind until she'd thoughtlessly spoken of losing a limb. Clearly, he did not need *her* to teach him about such loss. She deserved the harsh words he'd delivered to her last night during the storm.

With a heartfelt sigh, Siân gathered the children around her and they sat together on a blanket of dry leaves under an ancient oak tree. She had to stop thinking of Hugh and truly resign herself to her fate at St. Ann's.

Owen's decision was final. Siân had no choice in the matter.

"In my country, there is a place called Llanfabon, where the faeries like to make mischief," Siân said as one of the older girls sat down and began to plait her hair. Another child picked wildflowers and threaded them into Siân's russet tresses. "And in Llanfabon, there once lived a widow woman and her small son, Pryderi."

By telling the old tale, Siân hoped to get her wayward thoughts under control. It was no use thinking of Hugh Dryden or his heroic rescue—not only of her, but of Clairmont itself. He was remote and aloof, always so serious, Siân thought. Surely *he* had not been afire the night he'd gotten her out of her wet clothes. Siân knew she was not likely to inspire any sort of longing in a man.

Siân tamped down her irrational sense of defeat and continued her tale. "One day, while the widow was making her little son's breakfast, she heard a commotion outside. The cattle were lowing down in the byre. Pryderi's mother was afraid something was amiss."

"What could it be?" a little girl asked.

"'Twas a wolf!" cried one of the boys.

"No…" Siân said dramatically. "Remember, there were faeries in that part of the country…"

Which started a flurry of questions about faeries and whether or not they could be seen nearby, and if ever they caused mischief among the cows and pigs at Clairmont. The children crowded around her and plied her with their queries, so preoccupied that none of them took note of the knight who'd walked up behind them.

Hugh delayed his return to Clairmont to tell Siân to move in closer to the town with the children since there could still be danger lurking in the outlying forest. He'd intended to speak to her right away, but instead, kept his silence as he approached her and the children, unwilling to put a stop to the sound of her engaging voice and her pleasing Welsh accent.

She continued her story as the children sat spellbound. "When the poor mother returned to their cottage, she was suspicious that something had changed. '*Och,* child,' she cried, 'you look like my sweet Pryderi, yet you are somehow different. I fear it is not really *you* I see before me.'

"The child, who *was* different, awakened. He said, 'Of course it is I, Mother. Who else would I be?'"

One of the little girls interrupted the story. "Did the faeries take Pryderi from his mother?"

"Did they give her a changeling?" another asked.

"The poor old mother did not know for certain," Siân replied. "But the only way she knew to find out, was to ask the wise man of the village…"

Hugh leaned his back against a tree and watched as Siân wove her magical spell for the children. She was a gifted storyteller, he thought as she changed her voice and moved her delicate hands to emphasize parts of the story. His earlier impression of Lady Siân as a faerie sprite was not too far from reality, and he found himself falling under the spell of that voice, those hands.

And as he stood there, enveloped in the enchantment of the moment, Hugh wondered how it would feel if she were to touch him. Not the competent touch of a healer to his wound, as she'd been last night, but the soft caress of a feisty red-haired woman who wept with abandon in private, and laughed without restraint in the company of children.

"…and the boy's mother sought the counsel of the old wise man once more," Siân continued. "'You must perform a difficult task,' the old man told her. 'Search out and find a hen as black as night, whose feathers reflect no light. Close up your cottage, block the doors and windows, but leave the chimney open. Make a fire, and cook the hen over it…'"

The tale went on to its happy ending, and it wasn't until Siân had reunited the hapless Pryderi with his mother that the children noticed Hugh in the shadows near the oak tree. They were instantly wary of the man with the black eye patch.

"'Tis Lord Alldale," Siân said, as startled by his arrival as the children. Recovering quickly, she arose from her seat beneath the spreading oak tree. "'Twas he who saved me from the fierce boar who would have *gored* me with his tusks…" she grabbed the smallest boy and twirled him around as he giggled with glee "…and eaten me all up!"

Hugh warmed inexplicably as he watched Siân spin with the child, her face flushed, her skirts billowing out all around her. He cleared an odd thickness from his throat and approached the small group. "Lady Siân, it would be well for you to stay closer to the town."

"Why, my lord?" she asked, her innocent eyes full of questions.

Hugh hesitated. He saw no reason to take the joy out of her day. "Only because…it looks as if it wants to storm again," he finally said.

Siân looked up at the sky.

He was right. Rain *was* coming. She smiled warmly. It was considerate of him to come out and forewarn her.

"*Vraiment,* I am flattered, Lord Alldale," Marguerite said in response to Hugh's proposal of marriage.

And flustered, Hugh thought, although her excellent breeding was evident in her tact and poise. There was hardly any indication that she found his offer of marriage untoward. A mere flaring of nostrils, a twitch of the lips, a slight flush of color on those high cheeks… Hugh only noticed these subtle signs because he was more aware than most, after enduring so many politely averted gazes and disdainful glances.

Hugh's face had once been a pleasing one. In those earlier days, he'd been satisfied with his lot, quick to meet a challenge or to stand for his friends. His company had been sought in battle as well as in the public house.

Though he'd never had the kind of looks that made women swoon, there had been no dearth of beauties to grace his bed in those days, he thought morosely. Not that he'd want any of the shallow and vain creatures near him now. He'd seen too many women pale and weaken at the sight of his scars and the leather eye patch. He knew their grimaces came with the mere thought of a touch from his mangled hand...and how he'd gotten it.

Marguerite sat on a comfortable chair in her solar, while Hugh remained standing, free to wander the room as he chose. He refused to be discomfited by the situation, by her reserve. He was certainly aware that he was no longer pleasant to look upon, that a beautiful woman like Marguerite would have some difficulty with the notion of spending her future shackled to a man with his disfigurements.

Hugh had adjusted. He would never again be the man he was two years ago, but he was a man, nonetheless. Strong again. Capable. Marguerite could do worse for a husband. He was no pauper, to go begging for favors of a wealthy widow! He had Alldale, a prosperous estate that belonged to him alone.

The lady took a sip of wine from a delicate silver chalice, biding a few moment's time. She cleared her throat before speaking again.

"As you might know," she said haltingly, "I have received two, um, additional offers of marriage."

"I'd heard." And didn't particularly care. *Just choose,* he thought, *and we can get on with it one way or another.*

"My parents are dead," Marguerite added. "I have no one close by to advise me."

"Her Majesty, the Queen?"

"We are good friends, yes," she replied, "but she has counseled me to write my uncle in Lyons for his advice and...perhaps his consent."

"I see."

"And, um, I must also request the permission of the council in London. They have certain requirements—"

"Yes, I know all about the council's requirements," Hugh said, standing now with his back toward Marguerite. *This was impossible! Why had he ever agreed to coming to Clairmont?* He turned to face her, and managed to speak calmly. "I doubt you will find any objections from that quarter, but I grant you time to make your wishes known to them."

"Thank you, my lord," Marguerite said timidly. "You are most generous."

"If you do not mind," he said, "I will remain here at Clairmont until you have made your decision."

"It is not entirely my decis—"

Hugh held up one hand. "Whatever the case may be," he said, "if it is of no inconvenience, I will stay."

"You are welcome to remain here, my lord," Marguerite said, regaining her usual courtesy and aplomb. "Of course."

Hugh was well aware that Marguerite considered his marriage proposal only because he'd proven himself in battle, not because of any desire to wed him. Though her etiquette had been impeccable, Hugh knew the lady had won herself some time by requesting his patience as she asked her uncle and any other counselors for advice—time in which to prepare herself for a marriage that Hugh knew would be nothing but distasteful to her.

In spite of what Hugh sensed of Marguerite's feelings toward him, he resolved to stay at Clairmont to await Marguerite's decision, rather than returning to Windermere, or going to his own estate at Alldale. He and Nicholas would begin training with the Clairmont men, working with sword and lance, on horseback at the quintain, and with bow and arrow. They had already organized patrols to scour the countryside to ensure that all was secure, and had gone back to spend the rest of the day in town, helping the men with some of the heavy tasks that needed doing before rebuilding.

It was late afternoon by the time Hugh returned to Castle Clairmont, and he walked out to Marguerite's garden to enjoy the last minutes of sunlight in peace. The open spaces, the unlimited sky above, were comforting to his soul, as always.

There was much to do in Clairmont and the activity invigorated Hugh. It was an unfamiliar sensation—working toward a purpose, pursuing definite objectives. He was bone-tired, and it felt surprisingly good.

Sitting down on a stone bench, Hugh enjoyed the whisper of a cool breeze on his face. The busy sounds of the castle and all the activity on the grounds were distant now, and Hugh relaxed, shutting out his past completely. He tried to imagine Clairmont as his home. He thought of walking these parapets, patrolling these borders for the rest of his life. Of living here with Marguerite.

"Maman! Regarde!"

Hugh looked up sharply and saw *petit Henri* running toward him, smiling happily.

The little fellow ran across the lawn ahead of a group

of adults, and climbed up onto Hugh's lap, making the weary man sit up and brace himself against the little king's sharp knees as they dug into his thighs.

"Lord Alldale," the queen said, arriving with her entourage. "Do not rise," she added, noting her son's contentment on Hugh's lap. "It is a beautiful afternoon for a stroll, *non?*"

Hugh agreed with Her Majesty. The sky had cleared after the earlier rain, and the breeze was comfortably cool. He was fatigued, but satisfied after a productive day. However, the peace of the afternoon was now gone with the crowd of courtiers upon him, including Owen Tudor and his sister.

Lady Siân wore the bright yellow gown she'd ripped in the woods on the day of her encounter with the boar. The bodice—where it had been torn—had been cleverly repaired, so as to be hardly noticeable at all. Except that Hugh could not forget the way it had appeared that morning, torn to expose an exquisite wealth of tempting but forbidden skin.

Calming his wayward thoughts, Hugh decided that the color suited her—it was bright and sunny, innocent and open. Just like the woman.

Her hair was tamed this afternoon, as well, though Hugh doubted there were any pins in the kingdom that could hold those riotous coppery tresses in place for long. He wondered, in passing, what had happened to the crown of flowers she'd been wearing in the copse that morning.

"There is much training to be done with Clairmont's knights, *non?*" the queen asked as she sat down on the bench with Hugh.

"They're in good shape, Your Majesty," Hugh said, "but they lack leadership."

Catherine's appraisal of him was speculative. By now, Hugh figured she knew of his marriage proposal. She knew his history, his strengths. Marguerite Bradley was Catherine's very good friend, and it was certain that the queen wanted to see the lady well married. Mayhap even happily married.

"You, Lord Alldale, could provide that leadership for Clairmont."

Hugh acquiesced wordlessly.

"I have no doubt that your knightly skills are excellent," Catherine said. "You were one of my husband's premier lieutenants in France. *Henri* could never abide incompetence."

"Siân!" the little king cried out when the lady came into his line of vision. The boy wriggled around on Hugh's lap and raised his arms to be picked up by the young Welsh woman who suddenly caught his fancy.

Siân smiled and took the child from Hugh's arms, using the Welsh pet name she'd given him. *"Parry!"* she said as she hugged him while the king giggled with glee. Hugh could not tear his sight from Siân as she kissed the little boy's neck. His own neck heated unaccountably.

"You have healed from your ordeal at Windermere?" Catherine asked, drawing Hugh's attention sharply away from the lively young woman and child.

Emotions warred within him. No one spoke of the atrocities committed at Windermere, at least not within his hearing. Nor was he interested in discussing them *now*. Not while Siân Tudor's hands tickled, and her lips nuzzled the little boy in her arms.

Hugh finally gathered his composure, inclined his head slightly, and replied, "Yes, Your Majesty. Fully recovered."

Petit Henri chortled merrily and buried his face in Siân's well-rounded bosom.

Blood pounded in Hugh's ears. He stood abruptly. "My injuries were mostly superficial. As you can see, I have adjusted."

"Of course, Alldale," the queen said, frowning, looking up at Hugh. "I would never imply otherwise."

"Your Majesty...I...apologize," Hugh said uncomfortably, "for being brusque—"

"Nonsense," Catherine interjected as she rose from the bench to stand next to Siân and her gleeful son. "You are quite obviously fit. I should never have questioned it. Tell me," she said, changing the subject abruptly, "what is your assessment of Clairmont town?"

"They lost many men, Your Majesty," Hugh said. "And—"

"Rebuilding will be difficult, Your Majesty," Siân interjected as she moved closer to the queen and Hugh. "Robert Beak—the master carpenter—was killed in the battle."

"Oh? Does Lady Marguerite know of this?"

"I don't know," Siân said. "But so many other men were killed that the fall plowing will be difficult. There is still a great deal of autumn work to be done to ensure enough food through the winter. Threshing is not an easy task. Nor are plowing and planting the winter wheat."

"Siân, what do you know of this work?" the queen asked, furrowing her brow curiously.

Siân, embarrassed for speaking out, realized it was too late to stop now. Owen would surely take her to task for her forward manner, and for telling the queen of her humble background. "Everyone in my village worked, Your Majesty," she said. "Even the men from the manor house. When *we* were attacked...and men were killed..." There was a flash of something sharp and angry in her eyes. "...the people suffered a lack of food, for there was no one to work the fields, mill the grain."

"And what then, Siân?"

No point in holding back now, Siân thought as she dove right in. Bluntly. "People starved to death, Your Majesty. Especially the little ones," she said sadly as her hands unconsciously caressed Henry's head.

The dream was never far away.

Hugh felt the chains around his wrists, the manacles that held his ankles to the cold, dank floor. It was dark and smelled of death in that place, that horrible place where pain and terror ruled.

Waiting.

Burning.

A light skittering across legs and feet. Tiny yellow eyes peering, razor teeth nipping, tearing.

Burning. Sharp pain. Exquisite pain!

A voice nearby...always the voice of the old woman...unintelligible gibberish. Moaning, crying. Reciting nonsensical verse.

Blood. It was everywhere. He could smell it, taste its metallic character. Feel its sticky sweetness as it flowed.

Fingers...smashed. Oh, Jesus, Mary and Joseph...his hand!

Eyes now... Please, no! Not the eyes!

Hugh gave a strangled cry and sat up in his bed, sweat pouring from his face, dripping off his chest. Swaying now, panting, working to catch his breath, he pulled the bed curtains back and lit a candle, only to cause ominous shadows to be thrown about the room.

He stood up, took the bedside taper and lit every other candle he could find, finally dispelling most of the shadows. Shivering, Hugh picked up a cloth and wiped himself dry, then threw some wood on the fire, lighting it once again. After the fire caught, he sat down in the comfortable chair near the hearth, and tried to call up pleasing thoughts to dispel the terrible aura of the dream.

Siân Tudor came to mind first.

Bright, coppery hair. Dazzlingly sunny smile.

Hugh had thought her merely a whimsical child. Her words the previous afternoon, however, had shown that she was not. There was more to Siân Tudor than misty forests and faeries, though. In spite of her words about attacks on her village, and starving children, Hugh could not imagine any darkness resting within the untouched purity of Siân's soul.

Chapter Five

At eventide the following day, Nicholas persuaded Hugh to join in the formal supper that had taken two days for the castle cooks to prepare, and would be attended by the queen and all her retinue.

"You cannot continue going about ignoring Lady Marguerite," Nicholas had said with irritation. "You just proposed marriage. At least *appear* to be interested."

"I *am* interested," Hugh protested darkly. "I asked for her hand, did I not?"

Nicholas, seeming to Hugh to be unduly perturbed, turned and skulked angrily out of the room. Nick was giving far too much weight to this whole proposal, Hugh thought.

While a close allegiance with the new lord of Clairmont would be beneficial to Nicholas, and Wolf Colston, and several other neighboring lords, it was not essential. If Marguerite accepted another proposal, another husband, then so be it. The neighboring landowners could make an ally out of Marguerite's new choice. And Hugh would then make the journey to

Alldale—a trip he now realized he'd delayed too long already—and become lord of his own demesne.

Grumbling anew over his "command performance" in the great hall, Hugh dressed in clean doublet and chausses. He knew Marguerite could deal with the festivities very well on her own. She had no need of him, nor would she, he imagined, after they were wed.

Once he took Marguerite to wife, and Hugh had no doubt that the lady would be advised to choose *him*, Hugh would put an end to all this frivolous nonsense, as there was no need for it. The incessant parties at Clairmont would stop.

He would fulfill his husbandly duties, and his lady wife would be required to ask no more of him.

Siân loved a party.

All of the queen's ladies were dressed in their finest gowns, and one of them lent Siân a beautiful violet kirtle. The gown was exquisitely detailed with fine, white bone buttons that fastened up the front, fitting it tightly to her torso and hips. Its long, flowing sleeves were lined in multicolored, contrasting stripes. Siân had never owned anything so fine or stylish, and she savored every moment wearing it, vowing to be careful not to spill anything, or to trip over the hems of her sleeves.

One of Queen Catherine's maids arranged Siân's hair in a simple but elegant coif, and placed small tufts of dried flowers in the shining, russet mass. The queen herself gave Siân a fine gold pendant to wear about her neck, and Owen grudgingly allowed her to wear their father's ring which bore the Tudor crest on it. Owen had to admit that his sister was lovely, even if she *was* destined for the nunnery.

That was a fact that Siân intended to forget for the evening. It would be her last soirée before going to St. Ann's, and Siân intended to enjoy every minute of it. She would feast on Clairmont's superb cuisine, join in the card games and other amusements, and dance to her heart's content. Afterward, she would go to her bed knowing she had savored all the small joys she was to be allowed in this lifetime.

Owen escorted her into the hall, which was brightly lit and festively decorated. Queen Catherine's minstrels were already playing fiddle and lute, psaltery and harp. A couple of handsome young men sang in harmony to the musicians' accompaniment as the lords and ladies began to gather for the victory feast.

Nicholas soon escorted the queen into the gathering, then Siân's breath caught as Hugh Dryden appeared with Lady Marguerite in hand.

"What is it?" Owen asked.

"Ah… 'Tis nothing, Owen," Siân replied evenly, averting her eyes from the noble pair. Hugh was so striking tonight, so dangerously appealing, her heart pounded just at the sight of him. Nothing could come of her attraction to that dark and solitary man and Siân did not intend to invite further censure by saying anything of it to Owen.

It would be enough just to spend the evening here, in the great hall with Hugh, perhaps to speak to him later. Siân knew that a person of her own lowly stature could not hope to gain more than the passing attention of the devilishly intriguing hero of Clairmont.

The evening progressed satisfactorily for Siân, with no serious mishaps at table and no awkward breeches of protocol. Siân's tablemates were pleasant enough, though she felt the young men from London were still too forward with her. In the past, whenever she mentioned their behavior to Owen, he accused her of overreacting, of making more out of their actions than was warranted. He'd questioned how she could fault them for wanting to be friendly.

And perhaps Owen was right. Mayhap she was being unreasonable, for she knew so little of courtly ways. Nor was she accustomed to much male attention—the families of Pwll had painfully learned the cost of friendship with a Tudor. Though they hadn't completely shunned her, they'd certainly made sure no one became overly friendly. And Siân herself knew enough to keep herself apart after the tragic deaths of Idwal and Dafydd, not wanting to further endanger the townspeople who'd taken her in after her father's death.

As a result, she didn't really know what to make of these courtiers' attentions. She'd taken pains to avoid them since coming to Clairmont, but that wasn't possible tonight, since she was seated with Dwayne Morton, the worst roué of them all. Fully aware that it was up to her to avoid any trouble this night, and to overlook her companions' boldness, Siân was determined to make the most of the evening.

After all, she had not much time until St. Ann's claimed her.

The seating formalities at the main dais were complex, with Queen Catherine at the center of it all. Lady Marguerite was situated between Nick and Hugh. The other lords and ladies of Catherine's party were then arranged according to rank, all the way down the table.

Hugh gave his attention to his meal, indifferent to the French chatter going on all around him, leaving Nicholas to tend to Marguerite's needs since she was seated on his blind side and he couldn't easily see her. Siân Tudor was seated right in his line of vision, along with two noblewomen and three of the useless dandies who'd traveled from London with the queen.

Hugh's brow furrowed in puzzlement. Why had he never before noticed the elegant line of Siân's neck, or the delicate hollow at her throat? Why did she look so graceful and refined now? Had her hair ever glinted fire the way it did just now, or did its intricate style make it glow that way? He frowned. Why did she not tame those undisciplined wisps of hair that sprung loose over her brow and before her ears?

He turned away, taking a long draught of ale, and tried to remember if she'd had those small dimples next to her mouth the other times he'd seen her.

He didn't think so.

The meal went on interminably for Hugh, who cast quick, assessing glances Siân's way. He didn't particularly like the way the young dandy sitting opposite, leered at her. And the other two fellows were just as bad, their eyes wandering where no chivalrous knight's should go.

Where, in the name of Christ, was the woman's brother? Hugh looked around for Owen Tudor, but the man was nowhere to be seen. Shouldn't he be keeping an eye on his sister? Shouldn't he have sent her back to her chamber to change into a more demure gown? One that did not show so much bare, sculpted shoulder, so much…chest?

The angry red scrape Siân had gotten the day he'd killed the boar was now merely a mild red abrasion. It did nothing to detract from the beguiling expanse of lush skin exposed above the closely fitted bodice of the gown she wore.

Hugh shifted uncomfortably in his chair. His mouth went dry. If the lady moved any farther forward, he had no doubt she would fall out of her gown. How could her brother allow her to dress in a manner that was so...

Hugh swallowed his mouthful of ale and removed his attention from Siân Tudor. How she dressed, and what men attended her, were not his concern. He would do well to try to participate in the conversation at his own table. Glancing over at Marguerite, however, he realized belatedly that his own lady fair wore a gown with a bodice cut similarly to Siân's. So did Queen Catherine. Yet the clothing of Marguerite and the queen did not seem nearly as revealing. The expanse of bared skin was not as provoking, not as...as disturbing...as Siân's.

Siân's eyes sparkled happily, naively, flashing deep blue. Hugh simmered unreasonably each time one of the courtiers at her table cut meat and offered it to her from his knife. *She had her own utensil, did she not?* he wondered with inordinate irritation as he watched her take the morsel between her full, moistened lips.

Hugh used one finger to pull the collar of his doublet away from his overheated neck and wished for an end to this interminable meal. He could see no reason for the footmen to continue stoking the fire, as it was plenty warm in the hall already.

The overdressed peacock sitting next to Siân grinned flirtatiously at her, then touched her chin and slid an arm around her waist as the toasting began, finally pushing Hugh's patience to the limit. He stood abruptly to leave the dais and protest the untoward familiarity of Siân's companion just as the applause and cheering started.

He looked at the faces around him and realized with dismay that *he* was being lauded as a hero. Looking back in Siân's direction, he saw that she was now standing with the rest of the assemblage—well out of the reach of the lecher next to her—and was holding up her goblet to him and smiling openly with utter delight.

To satisfy the crowd, Hugh took up his own drink and swallowed, disquieted by the homage of the unpretentious young woman who stood before him.

Several more toasts followed the first, and soon afterward, people followed the queen's lead, arising from their seats to mill around the hall. Finally, when Hugh was about to make his escape, he was waylaid by Sir George, who plied him with detailed questions regarding the battle.

Tables were cleared away and the musicians began to play a carole, spurring the guests to arrange themselves in a circle for the dance while Hugh spoke at length with Sir George, outlining plans for the future defense of Clairmont.

"I beg your pardon, my lord," Lady Marguerite said as she interrupted Hugh's discussion with the steward.

Hugh turned to give his full attention to the lady. He knew he'd been remiss at supper, but did not believe Marguerite minded his inattention. After all, there had been plenty of others at their table who could engage in the kind of lively conversation upon which courtly ladies thrived.

Hugh was not one of them, nor would he pretend to be.

"Please excuse me, my lord," she continued, quite uncharacteristically ill at ease. Her eyes did not rise to meet his, and she picked at a nonexistent flaw in the sleeve of her gown. "The hour grows old... Her Majesty and I would retire to our chambers now."

"I will escor—"

"S'il vous plait," she begged hurriedly, as though reluctant to spend more time in his company than necessary. Hugh cautioned himself not to jump to that conclusion. "Please. The queen's guards accompany us. It is not necessary for you to shorten your talk with Sir George."

As Marguerite made her retreat, Hugh clasped his hands behind his back and resumed his discussion with the steward, not unaware of the undercurrent of discomfiture between himself and his intended bride. The lady would have to come to terms with the idea of marriage to him, he thought, as he would to her. The notion was no more appealing to Hugh at that moment than it was to Marguerite, nor did Hugh believe it would ever be.

But his proposal was given, and he was committed. There would be no withdrawal of his offer.

The music and revelry continued about him. Many of the castle guests retired to smaller rooms and alcoves to play at cards or to gamble over the throw of the dice. Servers refilled his goblet with mulled wine.

In the glittering light of hundreds of candles, dancers arranged themselves in two long, graceful lines with partners across from each other, making intricate steps apace with the music, meeting in the center, then moving down the row.

The bright, lively music brought Siân to mind again. Hugh glanced about for her, but could not locate her among the throng. He did not see her brother, though it occurred to Hugh that Owen may have escorted Siân to her chamber. It was late and she was likely weary.

Just because she so openly enjoyed the celebration
didn't mean she wouldn't use good sense and hie herself off to bed.

Did it?

"Please let me by, Dwayne," Siân said to the young
nobleman who had become more of a pest this night
than he had in all the time she'd spent in London or
during their journey to Clairmont. He'd hovered over
her all evening, touching her improperly, and ignoring
her protests. She knew with a certainty now, that Owen
had been mistaken about him. His was no mere over-
ture of friendship. Though Siân sidestepped him every
time, it was becoming more and more difficult to be
civil as the evening progressed and he refused to leave
her alone.

Escaping Dwayne yet again, Siân tried to locate
Owen among the crowd, but he was not in sight—
nowhere near to help her. She did not want to leave
the gathering so early, but this persistent young man
was making it impossible for her to stay.

Downcast and resigned, she took a last sip of wine
before turning to leave, only to find Dwayne in front
of her yet again.

"Come outside to the courtyard with me," Dwayne
said, taking her arm.

"No, Dwayne," she protested, resisting his pulling.
"I will not leave with you."

"You wound me, Siân," he said over the music and
laughter in the hall. "Tease me all night, then say nay.
I—"

"No, Dwayne," Siân said, knowing full well she'd
only been polite—to him and everyone else. "Unhand
me, please, and let me by," Siân persisted.

He gave her what she supposed he thought was a seductive grin and tugged at her more firmly than before. "You're a saucy little minx," Dwayne mumbled as he pulled her out of the hall and dragged her into a darkened gallery. "Ever since you came to London, I've thought that you and I—"

"No! Leave me be!" Siân demanded as she dug in her heels.

Hugh felt he'd spent hours walking the parapets, inspecting the gatehouse and barracks, and looking over the armory with Sir George and a few of the Clairmont knights. He made suggestions for improvements and talked about new drills for the knights at the lists, and the men were anxious to implement his changes.

All the while, the lively music continued in the hall, making his skin prickle and all the hair on his body stand on end.

Hugh didn't know what had come over him. It wasn't like him to be so distracted, but he was having some difficulty keeping his attention on armaments and ramparts. He imagined the dancers in the hall, and visualized Siân Tudor dancing merrily with some courtly partner.

"If you wouldn't mind, my lord," George said, "I would ask that you speak to the men on the morrow. Explain the changes you recommend."

Hugh nodded once. That was a task he could handle with ease. Unlike putting Siân out of his thoughts.

"Until morning then, my lord," Sir George said as he walked toward his own quarters, leaving Hugh to climb the steps alone.

Hugh entered the hall and slipped through the crowd,

hoping to climb the stairs and reach his chamber before being stopped and diverted again.

But as he climbed the steps at one end of the hall, a disturbing sight met his eye. Lady Siân was being pulled along toward a far doorway, by the dandified peacock who had been at her table earlier. And Siân did not appear to be going with him willingly.

Hugh didn't give it a moment's thought, but acted instantly. Taking the steps with quick agility, he reached the landing and moved toward the arch where he'd last seen Siân. The music and dancing went on, and no one spoke to him as he made his way through the crowd.

With one hand on the hilt of his sword, Hugh exited the hall and stepped into the dim corridor. Five more steps brought him to the place where Siân stood fuming. Her companion suddenly lunged for her and Siân, just as quickly, threw the contents of her drink at the fellow.

"*Jésu* bloody *Christi,* Siân!" he bellowed. Then he took a swing at her.

Siân ducked, missing the blow, and started to make a run straight toward Hugh, who braced himself for their collision.

"Ogh!" she gasped as she crashed into him. Looking up at him, she quickly whispered, "*Mae'n chwith gen i,*" then darted behind him, holding on to his doublet and using him for a shield, muttering to herself all the while. Though none of Siân's thoughts seemed pieced together intelligibly, Hugh was able to hear a few disjointed words, a mix of English and Welsh.

There were tears in her voice, and anger, too. Hugh might even have found some humor in Siân's talent for trouble, but for the steaming young buck standing be-

fore him, the young scoundrel who'd have knocked
Siân flat with his fist had she not reacted so quickly.

Siân pressed herself up against Hugh's back,
wrapped her trembling arms around him from behind,
and said in a quiet, meek voice, "Don't leave me,"
she whispered, the desperate plea penetrating Hugh's
tough shell. "*Os gwelwch yn dda!* Don't leave me."

Hugh was immobilized for an instant by the impression of Siân's soft, womanly form pressing against his
back, her arms grasping his belly and chest. His breath
caught at once and he reined in a savage need to throw
her over one shoulder and carry her away.

Shocked by his fiercely physical response to her, and
damning himself for a fool, as a man who had risen
beyond such primitive needs and desires, Hugh braced
himself for the next threat against Siân's safety. He
would see to her defense, as would any knight worth
his armor, then remove himself from her presence.

The peacock stalked toward them, dripping of wine
and vengeance, until he saw that it was the earl of
Alldale whom he faced. Suddenly the courtier straightened up and smoothed out his ruined, multicolored
doublet as if there were nothing more than a speck of
dust on it. He began to speak, then apparently thought
better of it.

Hugh knew that even though Siân had the upper
hand now, by morning her reputation would be in
shreds. The fellow, clearly a man of very little honor,
would tell his cronies whatever suited him, in order to
assuage his pride. There had to be a way to keep the
brute from destroying her reputation.

Making the only decision possible, one that he did
not particularly relish, Hugh took hold of one of Siân's
trembling hands, placed it atop his own, then turned

and walked away from the man, escorting her back to the hall.

Siân glanced back over her shoulder to see Dwayne Morton's face contorted in rage. Frightened by his look, she quickly turned to face forward again, squared her shoulders and straightened her backbone. She had nothing to fear, after all, with Hugh Dryden to protect her.

Still, that didn't keep her knees from knocking or her eyes from welling with unshed tears. She'd been such an idiot again! Allowing Dwayne to ruin this special night—the last party she would ever attend! She blinked away the tears and proceeded through the dark corridor as she tried to compose herself. Siân knew she had no choice but to retire to her chamber for the night to avoid a scandal that would not only raise her brother's ire, but also make her an unacceptable candidate for St. Ann's.

With a heavily burdened heart, Siân followed Lord Hugh back to the music, to the dancing. She would have to walk through the hall to reach the stairs that led to her room but she was determined to hold her head high, to smile as though nothing untoward had happened.

When they reached the archway near the entrance to the hall, Hugh stopped her from going in. "Tame your hair, Siân," he said. "Else everyone will think I...that you and I..."

"Oh!" she exclaimed, surprised by his words. Her hair must be an awful sight for the earl to mention it, though it was terribly flattering that he believed anyone would mistake his interest in her. Scoundrels like

Dwayne Morton were the only ones who ever vied for her favors.

Siân turned away from Hugh and fumbled with the hairpins that held the unruly mass in place, then tried to draw it into some semblance of order. However, still shaken by the confrontation with Dwayne, her efforts were clumsy and of little avail.

"I—I don't think I can... It will not matter if I let it be..."

There was an impatient sigh behind her, and Siân suddenly felt Hugh's hands at her nape. Silently, he took over, and Siân let her own hands drop to her sides. His touch brought a sigh to Siân's lips, but she suppressed it, though she was unable to quiet the shiver that started in her scalp and radiated down her neck and across her shoulders.

His touch was gentle, and he took care not to pull any strands to cause her discomfort. Siân allowed herself, for the moment, to imagine that Hugh's kind touch meant more to him than a simple correction of her appearance. She wanted to believe that she was of some consequence to him...even while she knew that was a foolish fancy.

Hugh quickly realized that trying to repair Siân's coif was a mistake. As wild and untamed as it always seemed to be, he had never touched any silk as finely spun as the texture of her hair. Her loose curls smelled like wildflowers as they wrapped around his fingers, making him clumsy as he tried to pin them back in place, along with the little tufts of flowers that had shaken loose.

What did he know of women's hair, anyway? And what use would he ever have with the knowledge? His own lady wife would certainly have maids to attend her. Marguerite would never have any need of his assistance.

Exasperated, Hugh swallowed hard and tried to finish his task, even though he'd never felt so inept. Then Siân tipped her head in an unconsciously sensuous manner. Her elegant neck and a beguiling décolletage were now exposed to him from where he stood behind her, and Hugh bit back a groan.

He suddenly turned and pulled her into the hall. "Dance the farandole with me," he said, his voice gruff and abrupt.

Siân had no opportunity to refuse him, nor did she have any desire to do so. Dancing the steps, looking at the strong features of his face, basking in the touch of his hand…all these were things she had only dreamed of since she'd met him. But she was well past dreams now. Hugh had rescued her, and now he was making her the most important lady in the hall.

Hugh remained with Siân since Owen still had not returned to the hall. As Hugh watched Siân follow the intricate steps of the farandole, he thought her color improved. She was no longer quite so pale, and she'd finally stopped trembling. He sensed that she was beginning to enjoy the dance, even though *he* was exceedingly ill at ease.

At least none of the ladies cringed outwardly at his touch. No one gaped at his eye patch or his scars. The brute who'd accosted Siân was nowhere in sight, and if the man returned to the hall, Hugh doubted he'd attempt to try anything untoward again.

All was well for the moment.

Hugh only planned to stay a few minutes more. Owen would certainly return soon to keep track of his sister, then Hugh could reasonably leave. They might have a glass of wine together…perhaps another dance, but then he was going. There was no point in staying any longer. He didn't particularly *want* to stay any longer. After a long and trying day, he was weary, and he intended to seek his bed as soon as possible.

The only question was whether or not he'd be able to sleep once he got there. Hugh suspected that the fleeting scent of wildflowers might plague him throughout the night.

Chapter Six

All this excessive bathing would be the death of him, Hugh thought as he climbed the spiral stone stairs to Marguerite's solar. After a long, hard morning at the lists, he'd finally given in to Nicholas's coaxing. He would put some effort into wooing Marguerite.

Courtship. It was not a particularly appealing prospect, but Nicholas had nagged him about it like such an old woman that Hugh had finally resigned himself to getting on with it. He knew it would take some time for Marguerite to learn to be at ease with him, or at the very least, accustomed to him, so he resolved to spend more time in her company.

As Nicholas had very aptly pointed out—Hugh was not going to win Marguerite by avoiding her.

"Oh! Lord Alldale!" Marguerite gasped, dropping her needle as Hugh strode into the solar.

The minstrel stopped playing and the other ladies in the room looked up abruptly from the unfinished tapestry. Queen Catherine sat on a cushioned seat near the window, watching *petit Henri* as he played. She alone seemed unaffected by his arrival in the solar.

What was it? Hugh wondered as he looked at all the

startled feminine faces around him. Had he grown another nose? Or perhaps forgotten his eye patch? Was this always to be the reaction to his entrance into Marguerite's presence?

An awkward silence ensued until the queen spoke. "Lord Alldale," Catherine addressed him. "Come and join me."

Hugh approached the queen, and after bowing as courtesy demanded, sat down nearby on the rich, brocade cushion she indicated. The other ladies in the solar resumed their work and the minstrel began playing again. Serenity and order were restored. All was as it had been.

"Clairmont's soldiers are becoming much better disciplined," the queen said, "more agile, more… *raffiné*…euuh, refined in their skills. They needed a leader to give them direction."

Hugh shrugged in response. Plenty of men could lead Clairmont's troops. There was nothing particularly special about his own methods.

"Clairmont is quite pleasant, no?" she asked.

"Very…nice," Hugh replied with a shrug. He'd never been a great conversationalist, never having needed the skill before. He'd ridden with men all his life, lived with them, eaten and drunk with them. Fought with them. None had been excessive talkers.

Now, though, it seemed he had some adjustments to make. He was going to have to learn to deal with female company. Make conversation. Listen to chatter about needlework and fashion. Cooking. Babies.

Hugh didn't know if he was up to it.

"Lady Marguerite is a chatelaine whom any man would be proud to call wife."

"I am certain you are correct, Your Majesty." What

man in his right mind wouldn't want Marguerite? Beautiful, intelligent, charming. He supposed he should say something to that effect to the queen, but couldn't find the words that would express the thought correctly. Besides, Catherine already knew Marguerite's attributes. There was no need for Hugh to reiterate them.

"She always strove to be a good daughter and sister," Catherine said, "and, of course, a model wife to Richard Bradley. Now, though, Marguerite is in a position she has never enjoyed in her life."

Hugh raised an eyebrow. What in kingdom come was Catherine talking about now? He hadn't thought about Marguerite in any way other than as the chatelaine of a very wealthy estate. As an eligible widow in dire need of a husband with strong military skills.

"My friend has *freedom* now," the queen said, her voice soft and even. The French lilt was pleasing. "She is free—for the first time in her life—to make her own decisions. Free from the dictates and demands of a father or brother...or husband."

"Dictates?" Hugh asked, puzzled.

"You are a man," Catherine explained, "so it is difficult for you to understand, yes?"

Hugh frowned. What was there to understand? Men made decisions, ruled their families. Certainly a considerate and generous man would take into consideration the wishes of his wife and daughters when he made decisions affecting the family.

"You must be patient with Marguerite..." the queen said, interrupting Hugh's musings. "I do not doubt she will come 'round," Catherine added. "But it may take time."

Henry ran to his mother just then, and she picked him up. *"Il n'a qu'un oeil, maman,"* he said, pointing to Hugh's covered eye. Then he put two fingers into his mouth and gnawed toothlessly at them, drooling profusely all the while.

"*Oui*, little one," Catherine said. "But you must speak English. It is your duty to speak the language of our people." The queen looked up at Hugh. "Marguerite will also, no doubt, do her duty for *her* people."

Hugh thought about his discussion with the queen as he spent the next hour in Marguerite's solar, watching the ladies as they worked on the tapestry, exchanging stilted conversation with Marguerite and the rest of them.

He hated this. Hugh had no idea how to court his intended wife, or what to say to gain her interest. He supposed they could go over the account books of the demesne, but that would not really be appropriate until they were actually betrothed. They could speak of military matters, but Hugh didn't think Marguerite was more than superficially interested. As long as the knights were capable of defending Clairmont, that was all she wanted or needed to know. Management of the castle? On that subject, it was Hugh who cared little.

It made for a strained and awkward afternoon.

The days passed as Hugh awaited Marguerite's decision and he practiced tirelessly with sword and lance. Nicholas parried with him, as well as with Clairmont's other knights, as they all drilled and trained to be prepared to protect the town and castle from the next Scottish onslaught.

Men now regularly patrolled the perimeter of the demesne, and reported seeing ominous signs of intruders. Charred wood indicated small campfires. There were horse droppings. Matted grass. Hugh ordered an increase in the patrols.

Though the interlopers evaded being seen, Hugh warned the townspeople to be on their guard. It was hardly likely that a couple of stray men could do much damage, but caution never hurt.

Everyone in the castle knew of Siân Tudor's visits to town, and many marveled at her ability to engage the children in games, to keep them occupied while the adults made repairs, sorted foodstuffs, grieved. She helped many a young mother with her brood during those trying times, taking the little ones out to play in the late autumn sunshine. Many of Clairmont's aristocratic guests ridiculed her folly, criticizing her for engaging in such coarse and inferior activities.

The knights, however, seemed to enjoy seeing Siân with her group of little troopers on the hill, and the men whistled and waved to her whenever they were out in the countryside. Siân made sure to stay close to town, and the knights felt that she and the children were safe as long as they didn't wander too far afield.

While Hugh worked out with the other knights in the lists, his attention was repeatedly drawn to the hillside where Siân Tudor frolicked with the children. He forced himself to avoid thinking about the young woman, but unbidden thoughts of her entered his mind during unguarded moments.

He'd stayed away from her since the night of the celebration, the night he'd danced and drunk wine, and forgotten for a short time that he was a scarred man, an unworthy man, one whose only value lay in his ability to protect the Clairmont border.

Hugh wondered how long the queen's party, including Siân, would continue staying on at Clairmont. He hadn't heard of any plans for their departure, but considered that Castle Clairmont would become a rather dull place without the saucy Welsh redhead about.

The sound of her voice traveled fleetingly over the distance, catching his ear with her lively accent, and her expression of complete and utter abandon. Hugh couldn't remember how it felt to know such innocent joy. His own young life had been punctuated by a series of violent endings, then a continuum of drills, practice and military training, until he reached his majority and was knighted by Wolf Colston's German grandfather. He then joined Wolf and Nicholas to fight with King Henry in France, making his way by his sword and his wits. He'd returned to England some years later to help Wolf regain Windermere.

And lost all pride and honor in the process.

Turning away from the hillside with Siân and all the children, Hugh ran his hand across the whisker-roughened part of his face. He didn't have time for such foolishness. He gave orders to the men to pack up their equipment, and he returned to the castle with them for the midday meal.

The children were getting hungry. Siân had seen the signs of it, but she wanted to keep them away from town and out from underfoot for just a little while longer. As soon as the hammering and sawing stopped, she would take them back for their midday meal. For now, keeping them out of trouble seemed the least Siân could do while the townspeople rebuilt the structures destroyed by the Scots.

Besides, she enjoyed being with the children. She never felt isolated or alone when she was with them. They liked her, liked listening to her stories, and playing her games, laughing with her when she was silly, squealing when she startled them. She could be herself with them, and not have to put on the airs Owen wanted her to assume when she was with the high-and-mighty ladies of the castle.

"That's the way!" Siân called out to the children, laughing, clapping her hands with enthusiasm. "Catch those pesky butterflies in your hoods!"

"I've got one, Lady Siân!" little Meg cried.

"Is it really a faerie in disguise, Lady Siân?" another little girl asked.

"It's just all stories, muttonhead. There aren't no faeries," one of the older boys taunted the younger girl.

"Are, too!"

"See? They're all white, and shimmery!" Meg said. "They *must* be faeries!"

Sudden screams from the children behind Siân made her whirl around in dismay. A strange man—a warrior in plaid—had come out of the woods and sneaked up on them, only to grab one of the children and trot back to the woods with the boy.

Siân picked up a stick and ran after him, shouting for him to let the child go.

She was ignored by the Scotsman, who kept up his ungainly run toward the cover of the trees as he carried the kicking, screeching child.

Siân didn't think about any consequences, nor did she take note of the sudden, wild pealing of the church bell. She just continued her frantic pursuit of the man, whom she assumed had been one of the Scots involved in the skirmish of the previous week.

By the time the Scot got to the woods, Siân was practically upon him, and when he was finally within reach, she took the long stick she carried and used it to thwack him on the back of the legs. The Scotsman dropped the child. The man was not seriously hurt by her blow, merely taken aback, and he reached again for the boy, his dark eyes flashing dangerously.

"Run Davey," Siân cried, never taking her eyes from the massive warrior in front of her. "Run!"

The child scooted away and did as he was told, flying past Siân as fast as his short legs would carry him. Siân backed away from the Scotsman, but as she turned to run, she caught her foot in a mole hole and fell, giving the warrior the opportunity to grab her.

Instead, she rolled to the side and thrust the branch up again, swiping him brutally across the face. He reared back with a howl while Siân scrambled quickly to her feet.

The man recovered and made a grab for her, but Siân was too fast. She eluded him once again and darted in the direction of the town, but the big Scot blocked her way.

Clairmont's knights responded quickly to the alarm. When Hugh and the soldiers reached town, there was no need to stop for an explanation of the frantically clanging steeple bell. Tearful women hugged their children, and townsmen shouted and pointed to the woods. No further accounting was necessary.

Hugh led the men across the hillside, toward the dense forest, certain they would find the culprits who had been lurking in the area since the previous week's battle. They were unquestionably a threat to the townspeople, and it was up to Hugh and the rest of the knights to rout the interlopers from their hiding places and deal with them.

The ground showed recent signs of the intruders,

along with indications of a struggle. Assuming that one of the townspeople had gotten himself caught by the Scots, Hugh motioned the knights to spread out and blanket the area as they moved forward.

Deeper into the woods, a human cry pierced the silence. Hugh rode forward past a bramble thicket, and halted. He dropped from his horse, horrified to find Siân Tudor sitting crumpled on the ground, her skirts tangled in her legs, her knuckles scraped and nails torn.

"Siân!" he said, going to her.

She stifled a whimper with one bruised and scraped hand at her mouth.

"Siân, are you all right?" he asked, crouching next to her.

She nodded her reply, and added tremulously, "There are two m-men, my lord. One is on horseback, the other on foot."

"Sir John," Hugh said, turning to speak to the knight, "take the lead. Run them to ground."

"'Twill be a pleasure, my lord," the knight responded as he led the rest of the men deep into the forest.

"Siân, you are certain you are unharmed?" The color was gone from her face, even from her lips, and Hugh could not face the thought that she suffered from some unseen wound.

She shook her head again, denying any injury. "One of them c-came out of the woods. He grabbed little Davey Blue and I—I chased them."

"Siân—"

"He would have harmed the child, Hugh," she continued shakily, explaining her actions as though she expected a rebuke for helping the boy. "There was no one else nearby. So I h-had to help him get a-away."

Relief and tenderness flooded Hugh as he picked a dried leaf out of her disheveled hair. "Of course."

"Davey ran, but the S-Scotsman tried to get him again," she continued, a little confused by his apparent endorsement of her actions. "So I hit him. W-with a piece of oak."

"You hit the Scot?" Hugh repeated as he helped her to stand. She was shaky, but he resisted a foolish urge to hug her close to him, to share his heat and security. More appropriately for a betrothed man, he put a supportive arm around her waist and walked her to his horse. He gave her a boost onto the mare, then mounted behind her. Daring to hold Siân just enough to keep her steady, they rode slowly through the woods, toward town.

Her impulsiveness and audacity should not have surprised him. She was a brave and spirited lass with a great deal of heart, and he admired that in her. Not many women of his acquaintance would have gone off single-handedly to rescue the child.

"The boy got away?" he finally asked.

Siân nodded and fitted her body to his chest, relishing the warmth of his body, the security of his arms around her waist. A shiver went through her. "Aye," she said, a little breathlessly. "But the man managed to grab me. And then his cohort arrived on horseback. I—I thought I'd never... I mean, I didn't know if anyone would c-come in time."

"*Were* we on time, Siân?" Hugh asked. "You are truly unharmed?"

She nodded, and felt the air go out of him, and wondered if it was relief she felt in his body. The thought warmed her, though she knew better than to give too much importance to it. Still, she allowed herself to rel-

ish the heat of his breath on her cheek, the sense of his
strong thighs next to hers, even if it was just for this
moment. "When the Scots heard riders, they released
me and ran."

"On one horse?"

"No," Siân replied. "The man on horseback
brought a second mount with him."

He still hadn't berated her for running after the lad,
and Siân wondered when he would get around to it.
Instead, he held her close as they rode, steadied her as
she told her tale. She turned to look at him. His nose
was a mere inch from hers, his lips a breath away. A
slight sway of the horse could cause their lips to meet,
though he looked as if he might actually *want* to kiss
her.

"Do you hear riders?" Hugh asked softly, interrupting the thoughts and feelings coursing through her.

Siân realized then that she *did* hear them, although
she'd thought the sound was the pounding of her heart.

"There," he said, dragging his gaze away from her
soft mouth, "in the clearing up ahead."

"It's Owen!" she said, and Hugh felt her body
stiffen against his.

Owen Tudor, with a small group of knights, met
them halfway. "Greetings, Lord Alldale," Owen said,
frowning. If he had any concern about the well-being
of his sister, he did not show it. His expression merely
reflected disapproval of the condition of her clothes and
hair. "The queen and Lady Marguerite are anxious to
know the cause of that infernal bell-clanging."

"The Scots who were lurking in the woods came
out of hiding," Hugh explained. "Lady Siân rescued
a child from being taken by the men and was
nearly—"

"God's blood, Siân!" Owen groaned. "What in the name of—"

"Tudor," Hugh said calmly, but with a clear warning in his voice. "Your sister has just been through a difficult ordeal. I suggest you withhold your criticism for now, at least until she is safely returned to Clairmont."

The man's jaw clenched. He looked at his sister. "Dismount, Siân," he said, "and *I* will carry you back to Clairmont."

Hugh tightened his hold on Siân. "She is secure here, Tudor. We will ride as we are to the castle."

Owen's features darkened, but his tone remained polite and controlled. "My lord, as Siân is my sister and my responsibility, I must insist. It is unseemly for a maiden destined for the cloister to ride in this manner with a man who is of no relation."

"Cloister?" Hugh choked, unable to believe his own ears. "Siân is…she is to join a cloister?"

Owen gave a curt nod. "My sister is promised to the Abbey of St. Ann at Tyndale."

Siân seemed to sink in front of him.

"'Twas my intention to depart Clairmont in the morning, and begin our journey to the abbey," Owen continued. "But plans have changed."

Hugh's thoughts reeled. He was appalled. *A nunnery!* How could Owen Tudor have such little understanding of his sister? How could he sentence this vibrant, passionate creature to a life of silent penance behind cloistered walls?

If ever there was any woman unsuited to a life of quiet prayer, it was Siân. She, of all people, should wed a man who would appreciate her vibrancy, and be surrounded by laughing children. She should wear bright colors, run with the wind, sing and dance the caroles, the farandole....

Swallowing his ire, Hugh dismounted and assisted Siân to do the same.

"We've just received word," Owen said, "that the bishop of Winchester, Henry Beaufort, is due to arrive at Castle Clairmont either tonight or sometime on the morrow."

The news penetrated Hugh's dark thoughts. Bishop Beaufort was a cunning ecclesiastic, greedy for political power. His presence at Clairmont did not bode well for Queen Catherine.

Owen lifted Siân onto his horse, then mounted behind her. As Hugh stood aside and watched, part of a conversation he'd had with Queen Catherine niggled at the back of his mind. It had something to do with freedom...Lady Marguerite's freedom to choose her own fate.

It was a luxury Siân Tudor did not have.

Chapter Seven

Hugh stood before the fireplace in a small room off the great hall of the castle, and assumed that Siân had been asleep for hours. His thoughts returned repeatedly to the spirited young woman as the others in the room discussed Bishop Henry Beaufort's reasons for broaching Castle Clairmont, uninvited.

Still unable to adjust to the idea of Siân in a cloister, Hugh spent the evening in a dark and distracted mood, racking his brain to think of a reasonable option for her, an option that he might propose for Owen's consideration. The best alternative was marriage. Surely there was someone who matched Siân's noble rank, a man who had enough wealth that he would not require a substantial dowry as a prerequisite to marriage.

But who?

Hugh thought of several men, but dismissed each one as they came to mind. Only a particular sort of man could partner Siân Tudor. Her husband would have to be tolerant of noise and disorder, and be willing to sire a houseful of children. The man would need a lust for life, as well as a passion for his wife.

He would also have to be gentle with her, for Hugh

sensed a softness in Siân that she strove to keep hidden. The man would need to be patient, for Siân was not a particularly biddable woman. A sense of humor would be essential, as well as a strong physical constitution, for Hugh knew with a certainty that Lady Siân Tudor would likely try any man's endurance over time.

"...but you can rest assured he's not coming merely for a friendly visit to the farthest reaches of the kingdom," Owen said, breaking into Hugh's thoughts.

"My husband's uncle craves power," Catherine said. "It is what he lives to attain, nothing more, nothing less. But he is..." she searched for the word "...*malin.*"

"Devious," Nicholas said, and the queen assented.

"His aim is to control little Henry," Owen said.

"To what purpose?" Marguerite asked, her pretty brow furrowed in puzzlement. "The Parliamentary Council rules all England until Henri reaches his majority. What can Bishop Beaufort possibly hope—"

"The nobleman who weds Her Majesty will likely gain control over Henry," Owen said. "It is important that no man be given such power to wield..."

"But what nobleman would...? I am afraid I am lost," Marguerite said. "How does Bishop Beaufort's visit win Her Majesty's favor? She has left London on more than one occasion to escape his influence, and he knows it!"

Hugh knew the answer. "The bishop has chosen a husband for Her Majesty," he said, certain of his statement. After all, he'd just spent the better part of an hour ruminating on a suitable spouse for Siân Tudor. The idea was not at all foreign to him. "And Beaufort intends to see the marriage carried out before Council can object."

Everyone remained silent, as if in shock.

"I fear you are correct, Lord Alldale," Tudor finally remarked, clasping his hands behind his back in agitation.

"Well," Queen Catherine said. "He has never tried *that* before."

"I wonder who it will be," Marguerite pondered quietly, almost to herself.

"And whether His Eminence has brought the bridegroom along," Nicholas said.

The night was too cool to extinguish the fire completely, but Siân let it die down in the grate so there was less light in the chamber. Less light to see by. She didn't burn any candles, either, afraid of displaying her plainness and her ineptitude too clearly. For while she was determined in this endeavor, she was nervous.

Uncertain exactly how to proceed, Siân loosened her hair, allowing it to cascade freely down her back. It was clean now, and she'd rubbed it with some of the flower-water she made, so it smelled fresh, like summer. She sat down and removed her shoes, then unbuttoned the bodice of her gown, letting it drop into a dark heap on the floor. Then she stood near the fire in her fine linen under-kirtle.

And tried to keep from shaking.

Should she remove her underclothes and climb onto the bed fully naked, she wondered, or remain standing near the fire in her linens?

Perhaps she should stand near the fire *without* her linens.

Either way, she was determined to seduce Hugh Dryden, here. In his chamber.

Standing, as she was, on the threshold of an interminably solitary existence in the convent, Siân had decided to experience one night of passion. One night to experience the forbidden. She would ask for nothing more before she departed the secular world to enter the cloister of St. Ann's.

Only one night. With Hugh.

Hugh had decided that Nicholas Becker would be Siân's husband. Nick just didn't know it yet.

Becker was exceptionally good-looking, as well as patient and tolerant, and usually in good humor. Besides, as Viscount Thornton, he had no need of more land or possessions, so no dowry was necessary. He was a lusty fellow, too, so there was no doubt he'd beget children enough for her.

But that was the trouble. Hugh didn't care for the thought of any man—even Nicholas Becker—touching Siân. His harebrained idea of marrying her off settled about as well as sending her to St. Ann's. Hugh climbed the stairs and walked toward his chamber, and felt like punching something. A wall, mayhap. Why in kingdom come had she burst in on his life, with her reckless, frivolous ways? How had those damnable eyes of hers, with their mischievous glances and haunted looks, hooked him so?

And why did he feel so driven to set her future to rights?

If Bishop Beaufort hadn't been expected in the next day or so, Hugh vowed he'd have left Clairmont; left all and sundry to their own devices. What business did he have, anyway, thinking to meddle in the plans Owen had made for Siân? Owen was her brother, after all, the *only* man responsible for her. By all means, let her go to the nunnery! Let her live a long and pious life behind the—

A startled gasp and the crash of a shattered clay pitcher greeted Hugh Dryden as he thrust open the door to his chamber.

Hugh had his sword out and was on the attack before he realized that the intruder was none other than the woman who haunted his thoughts. Luckily, he halted before harming her as she stood half naked before him, in a puddle of spilled water and broken clay.

Standing a mere foot away from her, Hugh's physical reaction was instantaneous. Every thought and question drifted away as he gaped at Siân—her blushing cheeks and downcast eyes, her crown of defiantly unruly hair, lips that were full and soft, doubtlessly capable of giving endless pleasure. The hardened peaks of her lush breasts were clearly visible through the thin cloth of her shift.

Unable to resist her, Hugh groaned and took one step toward her.

Looking up, Siân's deep, sensual eyes met his hot, pale blue gaze. The muscles of her throat tightened as she swallowed nervously. Her hands knotted in the fabric of her under-kirtle and she took a deep breath, causing her breasts to move tantalizingly against the thin cloth that covered them.

Her lips parted.

Drawn, like a starving man to a feast, Hugh took another step.

Broken clay crunched under his feet.

"What are you doing here, Siân?" asked Hugh. With common sense dawning, his voice was quiet and dangerous; his visage dark.

Siân let out the breath she'd been holding and looked

away from him. What now? She hadn't planned on having to explain her naked presence in his chamber. She'd thought she was obvious. Hoped he'd understand what she had in mind without having to define her intent.

Embarrassment replaced nervousness and she started to step away, only to be stopped by Hugh's firm hand on her arm. "Don't move," he said. "You'll cut your feet."

Siân was quickly swept up into his arms. Without thinking, she threw her arms around his neck as he walked her away from the broken pottery.

"I thought you'd know…you'd understand…why I was here," she whispered haltingly, her breath stirring the hair near his ear.

A muscle clenched tightly near Hugh's jaw, but he remained silent.

"Don't be angry with me," Siân said, discouraged by his ominous silence. Her spirits sank. She should have known she was not comely enough to attract this man. That his heart would only be won by the fairest, the most beautiful lady of the realm. And that his integrity would not allow him to dally with a young, virginal maiden. "I only hoped…"

Hugh put her back on her feet near the chair where she'd draped her gown. "What did you hope, Siân?" he asked gently as he stood facing her.

Near tears with the painful reality of his rejection, Siân composed herself before she spoke. "I'd hoped," she said in a defeated tone, "that we…th-that…"

His face was so close to hers she could feel his breath on her face, smell the sweet wine he'd drunk earlier.

Should she stand on tiptoe and touch his lips with

her own? Press her body against his? How was a woman supposed to show a man that she wanted…more than polite conversation with him?

''Must I say it, my lord?'' she breathed, rising up on her toes and leaning toward him as if he were a magnet and she were made of iron. At least he didn't appear to be entirely repulsed, Siân thought, though he did seem somewhat torn.

A momentous interval passed, then she felt his hands at her waist, and gave in to the slight pressure he put on her.

''Siân,'' he said quietly, hesitantly, just before his lips touched hers.

It was not at all what she expected. The lightest feathering of touches, the faintest sensation of his mouth meeting hers caused thunder to roar in her ears and lightning to crackle behind her eyes. It was as if her soul and his had been seared by some passionate force that melded them together. She would never feel alone again. Never wonder what it was to hold someone in her heart, to be a true half of the whole.

She made a small, strange sound of yearning in the back of her throat, and Hugh increased the pressure, joining their lips together in an all-consuming kiss, drawing her body ever closer. One hand cradled the back of her head, but the other remained at her waist, and he spread his legs, in order to better fit her body to his.

Nothing else mattered. Every harsh word she'd ever received, every terrible day she'd ever lived, every excruciating moment of loneliness, melted away as Hugh's lips possessed hers.

His hand moved lower, and pressed them more closely together. His tongue invaded her mouth and

Siân shivered with the sensations caused by their intimate contact. She moved against him and heard his moan this time, while threads of pleasure unwound inside her and around her, binding them together in an ephemeral haze of arousal.

Siân felt his hands move again, then the ties that held her shift in place were gone. His hands were on her bare skin now, moving down, cupping her breasts, sending spears of pleasure through her.

All at once, she was on his bed, with Hugh poised over her. As his hands moved down her body, his mouth traveled to the sensitive skin below one ear, then down her throat while Siân trembled with the intensity of the sensations caused by his touch. His breath was hot as he circled one receptive nipple with his tongue.

"Hugh…" Her voice was a feather on the air, a gossamer plea for him to take her beyond anything she'd ever known. Beyond the realities of her life, her fate. All she knew, everything she was…was here and now.

Siân wanted to feel him against her, skin to skin. She pulled at his tunic, then he moved away for an instant, wrenching it over his head. When he came back to her, the crisp dark hairs of his chest brushed against her breasts, increasing her shivers of arousal. Siân touched his nipples and found, to her surprise, that they were beaded like hers, and craving her touch.

He groaned as she put her mouth to one. And pulled away from her. "Siân," he rasped.

Loud voices and a pounding at his chamber door brought Hugh to his senses.

"Dryden!" Nicholas's voice penetrated his haze. "Beaufort's arrived! You're needed in the hall!"

Beaufort. The power-hungry bishop from London had arrived.

What of Siân? He could not leave her this way. Bewilderment was clear in her eyes, those beautiful eyes so full of trust, full of...

He shook his head, trying to clear it. He couldn't stay. He had to be deranged to have allowed this encounter in the first place. What had she been thinking...coming to his room, undressing before him? He gritted his teeth and struggled for control.

God's Cross, he wanted her. Unlike he'd ever wanted anyone before. And she, apparently, wanted him. Flaws and all. She hadn't shrunk from the touch of his mangled hand, nor was she repulsed by his scars. She was truly a wonder.

And her intensity, her passion, would burn him to the core.

"Siân," he said, taking her hands in his, and drawing her up off the bed. His mouth went dry all over again as he viewed her innocent nakedness. "I must go."

A troubled crease appeared between her brows.

"It's not just Beaufort..." he began. She stood unmoving as Hugh pulled her thin linen shift down over her, covering her, and tied it in place. Then he picked up her gown and fumbled with it, unsure how to proceed. "We cannot do this. You're promised to the abbey."

"No," she whispered, her agony in her eyes, her voice. This couldn't be happening. A lump formed in her throat as reality dawned. He'd been making love to her only moments ago. Now he was turning her over to the nunnery.

"Siân," he said as he reached for his tunic. He held

it in one hand, and looked at her pensively, remembering how dejected she'd looked before, when Owen had spoken of taking her to the abbey.

She couldn't speak. She stepped down from the bed and moved away from him, hastily tying laces and fastening buttons, blinking away the tears that had begun to form. She'd been stupid and foolish again, hadn't *thought* before she'd acted.

"Siân," Hugh repeated.

"I apologize, my lor—"

"What if you were to marry?" he asked impulsively. "If a man offered for your hand, would your brother allow you to wed instead of going to the abbey?"

"I—I don't know..." she said dubiously. "My dowry is s-small. No one—"

"Would Owen allow a change in plans?"

Siân shrugged, wondering what he was getting at. There wasn't a man in all of Britain who would offer for her. Unless... A faint glimmer of hope arose in her breast. She turned to look at him. "I—I don't know," she finally answered, afraid even to begin to think what he might mean.

She must have been clumsy with her buttons, because as soon as he pulled his tunic over his head, he brushed her hands away and began buttoning up her bodice as if she were a child. His hands were gentle, and she could feel his piercing gaze, though she kept her own eyes downcast.

Siân knew her eyes would betray the hope and longing she felt, and she had no wish to embarrass herself any further. When she was put back together, straightened out and fully dressed again, she turned away from Hugh and took a few steps toward the door.

"Wait." Hugh was right beside her, preventing her from opening the door.

She looked expectantly at him.

"You are..." Hugh hesitated for a moment, then tenderly cupped her chin with one hand. "You are...unique, Siân. Special." A hint of a smile formed on his lips, touched his eye. "Never forget it."

He opened the door, keeping her behind him. When he ascertained that there was no one else in the gallery, he allowed her to pass around him, giving her one last glance as she walked toward her own chamber, and he headed for the steps.

The portly frame of Henry Beaufort, Bishop of Winchester, was ensconced in a large, comfortable chair before the fire, which had recently been stoked. His normally pale features were slightly flushed, as if he'd recently exerted himself, and the circular wen above his right brow was somewhat more pink than usual. His beady gray eyes were watery and, as usual, they missed nothing.

A trestle table had been set up near Beaufort, and was laden with food and drink. Several men were arranged around the prelate, some seated at the table, some standing. Nicholas was among them, as was Sir George.

The ladies were noticeably absent, though Hugh was certain that Marguerite knew not only that Beaufort had arrived but also the names and ranks of each man with him.

"Alldale," Beaufort said as he picked up a large chunk of fowl and sank his teeth into it. "Didn't know you were at Clairmont."

Hugh didn't doubt it. He was certain the bishop had

hoped to find Queen Catherine essentially alone. Unprotected from his political intrigues. "Your arrival is late, Your Eminence," Hugh said. He forewent the usual obeisance, not kneeling to kiss the ecclesiastic's ring. He'd known the old reprobate too long and too well to indulge in that particular formality.

Beaufort bristled, but did not remark on Hugh's breach of courtesy. Instead he merely commented on the coming storm. "Didn't want to spend another soggy night in tents on the road, so we pushed on. Wrexton!" he called, turning to his right.

A tall, sandy-haired man pushed himself away from the wall and came to stand next to Beaufort. His demeanor was disinterested but at the same time, his hazel eyes were cagey. A small sneer distorted what might have been a handsome mouth. Hugh had met many who wore that same sardonic look and he knew to be wary of the man. He would put nothing past him.

"Edmund Sandborn," the bishop introduced him, "Earl of Wrexton, meet Alldale."

Hugh nodded at the man. He'd heard of him, though he'd never met the earl. To Hugh's knowledge, Wrexton had never given service in the French wars, choosing instead to pass all his time at his estates near the Welsh border or occupied in various amusements in London. Though Wrexton looked as though he'd once been fit enough, there were lines of dissipation at the corners of his eyes, his mouth. To Hugh, he appeared to be a man accustomed to being indulged.

"I've brought Darly, as well, you see."

And Hugh did see. He was vaguely surprised Viscount Darly had made it all the way here from London on such an arduous journey. The man was skinny as a post and looked as weak as a hatched chick. His skin was pale and his hair thinning across his shiny pate. Hugh wondered if he'd ridden all the way to Clairmont in the back of a cart.

He caught Nicholas's eye as if to ask, "*This* is my competition?"

Nick shrugged.

"Her Majesty is well, I trust?" Beaufort asked.

Hugh gave a quick nod.

"And my grand-nephew?"

"Well enough," Nicholas answered, saying as little as possible about the child.

"It is rather dangerous, is it not," Beaufort began, "for the queen to be so near the border without adequate protection?"

"Your Eminence, there is more than enough protection here at Clairmont," Nicholas said. "In fact, it was only a few nights ago when…"

Hugh was content to let Nicholas spar with Beaufort while he sized up the bishop's companions. There were several very capable-looking knights-at-arms, as well as the two noblemen. Hugh had to assume that additional men had made the journey with Beaufort, as well. They were probably out in the barracks with the other soldiers, finding food and beds away from the wet weather.

What were Beaufort's plans? Hugh recalled that Darly had begun to press his suit for Marguerite's hand, so Wrexton had to be the bishop's candidate as a husband for the queen. Was the man as malleable as Beaufort must think, or did Wrexton have his own intentions? From the look of the man, Hugh didn't think Beaufort should trust him any more than he would rely on a defrocked monk.

A footman entered the hall and spoke to Sir George,

who then turned to address the guests. "Rooms have been made ready, Your Eminence, should you care to retire."

Beaufort stood and stretched. "I *am* weary," he said, wiping his thick lips on a cloth. "A real bed will be a godsend tonight."

And as Beaufort and his party made their way up the stairs and to their rooms, Hugh pulled Nicholas aside.

"I want to talk to you."

Chapter Eight

A gentle, thoroughly saturating rain fell steadily all night. Siân couldn't sleep. Terrified to let herself hope that Hugh intended to ask for her hand, she was none-theless unable to keep from doing so. So she sat up half the night, perched on a chair by the long, narrow window. She gazed out over the darkened Clairmont fields, and listened to the light rain as it fell, cleansing the earth, enriching it.

Siân wrapped a shawl snugly around her shoulders and pulled her knees up to her chin. It had been quite a day, she reflected. The harrowing confrontation with the two Scots had given her a whole new perspective on her life, and the things that were important.

Siân realized that life was full of alternatives. She didn't always have to choose the most expedient path, even if that was what Owen demanded.

She was not going to St. Ann's. Not now, not ever.

Nor would she be a burden to anyone ever again. After her parents' deaths, she'd been shifted around from uncle to uncle, then to her brother. Always just another mouth to feed, another body to clothe.

No more. Siân was a capable person, intelligent and

fit for employment in a noble house. Even if Hugh did not intend to wed her, Siân knew now that she would be able to make her own way in the world. Perhaps she could be a lady's maid, or a children's nurse, or even a companion to a wealthy lady. She was a Tudor, after all, descended from the councillors of David and Llewelyn, and the escheator of Angesley. Her own brother was the Keeper of the King's Wardrobe.

No one—not even Owen—could rightly scoff at her abilities.

And the other…though Siân kept trying to push *that* to the back of her mind, it just wouldn't rest. She'd never felt so alive, so much a part of someone as when Hugh had held her, kissed her. She would give almost anything to have the right to hold him always, to *belong* with him.

Siân knew it was too much to ask.

She couldn't remember the last time things had gone well for her. From the time she'd been shipped off to Pwll after her father's death until now, Siân could not remember a single time when her own wishes had come to fruition. In the past, she had always accepted her lot in life, never expecting anything more. But now that she knew Hugh's caress…had felt his arms around her, his mouth on hers….

She sighed. No wonder she couldn't sleep. At this rate, it would be hours before she found any rest at all.

"Your pardon, my lady," the young maid said as she shook Siân early the next morning, "but the queen would like you to attend her—as soon as possible!"

Siân dragged herself from the bed and dressed quickly. There was nothing she could do about the circles under her eyes. The queen would just have to ac-

cept her haggard appearance, she thought as she traversed the gallery that led to Catherine's chambers.
Siân couldn't imagine what the queen wanted with her
so early, especially when Clairmont was host to important guests from London. Not that the guests were
stirring yet. It was likely they would sleep several hours
more.

After a quiet knock, Siân was given leave to enter
the queen's chamber.

"Siân!" the queen exclaimed, her face flushed and
pretty. "You are so prompt!"

Movement from the far side of the room gained
Siân's attention, and she saw that it was Owen, sitting
in a chair by the fire.

"Owen...?"

"We need your help, Siân," Owen said as he stood
and approached his sister. Siân thought he moved about
Catherine's chamber in a rather proprietary manner,
considering that he was a mere servant of the queen.
Though his post was an important one, Siân was surprised at what appeared to be a casual familiarity between her brother and the queen. It was odd she hadn't
noticed it before.

"What can I do?" Siân asked.

"Our plans are not entirely complete," Catherine
began. "But—"

"We need you to take Henry away from Clairmont," Owen said.

"Away?" Siân asked, confused and taken aback.
"Why? Where?"

"It will only be temporary, Siân," Catherine said.
"The presence of the bishop of Winchester does not
portend well for me...or for my son..."

"He's brought with him a nobleman," Owen said,

"…a likely husband for Her Majesty. If Beaufort doesn't succeed in coercing the queen to marry this earl, then he will endeavor to remove Henry from Catherine's custody, and get the council to appoint a guardian for him."

"Either way, His Eminence will gain a great deal of power."

Siân exhaled slowly. A thousand questions ran through her brain, but she could put words to only half of them. "Your Majesty…"

"I know this is a difficult…unusual request, Siân," Queen Catherine said as she walked to the open window where rain continued to fall upon the garden. The sun was not yet up, but when it finally dawned, Siân doubted there'd be much light.

The queen twisted her hands in front of her, showing a nervousness that Siân had never seen in Catherine of Valois. The young queen had always struck Siân as completely calm and poised. Circumstances never seemed to ruffle her. "I know that if I am to succeed in thwarting Beaufort, I will need the help of someone as spirited and as…audacious…as you."

"Where will I take him?" Siân asked, overwhelmed by Catherine's confidence in her. "And how…?"

The queen's shoulders relaxed as she realized that Siân's questions indicated her agreement. Catherine embraced Siân lightly. "Thank you, Siân," the queen said. "You have no idea…"

"You will take him to Windermere Castle," Owen said. "But tell no one."

"How will I get to Windermere?" Siân asked, even more confounded than ever. She'd heard of the place, knew that Hugh Dryden had come from there. "I know nothing of—"

"One man will escort you."

"Alldale," Catherine said. "He must be the one to go, even though he is betrothed to Marguerite."

Siân's knees buckled. *Hugh was betrothed?* To Lady Marguerite?

"Nicholas Becker will stay here," Owen added, unaware of his sister's shock and dismay at the news that Hugh was betrothed. He and Catherine were so fully preoccupied with their own plans and schemes that neither one noticed Siân's sudden pallor, nor her sharp intake of breath. No human eye could see the shaft that pierced her heart. "Nick is more of a talker than Dryden anyway… We'll need that skill to keep Beaufort off your trail."

"And you'll need Dryden's survival skills on the road to Windermere to keep *Henri* safe."

"Your Majesty," Siân said, somewhat breathlessly. She needed to speak, to ask questions, with a clear voice. She would not succumb to tears, nor would she allow her brother to see the slightest weakness in her. "Would it n-not be better if Henri's nurse accompanied him? It would be—"

"*Non*, Siân," Catherine said abruptly. "She is becoming…" She looked to Owen to supply the word.

"Elderly."

Catherine nodded. "That is correct. Her age… She will not be able to withstand a long, hard ride with *mon petit Henri*."

"Henry likes you, Siân," Owen said. "He is familiar with you and you have a…a facility with children. You are our best choice."

"But Lord Hugh…" Siân protested. "If he is to wed Lady Marg—"

"It is not official yet, Siân," Owen said, "but it

matters little. Dryden is the most qualified to escort
Henry to Windermere. You are the best nurse for His
Majesty. The two of you will go.''

''And the earl…Hugh…has agreed to this plan?''

''Siân,'' Owen said with exasperation, ''do not be-
labor the point. Even now, Dryden is preparing for the
journey.''

Siân swallowed and looked away. She didn't know
how far away Windermere was, how many days she
and Hugh would have to journey together. Yesterday,
she'd have gone anywhere with him. Now, it would be
sheer torture to be near him, to know he belonged to
another. To know she'd made a fool of herself with
him the night before.

''Just the two of us, then…with little Henry?''

''Siân, it is the way Alldale functions best,'' Catherine said. '''Travel lightly and quickly,' he said.''

What choice did she have? She liked Catherine and
adored little Henry. Siân glanced around the room, as
if she would be able to somehow find a way out.

But there was no escape. She would have to go to
Windermere with Hugh.

Siân packed her things in one bag with the help of
a talkative little maid. The girl spoke of all the extra
work to do in the castle, now that so many more fancy
lords had arrived from London. ''I'm glad I have the
bishop under m' care,'' she said, ''and not that awful
Wrexton.''

''*Wrexton!* The earl?'' Siân gasped. ''Edmund Sandborn?''

''Aye, m'lady,'' the maid replied. ''Handsome fella
he is, too, for an older gentleman.''

Older gentleman? *Older?* Siân's senses reeled.

Wrexton here at Clairmont? It couldn't be! But yes, he would be an older man now. Probably close to forty.

Siân couldn't possibly leave Clairmont now, not when she had such a clear opportunity to kill the man. He wouldn't recognize her after all these years, would never dream of an intruder breaching his chamber and putting a knife between his ribs. It would be a quick, clean death, with Wrexton barely aware that it was Siân Tudor herself who wrought her revenge.

Or should she let him suffer? Make him die slowly and painfully for all the agony he'd caused to the people of Pwll?

"Where have they put all the new guests, Aggie?" Siân asked, careful to keep her voice even, controlled. "I didn't think there were any chambers left at all with—"

"No, no, m'lady," Aggie replied with a chuckle. "There's still plenty o' room. The bishop has the rooms to the north end of the wing. Wrexton is just to his east. He has a lovely view o' the garden...none of the stink o' the stables."

It was just what Siân needed to know. Now all she had to do was find a suitable weapon, deal with Wrexton, and be off. No one would be the wiser, and she would be well on her way to Windermere before anyone realized the evil earl was...

Siân swallowed hard. She wondered if she could do it. She'd never killed anyone before. She wasn't prone to violence, though she knew she could do what she must in order to survive. Siân hated Wrexton with every drop of blood that coursed through her body, but she didn't know if she'd be able to deal a killing blow to the man, unprovoked. She thought about creeping up on Wrexton whilst he slept, and jamming a knife through his...heart? His neck? His back?

"I'm about through, Aggie. You can go," Siân said abruptly, closing the straps on her canvas bag. She had few belongings, so there was not much to pack. She was all nerved up now, thinking about Wrexton, and how she would manage to murder the man.

And it would be *murder.* Cold-blooded, too. Just like the murders of Dafydd and Idwal. Perhaps more justified, but murder nonetheless. Oh, heavens. The murder of an earl.

Siân shuddered as if a chill wind had just blown through the room.

"Well, I'm sending all m' prayers wi' you, Lady Siân," the maid said, causing Siân's heart to jump to her throat. "And asking that you offer some up for me when you reach the abbey."

Siân bit her lip. The prayers of a murderess? Dear God.

They'd given out the story that she was off to St. Ann's with the earl of Alldale instead of her brother. Siân was reluctant to lie to Aggie, especially about prayers from the abbey. But it couldn't be helped. For Henry's sake, and for her own, they had to throw any possible pursuers off the trail, if only for a couple of days. "I'll...always keep you in my prayers, Aggie," Siân said finally, feeling desperately guilty even before the deed was done.

The maid left and Siân looked around her room. Everything was packed. The room was clean. There was no indication she'd ever been there at all.

Just like her life, she thought. Never a sign that she'd been anywhere at all.

* * *

Though he had only the skeleton of a plan, it didn't bother Hugh. That's the way he'd always worked, and what had worked best for him. He knew his goal, and he'd use his instincts to get to it. Going back to Windermere was simple.

Traveling with Siân would not be.

Hugh supposed he couldn't avoid it. He couldn't carry Henry the entire way to Windermere himself, and he didn't know anything about little children. What did they eat? When did they sleep? And what about their, er, bodily functions? He supposed he should be grateful that a woman was coming along to deal with all that, but still…Siân.

Siân. Just the thought of her made every fiber and muscle in his body clench.

For the hundredth time, Hugh shoved thoughts of what had transpired between them to the back of his mind, and continued packing the food and other supplies they'd need into the leather saddle packs. He couldn't afford to think of her in that way, nor could she continue thinking of him as a would-be lover. He couldn't be. He would soon be the husband of Marguerite Bradley, stepfather to her son, John. He would not dishonor the vows he would soon make to Lady Marguerite, nor would he sully Siân.

But thinking of the two women at once made Hugh wonder how the rest of his life would be with Marguerite. Of a certainty, she was beautiful and well versed in the womanly arts. She could keep house and order the servants, present herself and her household well. Those were important things. Those had been the *only* things Hugh had considered before, when Wolf convinced him to offer for her hand.

Hugh's perceptions were rather different now. He'd

experienced Siân's passion, her extraordinary respon-
siveness to his touch. Was there another woman in all
of England who was so free and open with her affec-
tions as Siân, yet so faithful and devoted?

Would Marguerite ever learn to suffer his touch
without being repulsed?

Hugh doubted it, but it was irrelevant now. He had
offered for Marguerite and when he returned to Clairmont, she'd be his bride.

His thoughts were interrupted by the arrival of two
knights on horseback. Hugh was near the courtyard,
behind the stables with his own horse, as well as the
gentle mare Siân would ride. Dawn approached and the
light was weak. Luckily, the rain had stopped.

"My lord," one man said as he dismounted. "Sir
George gave us orders to report to you here."

"You are prepared to travel for several days?"

"Aye, my lord," the other man said. "Just give us
our destination and we'll be off."

Hugh told them to hie themselves to St. Ann's, and
to stay in the vicinity of the abbey for a few days before returning to Clairmont. He also suggested that they
keep to themselves and avoid towns and other travelers
along the way.

The two knights departed Castle Clairmont as part
of a patrol so as not to arouse suspicion if anyone asked
about the comings and goings through the gate. Hugh
had yet to figure out how he was going to get the little
king past the castle walls.

He secured the horses' reins to a post, then headed
toward the rear of the stone fortress. Siân should be
ready by now, he thought as he walked through the
great hall and toward the steps of the castle. "Lord

Hugh,'' came a voice, along with the sound of footsteps behind him.

It was Sir George.

"When do you depart?" the steward asked.

Hugh glanced up at the windows toward the early morning sunlight that was just now creeping up over the horizon. "As soon as possible," he replied. "I just have to gather Lady Siân and...the, uh—"

"Your lordship, I will be going to the gatehouse presently. I've spent a restless night and did not sleep well," Sir George said, as if for an audience. "The insomnia...often plagues me and it will surprise no one when I relieve the guard at the gate."

Hugh nodded, taking the steward's meaning. Neither man was about to speak frankly of what Hugh was about to do, for fear that an outsider might inadvertently hear what was afoot. Very few knew of the plan, not even the knights who were, even now, on their way to St. Ann's.

It was good news that Sir George Packley would be at the gate. Hugh knew he would still have to conceal Henry, but not to the extent that would have been necessary had the gate been manned by another knight.

"I bid you farewell, then," George said, "and God speed you on your journey."

Hugh thanked him, then turned and walked up the stairs in order to find Siân and to take Henry from his mother, the queen. He assumed it would be difficult for Catherine to bid adieu to her child, and hoped she managed to have it done before he arrived to take the boy from her.

When Hugh arrived at Siân's room, he gave a light tap on the door. Receiving no answer, he went in and found the room empty of her belongings but for a canvas bag on the floor, all packed and ready to go. Momentarily puzzled, he stepped back out of Siân's room and started toward his own chamber. Perhaps she'd gone there to meet him, he thought, thinking again of their encounter in his room the night before.

He doubted he'd ever be able to forget her wild mane of shining hair, or those glistening eyes. The fullness of her breast in his hand, the softness of her lips on his were memories that would be forever burned into his mind. He wondered if Marguerite would give so freely of her body, her soul, as Siân Tudor did.

An odd glint of light caught Hugh's attention as he approached his room. There was someone in the corridor near Beaufort's chambers. Hugh moved closer and saw that it was Siân.

Mystified by her presence here, and her stealthy movements, Hugh approached her quietly.

As she put one hand on the door latch to Wrexton's chamber, Hugh saw that she carried a long, wicked-looking kitchen knife. She lifted the latch and crept silently inside.

"Siân!" he whispered fiercely as he approached her, but she didn't hear.

Hugh knew it was madness, but he followed her into the chamber. The bed curtains were pulled aside to reveal a sleeping, loudly snoring Wrexton. The stale, putrid smell of old ale permeated the room and the earl was quite obviously in a drunken stupor.

A woman slept alongside Wrexton, but Hugh did not recognize her. She may have been one of the serving maids, or someone from the village... Hugh did not know. Nor did he know which of the pair was Siân's intended victim.

As Siân approached the bed, Wrexton snorted and

turned, but did not awaken. His movements startled Siân, and gave her a moment's pause, but then she crept closer, her hand in a death grip around the knife. The sleeping woman moaned and then quieted, and still Siân moved toward them.

Hugh gained on her. Siân raised the knife, and held it with a shaking hand, poised to strike. She hesitated long enough for Hugh to grab her knife hand. As he did so, Siân gasped and dropped the knife, momentarily awakening Wrexton. The earl opened his groggy eyes, lifted his head slightly, looked at her hazily and dropped his head back down onto the bed.

Hugh grabbed Siân around her waist and covered her mouth with his hand, then pulled her silently out of the room. He let go long enough to pull the door closed behind him, then half led, half dragged Siân down the gallery until they reached her room.

"Are you mad?" he demanded in hushed tones.

Siân shook her head defiantly. Her cheeks were pale, and her lips absolutely colorless.

"Then what is this about?" he continued fiercely but quietly, pacing the room, raking his hair back with one hand. He was dumbfounded. "Why? Why in kingdom come would you…?"

"I—"

"You thought to murder Wrexton in his bed!" he answered for himself, hardly able to believe the vision of his one good eye. He'd never have thought her capable of it, never have believed there was a murderous bone in her body. And Wrexton! Of all people, she'd attempted the murder of an earl!

Siân nodded. Her chin, though she'd raised it bravely, trembled. One tear spilled over. She looked terrified, yet resolute.

It seemed a natural thing for him to pull her into his arms, but Hugh held back. He would not be swayed by her tears. He'd resolved to keep his distance from Siân Tudor, and he would satisfy his vow.

"There is no time for this," Hugh said more gruffly than he intended as he bent over and picked up Siân's bag. Whatever her reason for wanting to kill Wrexton, there was no time to dwell on it now. "We must leave right away. Before the guests stir. And before *you* can get into any more trouble. I don't think Wrexton saw my face, but we can only hope he didn't see *yours*."

Chapter Nine

Henry was a sleepy little boy that morning.

Not at all did he seem to mind the game he was about to play with Siân and Hugh. He hugged his mother, who remained stoically poised as she said goodbye, then crawled into a blanket-lined basket, put his thumb in his mouth and pretended to sleep. Siân hoped the boy would remain quiet as they carried his little basket out to the courtyard and hoisted him onto the back of her horse.

Hugh hoped they could get away without Wrexton calling an alarm. With any luck, the earl's drunken stupor would prevent him from realizing how close he'd come to losing his life that morning.

All they had to do was get past the gate without Henry being seen. As far as everyone knew, Hugh was taking Siân to St. Ann's as planned, and the two knights who'd left Clairmont earlier would provide the tracks to substantiate that story.

Hugh and Siân mounted their horses and rode slowly toward the gate, careful not to rouse anyone's interest. The rather large basket that hung from one side of

Siân's horse roused no suspicions—it appeared to be just another piece of her baggage.

It wasn't until they were outside the gate and well past the edge of town that Siân allowed herself to breathe easily. The morning had been fraught with tension, and their "escape" from Clairmont had been nothing short of miraculous. Besides all else, Siân had had difficulty believing that the toddler in the basket could manage to remain quiet for that entire stretch of time—a stretch that had seemed an eternity to her.

When they reached the woods on the northern edge of town, Hugh rode abreast of Siân and told her to halt. He reached over and unfastened the basket from her saddle, pulling it onto his lap.

Inside, Henry slept, his thumb still firmly tucked inside his mouth. Siân might have smiled had her mood been different, but with all that had happened that morning, she could not. She was frustrated and angry with Hugh for thwarting her plan.

Yet she felt strangely relieved.

She'd fully intended to kill Wrexton. She had purposely gone down to the kitchen and found a suitable knife, then crept back to his chamber without being seen. At least, she'd *thought* no one had seen her. She'd had every intention of rendering the fatal wound as Wrexton slept, then slipping away with no one the wiser.

Siân conceded that seeing the woman in Wrexton's bed had thrown her off. What if the woman had awakened? Had started screaming?

And the killing itself… *Could* she have done it? Siân chewed her lip. She felt shaky and nauseated all over again. Her palms were moist. Could she have taken the life of that horrible man?

Wrexton truly was evil. He deserved to die for what he had done all those years ago to Siân's friends. And who knew what other vile crimes he'd committed since then for which he deserved a death sentence? With a man like Wrexton, there had probably been plenty. Never before had Siân been in a position to do anything about him, and now she'd missed her chance.

And after all was said and done, she didn't know whether to thank Hugh or curse him for obstructing her in her purpose.

"Shouldn't we be going?" Siân asked peevishly. "I thought haste was imperative."

Hugh said nothing, just gritted his teeth and fastened Henry's basket in front of his own saddle. He had no interest in catering to Siân's mood this morning, as they had quite a number of miles to cover before reaching their destination at the end of the day. He was still baffled and astounded by his discovery of Siân with a knife in Wrexton's room, but could not afford to get into a discussion about it now. Nor was he inclined to speak with her about what had transpired between them the night before. He wanted *that* pushed back to the farthest reaches of his memory, never to be thought of again.

"We'll continue north for a few miles until we reach the river," he said.

Siân silently acknowledged his words. She knew the plan was to make tracks toward St. Ann's, then ride through a shallow stream that bordered Clairmont land, and double back through the water so their tracks would not easily be found. Then they would be free to head southwest, toward Windermere.

Beyond that, she didn't know what to expect. She'd only been told to trust Hugh.

Luckily, it seemed neither of them was in a mood for talk.

The little king slept over an hour. They'd gone several miles by the time he was up and asking for his *maman.*

They stopped while Siân soothed him and got him food and drink. The little toddler didn't understand why he could not see his mother, why she had not come with him. Then Hugh disappeared into the woods and Henry started to cry, so Siân held him. She patted his back and called him *"Parry,"* the pet Welsh name that used to make him giggle.

It was a ploy that didn't work this time.

Then Hugh reappeared. "Henry," he said as he squatted down next to Siân and the tearful child. "Look." He held a small toad in his cupped hands, and showed the boy. Henry's crying slowed down slightly to a pattern of shaky breathing and hiccups. His tear-filled eyes took interest.

Siân took an interest, too, but not in the toad. It was Hugh, and his instinct for giving gentle attention to the child. Many a man would have cuffed a two-year-old and been done with it, but not Hugh. He spoke softly to Henry and told him all about toads and how if you weren't careful, they'd make warts grow on you.

"Hew don't have warts," Henry said, pulling his thumb out of his mouth long enough to speak. "But your finger's gone."

"That's true," Hugh replied. "But toads didn't do that."

"What did?" Henry's big hazel eyes looked innocently up at Hugh. "A snake?"

Hugh shook his head. "It was a bad accident," he

replied without hesitation. "And it happened a long time ago."

"I sorry, Hew," Henry said, sniffling. "Can I hold him? I don't get warts, either."

Siân wondered how Hugh had lost the finger. In an accident? Not in battle? She couldn't imagine what kind of accident would cause him to lose an eye, too, and make all the small scars she'd seen. She wouldn't ask him, though. She didn't really want to speak to him at all. Not after what he'd done that morning. And especially not after what *she'd* done the night before.

She should have been dying of embarrassment. Siân had avoided thinking about her blunder of the night before, her awkwardly attempted seduction. She should have known a man like Hugh Dryden would have no interest in her—even for one night. Betrothed to a woman like Marguerite, Hugh had no need of a—what did Owen always call her?—an ill-kempt *minx*. A regretful laugh slipped out and Hugh glanced up at her. She turned quickly away, unwilling to let him witness her anguish.

Why hadn't she guessed? In retrospect, it should have been obvious that Hugh and Lord Nicholas had arrived at Clairmont for some reason. She just hadn't stopped to think what it was.

Now she knew. All those evenings he'd sat next to Marguerite at the dais…the afternoons spent in her solar… How could she have been such a dunce? Thinking he might care…finding that he was betrothed to the most beautiful, most cultured woman in all England. They were perfectly suited to one another. Both were quiet and reserved. Hugh was the perfect masculine foil to Marguerite's stunning femininity.

Why hadn't she realized it before she'd made a fool of herself?

They spent some time fooling with the toad. Henry calmed down enough for Hugh to talk to him, and explain that he was going on an adventure, that he would soon visit a little princess at her castle. The things he said seemed to pacify the child enough to allow them to continue on their journey, which they did. Hugh carried the king on his lap and they increased their pace, hoping to reach the manor house of a friend before nightfall.

Siân felt worse after the short interruption of their journey. She was on edge, having spent too much time thinking. She'd forced the door closed on thoughts of Hugh, but that left her preoccupied with memories of the incident in Pwll, her guilt over the deaths of her young friends.

Siân's blood boiled anew. How had she allowed herself to be foiled in her purpose? If anyone in the kingdom deserved killing, it was Wrexton, and she'd had the perfect opportunity. Siân knew she could have done it quietly, with no one the wiser. She could have rid the world of that awful man, then sneaked back out of his room and left Clairmont forever.

Why had Hugh interfered? Why couldn't he have let her complete her anointed task? Now, she would just have to return to Clairmont when she was through at Windermere, and finish Wrexton off as she should have done that morning.

With her return in mind, she kept careful track of the road and all the landmarks. Since she would return to Clairmont alone, Siân would not be able to rely on Hugh's sense of direction.

The day's ride was difficult for Siân, who was unaccustomed to riding horseback for such long stretches of time. Naturally, her physical discomfort did not work toward abating her ill temper.

It was not easy for Henry, either, a typical child who needed freedom to play and exercise his little legs. By nightfall, he was squirming and whining so much Siân didn't think they'd be able to go any farther.

But Hugh cajoled Henry into riding just a little longer, and soon they came upon a large, gracious house with a thatched roof. Lights were burning in the windows and, though it looked warm and welcoming, Siân was leery of approaching. They had to be cautious of who saw them, even if they had to eschew a warm bed indoors.

Not that *that* would have been the best thing for Henry—or herself, for that matter. It was quite cold now that the sun was setting and Siân knew it would become much colder as the night progressed. A warm and cozy bed was nothing to scorn when she was cold as well as sore.

"What place is this?" she asked Hugh.

"Down!" Henry cried.

"All right," Hugh said to Henry, "you can get down soon." He looked at Siân. "This is Morburn Manor. It's the house of Chester Morburn, an old friend. We'll be able to stay the night."

"Shouldn't we avoid—"

"Chester can be trusted," Hugh replied. "No one will ever know we've been here."

Siân had her doubts about that, but she followed Hugh into the yard. She'd been told to trust Hugh's instincts, and at this point, she had little choice. There was no further thought about it, though, when the front door opened and a tall, thin fellow with light hair appeared, carrying a branch of candles. He had the bearing of a soldier and an attitude of wary welcome.

"Morburn!" Hugh called as he urged his horse forward.

"Dryden? Is that you, man?"

"It is," Hugh replied. He rode up to the front of the house with Siân right behind him. "I've brought friends."

"So I see," he replied, stepping back in the doorway and setting the candles somewhere inside. "Joan!" he called, then walked down the steps to greet his guests.

Morburn first helped Siân dismount, who immediately went to take Henry from Hugh.

"Where is the princess, Siân?" Henry asked after Siân had let him down.

"Come, little *Parry,*" Siân said, taking the little boy's hand, "let's visit the privy, then we'll talk about the princess." She had no idea what princess Henry was talking about, and glanced suspiciously back at Hugh. Had *he* been telling tales of princesses?

"Never thought to see you outside Windermere's gates," Morburn said when Siân had left.

Hugh did not reply. He'd never thought to find himself out in the world again, either, much less caught up in the intrigues of court. Yet here he was, stopping murders in the morning, harboring a runaway child-king in the evening.

"You are well, then?"

Hugh gave a quick nod as Morburn's wife came out to welcome the guests. Chester introduced his wife to his old friend. "You're no more talkative than you ever were," Morburn said.

Hugh shrugged as he pulled saddlebags off the horses and handed them to Chester, who set them inside the house as if it were a common occurrence for old friends to drop by of a night. "We're on our own here, Hugh," Morburn said, "no servants yet. So you'll have to help me with the packs and the horses."

Siân soon returned with Henry. Hugh took charge of the horses, but before he and Chester led them to the stable to bed them down, he stopped to introduce Siân to their hosts.

"Siân Tudor, this is Baron Chester Morburn and his wife, Lady Joan," he said. "His Majesty is, without doubt, more interested in food than protocol."

"His Majesty?" Joan queried, understanding what had been said, but hardly believing it.

"Say hello, Henry," Siân said to the squirming toddler in her arms.

"No, Siân," Henry whined. "Down!"

Joan Morburn regained her composure quickly. "Would you care to come in? You'll pass the night with us, won't you?"

"Thank you for your kind offer," Siân replied as she followed Joan inside. "We will stay if it's no inconvenience."

It looked as if Joan and her husband had already supped. The table in the big room was clean, but there were tempting aromas emanating from somewhere.

"Eat, Siân!" Henry said, pulling on Siân's skirts.

"We will, *Parry*," Siân responded. She was hungry, too. "Soon."

"We have plenty," Joan said as she led the way to the kitchen in the back. She tied on an apron and took several pieces of covered crockery off a shelf, and began pouring the contents into cooking pans. "But we have no servants as yet. Chester and I only recently came to the manor, and there is still much to be done."

Joan was a pleasant-looking woman with light brown hair and freckles across her nose. Siân noticed a slight rounding of her belly under the apron, and felt a pang of jealousy which she quickly brushed aside. Joan was a friendly sort, and seemed glad for Siân's company. She said she had little contact with other women since coming to the manor and missed it.

"Especially now that I'm with child," Joan explained. "We have workmen coming in to make repairs to the house and stable, but Chester hasn't been able to hire any household help yet. I would dearly love to talk with another woman—someone who has born babies."

"Well, that would not be me," Siân said, hating the wistful tone of her words. "Though one of my aunts was midwife in my village. I attended many a birth with her," she added in a more agreeable manner.

"Oh!" Joan said, placing a hand over her heart. "Mayhap…we could talk some…later on… I have a question or two…"

"Certainly," Siân said. "I'll endeavor to answer them, but I'm not nearly as knowledgeable as a true midwife."

"Oh, but any talk will help," Joan pleaded. "I've had no one really, but my husband, and he is not inclined to speak of anything but the strong and fierce son he will have once I've birthed him."

Siân smiled. Morburn was like the men in her village, she thought. No care to the nurturing of the babe within, all hopes riding on the birth of a strong and healthy son. She supposed that was how nature intended it to be and wondered how Hugh would behave once Marguerite was with child. Would he be attentive to his wife, or would all his thoughts be directed toward the child once it was born?

These were not easy thoughts to entertain, and Siân was glad of the interruption when Joan spoke. "How do you come to be here? With…with H-Henry?" Joan asked, clearly baffled at how to treat the boy. As her monarch? Or as a tired and cranky toddler?

"It all has to do with politics," Siân answered, unsure of how much she was at liberty to say. "Very convoluted, very dull."

"More, Siân!" Henry cried, stuffing the last bit of bread into his mouth.

"Chew what you have, little man," Siân said.

The stew heated quickly, and while Henry was being fed, Hugh and Chester returned from outside and went upstairs. The two women listened to the footsteps from above, and Joan mentioned that the men were probably making up pallets to sleep on. Siân and Joan chatted amiably together and the little king soon fell asleep on Siân's shoulder. She finally carried him up the stairs to find him a bed.

Hugh was alone in the first room, building a fire in the grate.

Siân stood at the doorjamb, watching him, admiring the play of muscles across his back and shoulders as he added wood to the fire. The day's tension rolled out of her as she watched Hugh, replaced by a bone-deep weariness that settled into her.

Hugh turned and saw her caressing the little boy's head with her lips. He could hear whispered, loving words spoken in Welsh, words that held no meaning for him. Standing abruptly, Hugh stepped over to Siân and gently took the sleeping child from her arms. And without ado, he tucked Henry into bed.

"I think I'll retire now, as well," Siân said quietly. "I'm too tired to eat."

Hugh hesitated. She looked frail in that moment, her skin too pale, and dark circles under her eyes. There was no doubt she needed rest, but she needed nourishment just as badly.

"Is this to be my bed, too?" she asked.

Hugh nodded. "If you don't mind sharing."

Siân paused, feeling awkward with the moment. "N-not at all."

"You should eat something."

"I'll wait till morning," Siân said. Then she grinned sleepily. "By then, I will probably feel like eating one of the horses."

Chester's great room was comfortably warm, and Hugh's stomach was pleasantly satisfied. Joan was an excellent cook. He realized that she was with child, and the familiar, affectionate way the couple treated each other gave Hugh a moment's pause. For an instant, he wondered how it would be to enjoy the comfortable companionship of his own wife as his child grew within her.

Hugh discarded the thought immediately. Companionship and affection would have no place in his marriage, nor did they constitute good reason to wed. His betrothal to Marguerite would be satisfactory because she was an accomplished woman who would require very little from him, which was well and good since that was all he had to give.

"What do you hear of Nicholas Becker?" Morburn asked as his wife refilled his cup.

Hugh declined any more of the warmed wine. "He's

at Clairmont," he said, "trying to keep Beaufort from discovering that Henry's gone."

"How?"

Hugh shrugged. "You know Nick," he said. "Gabs like an Irishman."

"Yes, but—"

"He and the queen will buy us a day or two by telling Beaufort the boy's ill, or some such," Hugh said. "It's doubtful the bishop will insist on seeing him…"

"But possible?"

"Of course," Hugh replied. "Anything's possible. But I think we should be able to get to Windermere and have Henry under Wolf's protection before Beaufort or anyone else can overtake us."

"Wolf will protect him as his own," Chester remarked.

"Aye," Hugh replied. "He will."

"What about Wrexton?" Morburn asked. "Why was he with Beaufort?"

"Do you know him?"

"A little," Morburn replied. "His estate is well south of here, beyond Windermere. It borders Wales." Hugh gave no outward reaction to that news, but his ears perked up. "Joan can tell you. She's from down Stafford way so she knows more of him."

Hugh looked to Joan for confirmation. Joan blushed and lowered her eyes. She nodded quickly, nervously, her manner indicating she would prefer not to speak of him.

"Wrexton was…" She frowned a bit and looked to Chester for help, but none was forthcoming, other than the urging in his eyes. "He was…unkind to the nearby

Welsh towns. Well, perhaps a bit more than unkind. He was at times, brutal.''

"How so?" Hugh asked.

"Well, after the rebellion, and the Welsh were put down, there were some Englishmen who felt it was their duty to personally persecute the 'traitors'—meaning *all* the Welsh."

"Glendower's rebellion?"

Joan nodded.

"But that was what? Twenty years ago?" Hugh said, frowning. "Wrexton can't be much older than me. Mayhap ten years or so."

"I don't know, my lord," Joan said, "I never saw the man. But I know of Englishmen who, to this day, harbor resentment for the Welshmen who rose with Glendower against the king. Wrexton lost his family during the rebellion. It's why he hates the Welsh. And beyond that…Edmund Sandborn has a reputation for cruelty."

Hugh's thoughts returned to the woman he'd left upstairs. Had she experienced Wrexton's legendary brutality? He frowned. He couldn't imagine any other reason for Siân to attempt to murder the man.

Still puzzled, Hugh stood. He thanked Joan for the meal and both of them for their hospitality. Then he bid them good-night.

Climbing the stairs, Hugh's puzzlement changed to a certainty that Wrexton had committed some unforgivable cruelty against Siân or, more likely, against someone she loved. He couldn't imagine her committing a violent act against any man—unless that man was guilty of a crime committed against an innocent.

He tapped lightly on the door, gently enough not to

disturb her if she was asleep. She did not answer, so Hugh pushed the door open and went to the grate. Crouching down, he banked the fire, then stayed a moment, basking in the warmth of the room. He finally allowed himself to look at Siân, sleeping so peacefully with the little boy tucked protectively in her embrace.

One of her fine, delicate shoulders was exposed, with only the soft linen ties of her underclothes to shield her. The silky mane of her russet hair was loose about her face, framing its perfection with tiny, untamable tendrils.

Henry kicked in his sleep, and Siân sighed but slept on, raising one arm to rest above her head. And at the sight of that bared arm, everything inside Hugh urged him to shed his clothes and lie down with her. That vulnerable length of smooth, flawless skin made him think of the rest of Siân's body as he'd seen it, felt it, the night before—soft and smooth, warm and inviting.

He could spend the night just holding her there, keeping her warm and safe, sharing the intimacy of sleep. Their breaths would intermix once again, and he would relearn the sensations of her legs resting against his, her breasts against his chest.

As she slept, a small frown marred her perfect brow. Hugh reached over and lightly brushed a bit of hair from her face. An impossible tenderness filled him.

Could he lie with her and not want her? Was he just asking for torment in being so near, yet so impossibly far away? Hugh looked at her lips, parted in sleep, and remembered her taste, her passionate sighs.

He stood up quickly. This would never do. He had to get away from here and find his own bed before he made an irrevocable mistake. He walked to the door, then turned to look at her again.

No. He had not the power of will to be so close, and still resist her.

Knowing he must, Hugh left Siân to her slumber.

Chapter Ten

The nightmare woke her. Siâan hadn't had the dream since her reunion with Owen. Not that Owen had caused the dream, Siân thought. Common sense told her it was all the recent upheaval in her life that had brought the awful dream back.

It was still deep night and Henry was sleeping soundly, each of his breaths audible to Siân's ears. She got out of bed and shivered with the chill of the room. After adding more fuel to the fire, she ran her hands up and down her arms to warm them.

The unpleasant aura of the dream hung on. Her stomach growled with hunger. Now that she'd taken the edge off her exhaustion with a few hours' sleep, Siân realized she'd never be able to go back to sleep until she ate something. Intent on finding a slice of bread for herself, or perhaps an apple, Siân wrapped herself in an extra blanket, then lit a taper and quietly left the room.

Joan Morburn's kitchen was in perfect order. Siân remembered where everything was kept, so she took out the remains of a loaf, found a knife, and sliced a piece of bread. So intent on her purpose, she did not hear anyone behind her until she turned to reach for the butter crock, high on a shelf.

"Siân," Hugh whispered before she had a chance to be startled and perhaps wake the entire household.

Siân gave a little squeak of surprise anyway, and dropped her blanket. "Hugh!" she gasped. "You scared me!"

"I'm sorry," he said.

His form was cast in shadows, her flickering taper providing very little light. Siân could not help but notice, however, that he was nearly naked. Somewhere in her rational mind, she realized that her stirring about must have awakened Hugh and he'd come to investigate.

He was lean and taut, with well-defined muscles in his shoulders, chest, stomach. She remembered how the crisp hair of his chest had brushed against her own sensitive skin, how his strong arms had held her in their embrace.

She shivered.

"You're cold."

"I—I dropped my—"

He reached down and picked the blanket up for her. Then, when she thought he would wrap it around her, he seemed to change his mind. He handed it to her, keeping some distance between them.

"You…must be hungry."

Siân nodded. "It woke me, I guess," she said in a small voice, avoiding thoughts of the nightmare. She pulled the blanket around her shoulders and turned to reach for the butter crock.

"Henry's asleep?"

"Yes," Siân said. "He had a long day."

"So did you," he replied, watching her spread the

butter. He poured her a mug of water. "We never talked about the incident this morning…with Wrexton."

Siân shook her head and sat down on a hard, wooden bench near the fireplace. The fire was still smoldering and Hugh rearranged it to burn hotter. Siân took a bite of her bread.

"What did Wrexton do to make you hate him so?" Hugh asked as he took his place on the bench next to her.

"You won't understand," she said.

"You cannot know that," Hugh responded. "You might be surprised at the kinds of things I understand."

Siân realized that it was true. He had surprised her several times in the days since she'd met him, and perhaps it was time to speak of what Wrexton had done. She'd held the pain inside for so long…

"When my da died, Owen was sent to London," she said. "I was given to my mam's brothers in Pwll."

"How old were you?"

"When I went to Pwll? Ten or so," Siân said. "Pwll's a small village—it lies near the eastern border of Wales. It's just a hillock or two from Wrexton lands.

"The people of Pwll weren't exactly pleased to have a Tudor in their midst… My father's name was heavily associated with Glendower and the rebellion. I couldn't deny it. My uncles couldn't deny it. And Pwll had already had plenty of trouble from Wrexton.

"So I was supposed to keep to myself," Siân said. "I was to stay away from the other children in town, though that wasn't quite practical. I couldn't avoid them altogether."

Hugh got a distinct impression of a lively young Siân, being kept to a solitary existence and his heart clenched in his chest, thinking of the loneliness and isolation she must have felt. Though Hugh's own parents had died when he was young, he'd been welcomed into Wolf Colston's family like another son. And after Wolf's father and brother had been killed in ambush, Hugh had been taken into the house of Wolf's German grandfather. He had never wanted for companionship.

"Our families didn't know it, but I had friends...two young boys in particular. Idwal *ap* Rhys and Dafydd *ap* Dai. We used to run all over the hills and dales, getting into trouble as much as not, but careful not to let anyone know I was with them." She smiled wistfully, remembering the fun they used to have.

"It was late winter, about a year after I had gone to Pwll, when I found two young lambs lost in a narrow valley that lies between Pwll land and Wrexton land. They weren't any of *ours,* at least that's what Idwal said. Between us, we decided that if they were Wrexton's, he could afford to lose a couple of little lambs, being a rich Saxon."

Siân stopped to take a swallow of water.

"People were hungry. It hadn't been a good year, and we were in need of food," she said. "Dafydd butchered the lambs out in the woods and we took the meat home. Their mothers were suspicious, as were my aunts, but hunger won out and our families had several fine meals."

"How did Wrexton find out?"

Siân shook her head. "I'll never know," she said. "We never thought to bury the carcasses...never realized... In any event, Wrexton came to the village with some of his men, demanding that the thieves own up."

"And did they?"

"Not at first, of course," Siân replied. "We were children. Afraid. But people had figured it out…"

"What happened, Siân?"

"I—I came f-forward first," she said, her voice trembling now, her throat burning. "I told him I'd stolen the sheep and that I'd pay for them. The earl laughed in my face. He said he knew a measly *girl* hadn't taken his sheep and butchered them in the woods—even if I *was* a Tudor. He had me tied to a post and he beat me—"

"God's Cross, Siân!"

"—and tried to get me to tell who'd helped me."

Hugh pulled her to him and wrapped his arms around her.

"Idwal came out," she said. "Then Dafydd. They couldn't bear to watch what Wrexton was doing to me. His men grabbed them. Oh, Hugh!" she cried, burying her face in his chest. "They were only *boys!* Barely twelve years old! Their voices had not yet changed. They were still so soft, so gangly.

"Wrexton took them. He had them bound…"

"You don't have to finish," Hugh said quietly, but it was as if she hadn't heard him.

"The Saxons threw ropes over a tree branch," she said, weeping now, having difficulty getting the words out. "Wr-Wrexton said this was what they g-got for trusting a Tudor. And he…he h-hanged them. In front of me, in front of the whole town…everyone." Her voice was the barest whisper by the time she finished.

"I still see their faces sometimes," she said, sniffling, thinking of the nightmare.

"Siân, don't."

"And their mothers…I hear their voices…see their eyes," Siân continued. "And I know I was to blame."

"You weren't, Siân," Hugh said. "If there's any blame at all—it lies with Wrexton."

"Yes, he carries the blame," Siân said, "and that's why…this morning…why…"

"I see now."

"I promised myself that day—the day those boys died—that I would deal with Wrexton someday," Siân said. "I didn't know how or when, I just knew that someday I would end his life just as he ended Idwal's and Dafydd's."

Hugh let out a long sigh. Her head was nestled under his chin, so his breath ruffled the hair on top of her head. "Siân…"

"But even now, I don't know. Even if you hadn't stopped me, I don't know if I could have gone through with it," she said, pulling away and looking up at him with those luminous blue eyes, her nose red and runny, her lips swollen from crying. "I still don't know if I have the courage to hold to my vow."

Hugh tenderly caressed her face. It was no wonder she'd wanted to murder Wrexton. Her feelings for the man must have been akin to what he'd felt about Philip Colston, the deadly madman who'd captured and imprisoned him in one of the dark tunnels under Windermere Castle. The man who'd tortured him beyond all covenants of humanity.

Hugh didn't know if murder was ever justified. But he *did* know how it felt to want it more than he wanted his next breath.

"You were a child when you made that vow," he finally said. "You can't hold yourself to it now, Siân."

She didn't answer him, only sat close, in the shelter of his arms. Hugh didn't feel the chill of the room on his bare skin, nor the lateness of the hour. For now, it was enough to hold Siân Tudor.

They left Morburn Manor before daybreak, to avoid being seen by the thatchers and carpenters who would soon arrive. Henry was still asleep, a condition in which both Hugh and Siân wanted to keep him, so Hugh carried the boy for the first hour of the day's journey.

Siân rode quietly behind Hugh, thinking of the way he had held her the night before as she poured her heart out to him.

She couldn't remember ever receiving such comfort before, and it gave her an odd sense of belonging, a feeling of intimacy, that she'd never experienced before. No one had held her or spoken gently to her after the boys had been killed. Her uncles had untied and released her hands from the post where Wrexton had beaten her skin raw. They'd taken her inside her uncle Llwel's house where her wounds had been tended in miserly silence, without a thought to the grief and guilt she felt over the tragedy.

But now there was Hugh, who seemed to understand the depth of her anguish. And Siân's heart swelled with the wonder of it.

They rode on, following the worn little footpath as the sun crept its way above the horizon directly behind them.

"Hew?" Henry said as he awoke with a yawn and a stretch. "Hungry."

"You are always hungry, *Parry,*" Siân said with a laugh. She nudged her horse closer to Hugh's and handed the boy a slice of apple. "We'll stop in a few minutes, shall we, Hugh?"

Hugh's brow furrowed with incredulity. How could she smile and appear so carefree when the events of her youth had been so devastating? She might not be justified in murdering Wrexton, but how could she go on so cheerfully, knowing the man lived...prospered?

Siân chatted amiably with Henry as Hugh mulled things over. She was amazingly resilient, leaving all she knew in Wales to go to her brother in London, accepting Owen's decree that she go to the abbey, taking charge of the children at Clairmont, organizing activities for them during the repair and rebuilding of the town.

He knew of no ladies who could have endured all that Siân Tudor had, and still retain her sense of humor, her apparent delight in life. And courage? She wondered if she had the courage of her convictions.

Hugh almost laughed.

Just because she hadn't murdered Wrexton didn't mean she lacked courage.

He wished he could hand the despicable earl's head to her on a platter, then stopped to realize that it was not his place to become Siân's champion. He would find a suitable husband for her, and provide a decent dowry if need be, if only to see her satisfactorily settled. Nicholas hadn't declined to wed her, but he hadn't exactly agreed, either. In fact, his manner had been altogether unlike Nicholas. He'd been uncharacteristically quiet and pensive when Hugh had spoken to him about taking Siân to wife.

Hugh vaguely wondered what was amiss with his friend. It had been so long since the cares and worries of others had bothered Hugh that he didn't know what to make of Nicholas and his quiet, sober attitude of late. Something surely was not right, but Hugh dismissed the question for now, since there was naught he could do for Nick until he returned to Clairmont.

The day's ride was long and tedious again, with the threat of rain hovering over them all afternoon. The clouds were dark, low, and heavy, and Hugh worried that they would not make as many miles as were needed to get to their destination, and that they'd wind up staying the night somewhere along the road.

Though Henry started well, he ended up being difficult, and Siân insisted on stopping several times—too many times, in Hugh's opinion—to give the boy a chance to run and play.

But Hugh was only as patient as common sense would allow, and more than once he had to compel Siân and Henry back into the saddle, much sooner than either of them liked.

The rain started near dusk.

Hugh wrapped himself in his thick cloak and held Henry underneath it, close to his body as they rode. The boy snuggled against Hugh and allowed himself, finally, to be lulled to sleep.

"Do you suppose there'll be a cotter's hut or shelter of some kind where we can wait out this rain?" Siân asked, glancing fearfully at the faint flashes of lightning in the distance.

Hugh nodded and glanced around for landmarks. "We'll stop soon," he said as he nudged his horse to a quicker pace. Siân kept up behind him, wishing they'd soon find a place to stop for the night. She was exhausted, and her backside felt miserable from riding. She needed rest, and knew Henry needed it, too.

Soon, the aroma of a fire reached her nose, and before Siân had time to wonder about it, they came upon three ragged men sitting at the side of the road under the branches of several low-hanging trees. A small, smoky fire burned between them as they sat among the rocks and broken logs, eyeing the passersby. Siân held her breath. This would not be a good time for a confrontation, she thought, with Henry sitting on Hugh's lap and her riding behind, unarmed in any way.

Hugh appeared unconcerned by the soggy vagabonds, though, merely kicking his heels into his mare's sides and quickly moving out of range. The danger was past before it ever really amounted to anything.

They rode on as darkness fell and the rain increased.

"We must stop soon, Hugh," Siân said. "I fear I am too...sore to go on."

"Just over that rise, Siân," Hugh said, chagrined at having to keep her going. He knew she was uncomfortable, he'd seen her grimace the last time she'd climbed onto the mare, but there hadn't been any remedy for it. Tonight, at least, they would get a long night's rest, and tomorrow their journey would be shorter. Windermere was not far.

They veered onto a side path that led to a large manor house that was deserted, and horribly neglected. Hugh picked his way along the overgrown path, and rode up to the stable yard. Siân glanced over at Hugh, who was carefully dismounting with Henry. *"Maman?"* the boy said as he awoke.

"No, Henry," Hugh said, sheltering him from the rain as he went to help Siân down.

Her legs would hardly hold her when she stood. "Are you all right?" Hugh asked, frowning. It was unlike Siân to show any weakness at all and Hugh realized she must be more "leather worn" than she wanted to admit.

She nodded. "Just weary. What place is this?" she asked, stretching, shaking out her legs.

"Dryden Hall," Hugh replied, glancing warily up at the great, rundown house that was his boyhood home. "Come with me to the stable. I don't want to risk you going into the house without me."

"Why, Hugh? What do you—"

"It's been empty for a long time," he said as he led the horses away. Siân's legs felt marginally better now, and she was able to walk, so she caught up to him. "I just prefer to be cautious."

Siân asked no further questions, but followed him as he carried a whining Henry and led the horses to the stable. It felt good to get out of the rain, and the roof of the stable was intact. The old building felt positively cozy after so many hours in the cold and wet weather. She took Henry from Hugh, then walked back to the entranceway of the stable door to look across the yard at the house.

She realized this must be Hugh's family seat. Once a beautiful home, it was now a wreck and Siân wondered whatever had happened to the rest of the Drydens. Where were Hugh's parents, his siblings? Why had such an impressive home been left to ruin?

"Look, *Parry*," she said, pointing to the house. "There is no light at the house."

"Where the people gone?" Henry said as he lay his head on Siân's shoulder and stuck his thumb back in his mouth.

"Mayhap there are none," Siân replied quietly. "Mayhap we are alone here," she added as she repressed a wave of anticipation that she knew she should not even acknowledge. This would be her last night alone with Hugh, for he said they would reach Win-

dermere on the morrow. But Siân could not afford to
think of intimacies with Hugh, of comfort and affection
between them. Hugh was a man betrothed to another.
He would never betray Marguerite, nor would Siân
want him to.

"Where's *Maman?*"

"*Maman* is at Clairmont," Siân said, then she
changed the subject to divert his attention as well as
her own. "Soon we'll have supper, *Parry,* and we can
play in the house. I've got your wooden blocks. And
mayhap Hugh will let us explore the house."

After their arrival at Windermere, Siân did not know
what would happen. She assumed Hugh would travel
back to Clairmont right away to be with Marguerite.
That thought gave her pause, but she did not allow
herself to dwell upon it. Hugh's future was laid out.

As Siân saw it, her own choices were limited. She
could either beg a place at Windermere, taking a servile
position in the duke's household, or she could return
to Clairmont herself, and do what she'd intended on
the previous morning. Kill Wrexton. She wondered if
Hugh would escort her back if he knew what she
planned.

She doubted he would allow her to go through with
it, even though he said he understood her hatred of the
man, her need for vengeance.

Hugh stepped up behind her. "Stay here while I go
into the house," he said.

"But—"

"It looks vacant, but I want to be sure," he said.
"Siân, if anything should happen to me, there's a village a short distance down this path. Keep follo—"

"No, Hugh!" She startled him by reaching up and
hugging him to her tightly, with Henry squeezed be-

tween them. The child protested loudly, and Siân merely said in a quiet voice, "Just be careful...and there will be no need for us to go to the village."

Unable to keep himself from touching her, Hugh smoothed a wisp of hair from her forehead. "I will," he said, and then he was gone.

Hugh wasted no time in getting a fire going.

The house smelled of must and disuse, but it was empty for the most part—save for a few lucky mice who'd found a safe haven in the walls and under the floorboards. Hugh assumed there were bats upstairs, as well, but he was not inclined to go looking for them in the dark. It was enough to know there were no other, more dangerous, intruders about.

Hugh took no pleasure in meandering through the dark, cavernous hall where he'd spent his early childhood. He'd had his fill of dark, decaying places when he was taken prisoner by Philip Colston, and had avoided all dank and dismal places since then. But it couldn't be avoided now. He had to provide some kind of shelter for Siân and the boy, and Dryden Hall was the most likely choice. It was their best refuge, where they could stay the night and no one would be the wiser after they left on the morrow.

Henry started sneezing as soon as he came inside, but his reaction to the dust and mildew subsided after a few minutes. Hugh went back to the stable to get their packs, and as soon as he dropped them off, he disappeared again to take care of the horses.

From the look and smell of Dryden Hall, Siân knew it had been left empty for quite some time. It was doubtful that any of the rooms would be habitable, but at least the building seemed a good, sturdy shelter from

the rain. Siân was grateful they wouldn't have to spend
the night out of doors.

There were several tallow candles in pots, and Siân
lit a few. She knew it would be some time before she
could sit comfortably again on her sore bottom, and
Henry needed to exercise his little legs. So, as she
limped with discomfort, Siân took the little boy by the
hand, and together, they went exploring.

By the time Hugh returned, Siân had changed
Henry's and her own clothes, and had set the wet things
out to dry. The great hall looked fairly cheery, with
candles flickering all around, and Siân sitting by the
fire with Henry in her lap, already eating.

Hugh paused for an instant, taking in the scene before him, curbing the powerful sense he had of coming
home. It was absurd, of course. He hadn't been to Dryden Hall since his seventh year, not since he'd gone to
Windermere to foster with the Colstons. Any sense of
homecoming he felt would have been—should have
been—for Windermere.

"I didn't think there'd be any suitable beds," Siân
said, "so I just—"

"This is fine, Siân," Hugh replied, indicating the
furs she'd laid out near the fire. "The beds are likely
moldy. The house has been closed up since my father
died, years ago."

He joined Siân by the fire and sat down nearby, par-
taking of the food she'd unwrapped. Very sensibly, she
hadn't disturbed anything, not even the dust. Had she
started sweeping, the place would have become unin-
habitable.

"You'll have to get out of those wet clothes," Siân
said, unable to avoid thinking of his naked, muscular
chest, the mat of dark hair sprinkled across that broad

expanse, and how it felt against her own bare skin. "It f-feels much better to be dry. And warm," she added, cuddling Henry closer.

The little boy chafed at being held so tightly and he protested. Siân sighed, letting him loose to resume his meal.

"What's 'at noise, Hew?" Henry asked, standing up.

"Just a little thunder, Henry," Hugh replied. "Nothing to worry about."

"How far do we travel tomorrow?" Siân asked, feeling uneasy with the thunder. She knew she should feel secure within the shelter of Dryden Hall, but violent storms always unnerved her. A little thunder in the distance was nothing, she told herself. She was perfectly safe here. And she needed to rest and relax. She couldn't allow this storm to keep her from sleeping.

"Windermere's not far," Hugh replied. "Less than a day's ride."

Siân cringed with the thought of mounting a horse anytime soon. Her legs and bottom throbbed as if she'd been beaten with a wooden plank. Even now, she had difficulty finding a comfortable position in which to arrange herself. She eased onto one hip and asked, "Is Dryden Hall your family seat?"

He nodded. "Built a hundred years ago by the first baron."

"And your family?"

"Gone," he said. "Long dead."

Thunder rolled in the distance and Siân looked toward the high windows, thankfully noting that they were intact. Shivering, she reminded herself that it was warm and safe inside, that she would have *hours* of rest before having to mount up on her mare again.

She didn't want to think about that just yet.

Henry played for a short while before fatigue overcame him and he fell asleep among the furs and blankets Siân had spread out for him. It wasn't long before Siân and Hugh followed suit.

Hugh slept soundly for several hours before the dream woke him. Or was it the storm? For it was blowing wildly around them now, with rain blasting in horizontal torrents against the house. Cracks of thunder sounded closer now, and flashes of lightning illuminated the great hall intermittently, as if it were suddenly lit by a thousand candles.

His shoulder was sore. It had been dislocated at some point during his imprisonment at Windermere, and the cold, wet weather often brought about an inflammation of the joint. He reached into his pack and drew out a glass bottle of liniment that Kit Colston had made for him, then drew off his tunic and rubbed the ointment into the joint. Relief was almost immediate as soothing heat and comfort permeated his shoulder.

Siân stirred in her sleep, moaning. Hugh knew her muscles ached from riding, but he wondered if it was also the storm that was keeping her from resting well. He remembered her reaction to the thunder the night they'd been on the parapet together. She'd been terrified.

Hugh slipped the liniment back into his pack and went over to her. Lying prone, her kirtle had ridden up and she'd kicked the blanket off one leg, which now lay bare and exposed on her pallet. He tried not to look at that smooth expanse as he reached over and pulled the woolen cover back over her.

She muttered something. *Hugh?*

Was that what he heard? Or had it been the wind that made her soft murmur sound like his name.

Then her eyes opened. "Hugh," she whispered again, groaning in discomfort as she moved. Thunder roared at that instant, sounding as if it were right outside the hall, startling Siân and making her cry out in dismay. Even Hugh was taken aback by the sound. He got up quickly and went to the door, unbarring it, pulling it open a few inches to look outside.

It was an unusually violent thunderstorm, and Hugh could barely believe they'd been fortunate enough to have made it to the hall before the worst of it hit. Trees were dipping and swaying in the wind and more than one hefty branch littered the ground. Small hail pellets battered the ground, and when the thunder sounded again, it seemed that the tempest was right in the stable yard.

There was nothing Hugh could do. The horses were sheltered, as were the humans, and Hugh hoped to God they would not have to take refuge in the cellars of the old house. Just the thought of going down into that dark and clammy place made him shudder.

He barred the door and returned to where Siân lay, tense and frightened, near the fire.

"It's only a storm," he said, gazing over at Henry, who remained sound asleep and perfectly content, with his thumb firmly planted in his mouth.

"You are a master of understatement," Siân replied with a groan. "It sounds like lightning hit something nearby."

Hugh shook his head. "Not that I could see from the door. Was it the thunder that woke you?"

"No," she answered irritably, trying to make herself

comfortable. "It's these cursed muscles that don't like being curled over the back of a horse all day."

Hugh leaned over and reached for the bottle of liniment from his pack. If she was so sore she couldn't sleep, then she certainly wouldn't be able to ride on the morrow. That would mean another day at Dryden Hall, another day for Beaufort to catch up with them.

"What have you?" Siân asked, tipping her head toward the bottle in his hand.

"An ointment I'm going to rub on your legs," he said, ignoring the storm raging around them. He took the stopper out of the vial as thunder crashed nearby. "Turn over and lie down."

Chapter Eleven

Siân eyed him warily and gave a little shake of her head. She had her pride even though her modesty was not exactly intact. There was no way in heaven she was going to give him leave to stroke her, to tantalize her with his touch when she knew that his thoughts, his heart, lay with another. She couldn't bear it.

Besides, she'd always taken care of herself, and she would continue to do so now. It would not do to become dependent on anyone…especially Hugh Dryden. "I'll be all right," she said, "once this storm passes. They always make me nervous. Then I'll be able to sleep and all will be well."

A muscle in Hugh's jaw flexed and he poured some of the liniment into one hand. "Siân," he said. "You will have to ride tomorrow. But the look of you now, you'll be too tender and I'll have to go on without you."

"No!" she cried, despising the sound of panic in her voice.

"Then lie down and turn over."

"No, I—I can do it myself," she said, reaching for the bottle.

Hugh gave a derisive snort. "Siân, just lie down. Nothing untoward will happen."

She didn't know how he could say that. Untoward things happened each time he touched her. His very proximity wrought havoc on her senses.

Hesitantly, she did as she was told, then Hugh moved to kneel at her side. There was a long pause as she waited for him to touch her, but she soon felt his hand at the back of her knee. He reached under her gown, and, keeping her properly covered, began to rub, his hand slowly rising to massage the back of her thigh.

Before long, his other hand joined in and he worked the muscles of both legs. Siân's entire body turned to gruel as his hands kneaded her limbs. Heat permeated the muscles and relaxation followed as he worked, and Siân began to feel a measure of relief.

His hands were amazingly strong. He compressed and released with exquisite care, massaging, soothing, inching gradually upward to where she felt the most discomfort. It was also the place where she was most sensitive to his touch.

Siân hid her face in her folded arms as he worked her buttocks, first one side, then the other. His hands always moving, kneading, they created sensations akin to those she'd felt on that last night at Clairmont. She felt cool air on her legs, so she knew she was lying fully exposed to him, but she didn't care. She was well beyond caring about propriety with Hugh.

She bit her lip to keep from moaning out loud, but a small whimper of pleasure managed to escape from the back of her throat. How could he go on, not knowing, not understanding, what his touch was doing to her? Did she affect him so little? Was the touch of her intimate parts of no consequence to him?

Arousal churned in the pit of her stomach and she yearned for more. More touching, more closeness, a deeper intimacy. She wanted to feel the touch of his lips on hers, his hands on her breasts. She couldn't lie still any longer.

Hugh's movements slowed. His hands no longer massaged, but caressed, as if seeking to learn every inch of Siân's naked flesh. His fingertips traced her curves, grazed her exposed skin, teased her to a crest of agitation. She swallowed hard and surprised them both by turning around suddenly, her skirts bunching up around her.

"Hugh." His name was a whisper uttered on the peak of her desire. Thunder roared in the distance, and somewhere in the back of Siân's mind, she realized that the storm was moving away. She reached for him and he did not resist.

Hugh's hand continued caressing Siân's hip as his head moved toward hers, his lips warm and seeking. One of his legs slipped between hers as their mouths met. He kissed her with a slow heat that matched the sensuous movements of his leg.

"You are so beautiful, Siân," he said, his kisses tantalizing her ear, then her jaw, her vulnerable throat.

Siân was awash in a river of sensations. The pressure of his thigh, the hard intensity of his touch, made every muscle contract and quiver with pleasure. The only time she'd experienced such closeness, such intimacy, had been with Hugh. She felt as if she were part of him, part of a whole, never to be left alone or isolated again.

She loved him, though she knew how impossible it was. A wayward tear slid into the hair at her temple and Siân hoped Hugh wouldn't notice. She did not want his pity, she wanted his love even though she knew perfectly well that he was not free to give it. Even though she should not be seeking it.

And she refused to acknowledge the guilt that niggled at the edge of her awareness. Her heart clenched, knowing with a certainty that the memories of what happened between them tonight would have to last a lifetime, though it was wrong. Though he was not free to pledge his faith to her forever.

In desperation, Siân arched against his hard length and demanded more. They would be one in truth this time, even if he did belong to Marguerite Bradley and this one night would be all that she could ever have of him.

"Siân," he rasped, turning his head so that it lay quiet on her breast. An eternity of silence passed before he spoke, and Siân knew what he would say before he even uttered the words. "We...cannot. This is not—"

She stifled a whimper, her guilt refusing to stay suppressed. "Oh, Hugh," she said, with tears clogging her throat. She closed her eyes and turned her face away. "I—I know it. I know you have M-Marguerite to think of and you cannot break your troth to her. I should never have—"

"No," he countered. "'Twas was my fault. I should not have touched you...."

When it seemed that he would have said more, he stopped himself. Siân sat up and pulled away from him, straightening her clothes, making herself decent. She would fight the tears that threatened, never allowing him to know how deeply she needed him. How alone she was without him. Biting her lip, struggling to regain her composure, Siân drew her skirts down around her legs, covering her naked flesh, drawing herself into a compact, self-contained package of confidence and self-assurance.

She would never let him know how it hurt her to give him up to Marguerite.

"Siân, I—" He paused, listening. Then they both heard it. Voices, noises outside.

"The horses!"

Hugh was up in an instant. He grabbed his sword and bow, and threw his quiver of arrows over his shoulder. "Stay here and bar the door!" he ordered as he left the hall, slamming the door behind him.

The bastards were stealing the horses—their only means of traveling to Windermere! Hugh ran through the rain toward the sound of the agitated animals.

Luckily, the thieves were not competent horsemen. The horses reared and protested their rough handling. In a quick flash of lightning, Hugh saw that there were three men, likely the vagrants they'd passed on the road, and they were all trying to mount the two horses.

Without hesitation, Hugh nocked an arrow to his bow and let one fly, accurately striking his target. The man made no sound, but fell to the mud, leaving the other two for Hugh to deal with. But at least the odds had improved.

A lot of muttering and cursing followed the downing of one comrade, and the two remaining men split up, leaving the horses untended in the pouring rain. Hugh drew his sword and, seeing no choice, went after the larger man.

The thief was also armed with a sword, and they clashed as soon as Hugh was in striking distance. They parried for a few moments, but Hugh was the better swordsman. He would have finished the man off quickly but for his accomplice, who came up on Hugh's blind side and struck him with a broken tree branch.

Hugh was thrown off balance, but not off his feet. He turned and thrust quickly at the newcomer, who defended himself with the wooden bough. Hugh turned slightly to make a jab at the bigger man, but the rogue slogged through the mud and awkwardly dodged Hugh's sword, while the other fellow with the branch struck again.

The thieves continued attacking from both sides while Hugh successfully fended them off, though it was next to impossible to mount any significant offense against them. And Hugh knew he had to come up with a solution to this skirmish quickly. With the two men waging battle against him, he would tire faster, and they would soon overcome him.

Acutely, he felt the disadvantage of his narrowed vision, being unable to take his eye off his adversary to search out higher ground, or a better position of attack. If he turned just for an instant, he'd lose any slight advantage his skill gave him. He just hoped, that whatever happened, Siân would have the good sense to stay inside with Henry and keep the doors barred against the intruders.

Without warning, an opening came. Hugh took quick advantage of a miscue by his attackers, and lunged for the swordsman, spearing the man in the side. Unfortunately, at the same time, the fellow hacked and wounded Hugh in his upper arm, near the site where his previous wound had already begun to heal.

His arm went numb, and even so, Hugh considered himself fortunate that the rogue hadn't struck him in his sword arm. Reflexively, Hugh finished him off.

But he lost his advantage as the remaining thief blindsided him with the thick oaken branch, knocking him unconscious.

Siân could not leave Hugh out there so badly outnumbered.

She looked for a weapon in the house, but there were none. She finally settled on a big clay jug that she might be able to use in case of necessity. Then she let herself out a back door of the manor house.

The horses had more intelligence than she would ever have credited them. They'd wandered back into the stable, out of the rain. Siân hoped they would stay there for she had no time to bother with them now.

With the large jug in her hands, Siân crept through the rain across the yard where Hugh was beleaguered by two attackers. A third man lay dead on the ground with a sleek, narrow shaft protruding from his throat. Swallowing back a wave of nausea, she watched as Hugh held his own against the remaining men, but knew that the unfair advantage was multiplied by Hugh's lack of sight on his left side. She stole across the yard, undetected by Hugh and the men who continued their pitched battle.

Choking back a scream when Hugh's arm was savagely sliced by the sword, Siân watched with horror as Hugh finished off the rogue. Nearly paralyzed now, and choking on the bile in her throat, she was powerless to act when the oaken branch came down on Hugh's head, knocking him to the ground.

Without thought, she returned the favor and slammed the crockery on the rogue's head, knocking him unconscious, too. Disregarding the man she injured, Siân ran to Hugh's side, knelt in the mud and cradled his head in her lap. "Hugh!" she cried.

He did not respond.

"Os gwelwch yn dda, Huw!" she cried, terrified and desperate for him to react to her. He was breathing, though, and bleeding badly from the wound in his arm. Siân knew there would be a terrible lump on his head where he'd been hit.

She had to get him into the house, out of the rain, but he was a great deal larger than she, and would be impossible to carry. Nor could she pull him by the arms, only to do more damage to the injured one.

Siân quickly ran into the house and gathered up the largest of the furs, checked on Henry to find the child still sound asleep, then ran out again to where Hugh lay in the mud. She carefully rolled him onto the fur, then yanked and pulled and struggled until she managed to drag him into the manor.

First, she barred the door behind them. She doubted that the one surviving thief would be moving anytime soon, but she was unwilling to risk another dangerous confrontation. If the scoundrel regained consciousness and managed to go back and steal the horses, then there was nothing to be done about it.

She tore Hugh's tunic and used the material to make a tourniquet for the wound in his arm. Then she dried him as well as she could and felt his head for lumps, finding a nasty one right at his crown. Dragging him closer to the fire now, Siân covered him with blankets, then threw her cloak over her shoulders and went outside to secure the horses in the stable. They really couldn't afford to lose them.

For the next few minutes she wouldn't allow herself to worry about Hugh. She had to concentrate on taking care of everything else so that when it came time to leave for Windermere they would be able to do so.

Luckily, the animals hadn't wandered. They were still standing in the dry building, out of the rain. There were a few leaks that Siân noticed, but for the most part, the shelter was sound.

She dried the horses down and threw their blankets over them, then stood in the doorway, her arms crossed over her chest, and wondered what to do about the thief who lay unconscious in the yard. She assumed the other two were dead, and therefore no threat to them, but she couldn't very well leave the third man at large to try to steal the horses again. Nor could she leave him out to catch his death in the rain. Clearly, she had no choice in the matter. She had to get him out of the wet.

Glancing around the stable again, Siân spied a long, thin strip of leather. It may have been a whip at one time, or part of a bridle, but it was about to become the man's shackles. She picked up the length of leather and braved the rain to get to the unconscious man. Finding him facedown where she'd left him in the yard, Siân pulled his hands together and tied them securely. Then she pushed him onto his back and pulled him by the feet through the mud to the stable. Leaving him just inside, she shoved the door closed and barred it behind her.

Exhausted now, Siân went back to the house and, once inside, made sure the door of the manor was securely bolted against intruders. Then, leaning her back against the thick wooden door, she took a long, deep breath.

There was still much to do. Hugh's wet clothes had to come off and the wound in his arm needed tending.

It was doubtful that anything could be done about the lump on his head, but Siân thought she might lay a cool, wet cloth on it—not that it would do much more than soothe the injury.

Siân built up the fire, then returned to Hugh. He was still unconscious and unmoving. He was a mess. His clothes were soaked and covered in mud and the wound in his arm still oozed blood.

She started at his feet, and quickly pulled off his soft leather boots. Covering him with a thick blanket—to protect her sanity as well as for modesty's sake—Siân found the laces at his waist and released them. She grasped one side of his chausses and worked the wet cloth down his leg, then leaned across him and worked on the other side. By the time he was bare under the blanket, Siân's hands were caked in mud and she was breathing hard and fast.

Getting the doublet off was even more difficult. Hugh groaned when Siân moved his injured arm, and she shrank from causing him pain, but it was necessary to move it to get the doublet off. She pulled and stretched, then pulled some more, and finally managed to get it over his head and down his injured arm. When he was finally naked but for the cloth wrapped around the wound, Siân washed her hands, then started digging through her pack of belongings.

Certain that the sword wound would have to be sewn, she located her needle and some thread, then ripped another strip of clean cloth from the linen under-kirtle she'd torn for him once before. Returning to his side, she uncovered his shoulder and arm, then peeled away the cloth that bound the arm and washed the wound.

Hugh grimaced and groaned a few times as she

stitched, but didn't put up much resistance. Siân felt he was fortunate not to have awakened for the procedure.

By the time she was finished, Siân realized she was now shivering from the cold. Her own clothes were soggy and mud-caked, and she was anxious to remove them.

Only then would she be able to sleep.

The flickering firelight hurt Hugh's eye, and he mentally cursed whoever was pounding nails in his head. He was warm and dry, though for the life of him, he didn't know how he'd gotten that way. Last he remembered, he was out in the stable yard, battling it out with a couple of thieving vagabonds.

Where were the scoundrels now? And what had happened to Siân and Henry?

Dreading what he might see, Hugh glanced surreptitiously around the room and realized that he was back in the great room of Dryden Hall. The fire was going strong and little Henry lay sleeping peacefully next to him. It seemed that nothing was amiss, other than a deadly headache and the fact that his left arm felt as if it had been torn out by its roots. Those were things he would deal with later. Siân's whereabouts was something he needed to know *now*.

He moved his head slightly and surveyed the room again, but she was not visible. Where had she gone? What had happened to—

Then he saw her. She was in the shadows of the room, just close enough to benefit from the warmth of the fire. Standing next to a bucket of water, Siân bent over and soaked a cloth, then stood straight again and ran the wet cloth down her arms and across her naked breasts. Water trailed down her belly, and when she shivered, everything inside him flexed.

Siân was like an apparition, standing as she was, cloaked in shadows, enticingly visible one moment, then hidden from his view in the next. His throat thickened with arousal, as did other parts of his anatomy. Hugh knew he couldn't continue this way, wanting her, denying himself at every turn.

She would be *his* tonight, he thought fiercely as he moved to get up. He would claim her for his own, regardless of any other commitment, any other—

Pain exploded in his head and shot down the injured arm as he sat up. Then nausea and an alarming dizziness overtook him. He closed his eye and gingerly laid his head down.

Damnation! was all he could think before Siân rushed over to him and sank to her knees next to him.

"Hugh!" she cried, holding a blanket up to cover her nakedness. "You're awake! I was so worried!"

"What happened?" He ventured a glimpse at her once the pounding in his head subsided.

She told him everything, including what she had done with the unconscious thief. A crease appeared between his brows and Siân wondered if she'd done something wrong. Then the most remarkable thing happened.

A small smile appeared on his lips.

This was something Siân had never seen. He wore scowls, frowns, and impassivity on his face, but never smiles. And Siân's heart swelled with joy for she knew that it did not come easy to him.

"And you managed to carry me inside?" he asked. "All alone?"

"Not exactly," she replied. "I rolled you onto this fur, and then dragged you in."

A somber expression suddenly replaced his more relaxed one. "Siân, you should have stayed inside," he said.

Siân's brow creased this time.

"What if they...if Henry..." he said, when he was really thinking about the danger Siân had been in when she'd come outside to help him.

All her warm feelings fled.

She stood up abruptly and wrapped the blanket tightly around her, then grabbed clean, dry clothes and stepped into the shadows to dress. The surly earl of Alldale may have smiled, but *she* was exhausted, her emotions were in chaos and her nerves were frayed. There was no winning with this man! She'd saved his miserable hide, and all he could do was complain and berate her. Yes, she'd taken a risk when she'd gone outside to see what could be done, she knew it as well as he did.

But all he could think was that she'd left Henry.

She yanked on her linen under-kirtle—the one she'd ruined by using strips of it for Hugh's various wounds—and pulled her fur to the far end of the hearth where she lay down and forced herself to stay still. She *would* sleep. She *would* forget about that small smile he'd given her.

Swallowing back a pitiful thickness in her throat, she pulled her blanket up over her shoulders and closed her eyes.

Let her brood, Hugh thought as he carried the packs to the stable the following morning. His head ached abominably and his left arm was next to useless. But they were going on to Windermere today. They could not afford to dally.

Siân had barely spoken to him since the night before when he'd given her cause to believe he was ungrateful for her help. In truth, he was exceedingly grateful for his life and had no doubt that he'd be dead if not for her intervention.

In good conscience, however, he could not encourage her fond feelings for him. He'd been an addled fool the night before, thinking that he could have Siân, and the marriage, as well. The relationship he had planned with Marguerite suited him. There would be no emotional entanglements with Marguerite, no intensity of passion such as Siân roused.

Life would be well ordered and controlled at Clairmont. His role there was predetermined, predictable. It was the kind of life he needed.

A rough voice called out as Hugh pulled open the stable doors. "Unbind me, man!"

Hugh's vision adjusted to the dimness of the interior and he made out the shape of a man on the ground.

"Blighted wench went and tied me to—"

"The *lady* can run you through for all I care," Hugh muttered as he walked past the thief. He wasn't going to waste time on the villain, just get the horses saddled and packed and they would be on their way. The only problem was how he would manage to lift the saddles and throw them onto the backs of the horses. Hugh didn't think he had the strength in his injured arm to do it.

He would have to get Siân to help him.

He dropped the packs in the dust of the stable floor and went back to the prisoner. He was still securely tied.

"On your feet," he said, using one hand to haul the man up.

He half pushed, half steered the thief into one of the horse stalls and latched the gate, effectively imprisoning him.

"You can't leave me in here!" the thief complained.

Hugh ignored the man's protests. Getting the horses saddled while keeping Siân and Henry safe was going to be a logistical nightmare. He had to lock up the blackguard, at least until they were mounted and ready to depart. Otherwise, the man would be free to grab Henry. Or, God forbid, Siân.

Hugh stood outside the stable doors and deeply breathed in the morning scents. It was always best after a drenching rain, he thought. Clean and pure, open and free.

He looked up and saw Siân walking toward him, along with little Henry. She seemed so natural this way, with the little boy tagging along, talking incessantly, his tiny hand carefully enclosed in her own. The little king's speech was occasionally punctuated by her own, but for the most part, she let him chatter away.

Dangerous thoughts began to crowd him as he watched her move gracefully down the path. Thoughts he could not even begin to entertain.

"Siân," he said hoarsely.

Siân looked up, startled, as if she hadn't realized that he was standing there. She made no response at first, but swung Henry up into her arms before coming any closer to him. The little king shielded her like a suit of armor.

"You'll have to help me with the saddles," he said.

She glanced past him into the dark, gaping doorway of the stable, but didn't speak. Her beautiful eyes seemed tired and hollow, their expression decidedly unfriendly. Hugh could only be grateful she didn't berate him for asking for assistance now, when last night he'd scolded her for coming to his rescue.

Somehow, they managed to get the saddles on and the horses packed. Hugh was sweating profusely by the time they finished, and his head felt as if it had been wedged into a vise. His left arm was screaming in pain. It would be by sheer force of will if he managed to keep his seat all the way to Windermere, but Hugh had every intention of doing so.

Once they got there, Kit Colston could work her skills on him, the way she'd done after his imprisonment. Hugh was well aware that it was only because of Kit's knowledge and healing skills that he had survived his ordeal. Just as Siân's quick action last night had saved him.

Before they left the yard, Hugh returned to the stable and flipped a small knife into the stall with the prisoner. Having been brutally imprisoned himself, he could only be humane now.

He had every confidence that by the time the scoundrel got loose, they would be miles away.

It was just past midday when they reached Windermere Castle. Siân saw the high walls that surrounded the stone fortress and the three tall towers within. It was an impressive sight.

"See th' princess now, Hew?" Henry asked sleepily. He'd been courting sleep for the last few miles, but resisting a nap in anticipation of meeting the Windermere princess promised by Hugh.

Siân glanced over at Hugh when he answered, well aware that it took every ounce of his strength to stay upright and in the saddle, much less to speak. His weakened condition took the edge off some of her anger, but she would never allow her heart to be so vulnerable to him again. He'd made it perfectly clear—repeatedly—that he wanted no part of her.

It didn't change her plans, really. Though she was late in realizing it, there'd never been any hope of a future with Hugh. Owen had told her often enough that she was not the kind of wife a nobleman would ever chose. Besides her utter unsuitability, she bore the Tudor name…not something she could readily discard.

Besides, Hugh was promised to Marguerite Bradley and that was that. Siân would go ahead with the plans she'd made that night at Clairmont before they'd taken Henry and run. She was not some helpless, ignorant waif. After Henry was settled at Windermere, Siân would defy Owen and find employment in some noble house.

But first, she would avenge Idwal and Dafydd.

The road to Windermere was much better kept once they reached the town border. It seemed to Siân that there was a great deal of commerce going on, but Hugh's deteriorating condition worried her so much that she could not appreciate everything she saw. He was gray and drawn and she was anxious to gain the castle walls and get him to his friends where he could rest and heal.

"Lord Alldale!" a man called from the doorway of a large building. His voice registered surprise on seeing Hugh.

Siân turned to look upon two men who had been leaving the building when they'd spotted Hugh and called out to him.

"Juvet," Hugh replied, his voice strained and harsh.

Siân knew he was near the end of his endurance and she wanted to get him through town and past the castle walls.

"His Grace is here," the man named Juvet answered. "He will, no doubt, be pleased to see you."

"No doubt," Hugh muttered almost too quietly for Siân to hear.

"Where's th' princess, Hew?" Henry whined. He was tired and ill-tempered and Siân knew he was another one who needed to find a bed at Windermere Castle.

"We'll find out now. Her father is inside," Hugh replied, pulling up and dismounting. "Juvet," he called to the shorter of the two men, his voice sounding slightly stronger than before. "Help the lady, would you?"

"Certainly, my lord," the man replied as he gave a hand to Siân. "Are you all right?" Juvet asked, looking back at Hugh, who was not able to move his left arm at all now.

Before Hugh could answer, a tall, dark-haired man stepped out into the overcast day. Dressed in finely tailored clothes, with the dignified and imposing manner of a high-ranking lord, Siân knew this had to be the duke of Carlisle, Hugh's friend, Wolf Colston. His striking features were marred by a terrible scar that creased his forehead and traversed his brow and cheek. Siân knew that it was only a miracle that could have saved him from death after such an injury and she wondered about it.

The duke squinted against the brighter light outside and when they alighted on Hugh, his sharp gray eyes darkened with concern. In only a moment, he was at Hugh's side, questioning him.

Not wishing to intrude on Hugh's reunion with his friend, Siân stood waiting next to her mare, holding the fidgety child, when suddenly Henry whined impatiently, "Hew! Where's th' princess!"

The two men looked up and walked over to where she stood holding Henry, who was clamoring to get *down!*

"Lady Siân Tudor," Hugh said, his voice sounding strained, "this is Wolf Colston, Duke of Carlisle, Lord of Winder—"

"'Tis a pleasure, my lady," the duke said, bowing slightly over Siân's free hand. Siân made to curtsy as etiquette demanded, but Colston kept her from doing so. "Forgive me for being brief, but we must get Hugh to Windermere. He does not appear at all well."

Siân nodded as the duke took Henry from her arms, out of her charge. "That is so, Your Grace," she said distractedly. "He was badly wounded last night..." She hadn't anticipated giving Henry up just yet; she'd hardly adjusted to the idea that Hugh would never be hers. Now the little boy she cherished was gone from her, too.

"Can you mount, Siân?" Hugh said. "If not—"

Siân wiped all expression from her face when she saw Hugh glance her way. She was not about to let him see that she was completely bereft now. Not only was *he* lost to her, but her little *Parry* was gone now, as well, into the capable hands of the duke of Carlisle. She was really and truly alone again.

Blinking back pointless, idiotic tears, she climbed back on her horse and headed for Windermere Castle.

Chapter Twelve

It was difficult for Hugh to stay upright in the saddle. Fortunately, it would be only a few more minutes before they arrived at the massive stone steps of Windermere Castle and he could find a quiet place to deal with his headache and his wound.

Hugh suggested that Wolf return Henry to Siân as soon as she was mounted and, even through his haze of weakness, he could not help but note how her shoulders sagged with relief to get him back. Hugh hadn't realized how attached she'd become to the boy, nor how difficult it would be for her to give him up.

It was a wonder he could think of *anything,* though, with the pounding going on in his head. Somehow they made it to the castle, and Hugh managed to climb the steps and enter the great hall. Wolf preceded him, heading for the hearth where his duchess, Lady Kit, sat near the fire holding a small bundle. Two of Kit Colston's ladies stood nearby, looking quite pleased with the world.

Then the bundle let out a wail that pierced through Hugh's sensitive skull and understanding dawned. Kit's babe was born.

The lady greeted her husband with a flash of the eyes and a radiant smile, and for the first time, Hugh had some notion of what it was that bound Wolf and Kit together. He was able to perceive the love and passion the two shared on a level that he'd never sensed before.

And all from a look.

Hugh didn't know why it suddenly struck him *now*. After all, he was as close to Wolf as a brother, and Kit had become a sister to him, as well. It had been Kit who'd found him near death in the passage under the castle, and Kit who'd tended his wounds and nursed him back to health after Philip Colston had died. It seemed strange to him that he'd never before realized the strength of their devotion to each other.

It must have been the bash on his head. If he continued with these foolish notions, he'd soon be seeing the saints stepping out of their stained glass and joining them near the fire.

Kit turned slightly to greet whomever had arrived with her husband, and realized with surprise that it was Hugh who accompanied Wolf.

"Hugh!" she said over the noise of the squalling newborn.

"Yes, Your Grace," Hugh said, faltering slightly as he bowed. "I see you've been industrious in my absence."

"Hugh, you are not well," Kit said, frowning, ignoring the man's uncharacteristic attempt at humor. "What is it?"

"It's a long story," he replied, fading fast. "Too long to tell now. I...I'm afraid I—"

"Wolf," Kit said, "help him to his room. Maggie, fetch a footman to help and send a maid on ahead to turn down the bed."

"No footman," Hugh said. "I will manage on my own."

"Don't be surly, Dryden," Wolf said as he supported Hugh and helped him to the stairs. "You'll take whatever assistance is offered. Kit, don't get up," he added for the benefit of his wife, who'd just been allowed downstairs after bearing his son. "Someone can go for Will Rose as soon as we've settled him."

Hugh staggered slightly when he saw Siân standing alone in the shadows of the great hall, with Henry in her arms. She'd held herself apart, Hugh realized with dismay, as if she might not be welcome.

"Wolf…"

"Kit will see to her," Wolf said, noting the direction of Hugh's glance. "She will be made comfortable."

"Will you join us, m'lady?" the woman asked Siân. She was as plain as a sparrow, but more friendly than any flitting bird. "Lady Kit bids you to come and sit, and warm yourself."

Siân had felt alone many a time. And this was no different from any of those times, she thought, as she tightened up what little backbone she had left. She still had little *Parry,* and he was a comfort to her, snoozing with his head tucked under her chin, and his thumb firmly planted in his mouth.

"Thank you," Siân said as she watched Hugh make his way up the imposing stone stairs of Windermere.

"Maggie went to fetch the healer. Old William will take care of him," the woman said as she took Siân's elbow and led her to the hearth where the duchess sat with another young woman. "And he's very good at his craft, so you needn't worry."

"I—I'm not worried," Siân said, wishing she were

not quite so transparent. It was impossible not to show her concern, even though she knew it would be unwelcome. "It's not my place to…"

"Here we are," the woman said. "Her Grace, the Duchess of Carlisle—"

"Thank you, Emma," the duchess said as she cradled her infant's head against her breast. She was fair-skinned, with shimmering blond tresses intricately woven to crown her head. Green eyes as clear as glass greeted Siân, along with a charming, friendly smile. "I am Kit Colston. Please do not stand on ceremony," she said. "Join me."

"Your Grace, it is an honor to meet you," Siân said as she sat across from the duchess, feeling not nearly so alone any more. Lady Kit had a surprising ability to extend warmth and welcome, and a sense of belonging. "I am Siân Tudor," she said quietly in deference to the child sleeping in her arms.

"Of Wales?"

Siân nodded.

"I met Owen Tudor in London," Her Grace said. "A relation?"

"My brother," Siân said. "He was raised English. I stayed in Wales with my uncles."

"I see," the duchess said. The infant made suckling noises and its mother stroked its cheek. "What ails Lord Hugh? He was well when last we saw him."

"Your Grace—"

"Please call me Kit," the lovely woman said, "we are not so formal here at Windermere."

Siân nodded and shifted Henry slightly. She was unsure how much to say. "Lord Hugh and I…were sent to you from Clairmont."

"By whom?"

"Queen Catherine," Siân said quietly.

"Your Grace," Emma interjected tactfully. She'd been a close friend of Kit Colston's since Kit's arrival as a bride at Windermere over two years before, and she knew when the duchess needed privacy. "May I fetch Maggie to attend you? I am needed at home."

"Of course, Emma! I'm sorry, I lost all track of time."

"As well you should, Your Grace," Emma said with a laugh. "'Tis a fine and wondrous thing to suckle your firstborn son."

Kit smiled at her companion, and when she was left alone with Siân, she spoke. "You must tell me all. From events at Clairmont to Hugh's infirmity. Leave out nothing."

A hot poultice made the wound in Hugh's arm throb mercilessly, but the cool compress that lay across the lump on his head was soothing. He was shivering, but it didn't stop him from recounting the events leading up to his arrival at Windermere.

Wolf listened quietly, interrupting once or twice to clarify a point, then letting Hugh continue before he dozed off, which he did before very much time elapsed.

"'Tis a nasty wound," William Rose said quietly to Wolf, though Hugh could still hear them. "Just startin' to fester."

"Will it heal?"

Will shrugged. "He's lived through worse, I daresay, but who ever knows?"

After Henry awoke from his nap and broke his fast, he'd been pleased to meet little Eleanor Colston—the beautiful, blond princess Hugh had talked about. The little king was happy and very well situated, with Lady Kit doting on him as if he were one of her own children. Siân could see that Henry would be well cared for.

Hugh was in good hands, as well. The healer knew his business, it seemed, and along with Lady Kit, they decided what concoctions to use to draw out the poison from the wound in Hugh's arm. He was feverish and groggy, so he wasn't even aware of Siân when she came into his room to visit.

She sat with him for hours, making the most of this last opportunity to touch him as often as she could. She offered him sips of water, changed the poultice, freshened the compress for his head, and prayed for the fever to pass. And during the night, as Hugh lay with stuporous fever, Siân whispered all her hopes and dreams to him. She told him of wishes that could never be. She wept a little, too, and told him of her resolve to return to Clairmont and deal with Wrexton. Then she told him she loved him.

And when there was nothing left to say, she went to find her own bed, satisfied that he hadn't understood a single one of the words that she'd uttered in Welsh.

"Tell me, Siân," Lady Kit said, "how you came to be entangled in all this court intrigue." They sat together in Kit's solar, as Henry played with "Princess El'nor," and Kit's five-day-old son, Bartholomew, lay sleeping in his cradle near his mother.

Siân had been readily accepted as an intimate friend of the family, and honored as the one who'd valiantly saved Hugh's life. "I suppose I just happened to be available," she replied.

"Come now, Siân. I know Catherine would not trust

her son to *anyone*," Kit said with a smile. "She must hold you in high regard."

That statement surprised and puzzled Siân. For most of her life, she'd thought of herself as merely a burden to others. She assumed Catherine had chosen her to accompany Hugh simply because she was available. She had no other responsibilities, nor would she be missed at Clairmont when Bishop Beaufort realized that King Henry was gone.

"I—I suppose so," she said as one faint line creased her brow. Her value to the queen was something to think about.

"You certainly have a way with children," Kit added. "Henry is very fond of you. He doesn't like it when you're out of his sight."

"No, I suppose not," Siân replied. "But he misses his mother."

"That may be," Kit said, smiling, "but Queen Catherine chose a worthy substitute. Even Eleanor is at ease with you, and she does not readily take to strangers."

"She is a sweet child," Siân said wistfully, observing the way the two toddlers played. They played side by side, with Henry busily stacking blocks, and Eleanor rocking her own straw-filled "baby."

"And your spirit, Siân. Your courage... You know that Hugh Dryden would certainly have perished had you not intervened with the thieves as you did. He owes you his life."

"No," Siân countered. "Lord Hugh owes me nothing. He has been very...fair...with me," she said, hoping that the emotions she felt were not readily visible to Kit, who was studying her intently, though not unkindly.

"Tell me," Kit finally said at length, "how did

Hugh fare with Lady Marguerite? Have the banns been read?''

''N-no,'' Siân replied, keeping her voice as steady as possible, and swallowing the lump in her throat before she spoke, ''they have not. But as I have never been privy to the earl's marital negotiations…''

''So the betrothal is not yet official and binding?''

''I…I do not know.''

''Tell me of Lady Marguerite. Is she as beautiful as they say?''

''Oh, yes,'' Siân promptly replied, though she was unable to keep a slight tinge of bitterness from her voice. ''Even more so. She is perfect in every way.''

''Perfect?'' Kit laughed, a pretty sound that fit the warmth and caring atmosphere of the room. ''Who of us is truly perfect, Siân?''

Kit Colston had obviously not met Marguerite Bradley.

''We all have our imperfections,'' Kit explained. ''Even when everything *appears* exactly right, how can you ever know for certain that it truly *is?*''

These were thoughts that had never occurred to Siân. Her own shortcomings had always been pointed out to her, with her aunts and uncles, and now Owen, contrasting her with the paragons around her. She had never even been a contender.

''All any of us can really hope to do, is our best,'' Kit continued. ''We may fall short in one area, but excel in another.''

Siân thought of all the areas in which she fell short. The account was overwhelming. From her clothes to her hair, from housekeeping skills to piety, she was sadly lacking.

''I am fortunate that my husband does not expect

perfection from me,'' Kit said, ''for he would be sorely disappointed.''

''Oh, but—''

''By the same token,'' Kit proceeded, ''perfection can be a difficult thing to live with. What would I do with a husband who never erred? And what's worse, what need would he have of *me?*''

''I've never thought…'' Siân began, then stopped herself. She knew naught of what men and women expected of marriage. She only knew what *she* would want—a man who was kind and slow to anger. Someone she could cherish, and who would cherish her, and make her feel whole. Someone who needed her to the roots of his soul.

But the one man who could have been all of those things was pledged to another.

''I've never considered the question before, Your Grace,'' Siân finally said. ''But I don't imagine it will be difficult for Lord Hugh to live at Clairmont with Lady Marguerite.''

''Will she make him happy?''

''Happy? …I—I could not say,'' Siân replied, hardly trusting her voice not to betray the tumult of emotions going on within her. Whether or not Marguerite Bradley could make Hugh happy had nothing to do with her. He was bound to Marguerite, and he would honor his pledge.

The baby started to fuss and Kit picked him up, gently bouncing him in her arms. ''Can Lady Marguerite…accept Hugh's imperfections?''

What imperfections? Siân wanted to shout. A few old injuries? The man was fair and just. He had more goodness and honor in him than most men she knew. He was gentle and kind and he'd rescued her more times than she cared to count. "I am certain Lady Marguerite will accept Lord Hugh in every way," she finally said.

Kit seemed to ponder Siân's words as she attended the baby, and when she spoke again, it was on another subject. "What will you do now, Lady Siân—now that you've gotten Henry to safety?"

"M-my future is uncertain, Your Grace," Siân replied. "My brother arranged for the Abbey of St. Ann to take me as a postulant," she said without noticing Kit's look of surprise. "But...I've decided not to go."

"I cannot say as I blame you, Siân," Kit said as she sat down with her son in a comfortable chair by the fire. "You seem wholly unsuited to a nunnery."

"But I must find employment of some sort," she said, "to earn my keep." How and when that would happen, she did not know. She still felt compelled to return to Clairmont but did not know how she would manage *that,* either. There were so many details to consider, consequences to prepare for.

Kit opened her gown and put the baby to breast. "Then you do not care to marry?"

"No, it's n-not that..." she stammered, watching Kit perform a loving task that Siân had long since abandoned every hope of doing for her own child one day. "I m-might have considered it once, but..." But after she accomplished the murder of Wrexton, her fate was unsure. She would likely have to return to Wales to find refuge, somewhere far, far away from Clairmont.

Away from Hugh Dryden and his wife.

"Surely there is a man somewhere in the kingdom who would make a suitable husband for you," Kit said, apparently unwilling to let the subject drop. "Wolf and I know several marriageable men—"

"No!" Siân said.

Kit looked up at Siân's sharp rejection of marriage. "Then you are otherwise engaged? You...*care* for someone? Is he already married...or...betrothed?"

Siân shook her head and wished she were a better liar. "No," she replied, her voice sounding too breathless as she stumbled over her words. "It's just that I...well, I'm not well suited to m-marriage."

Kit's brows knitted together with disbelief. "Why would you think such a thing, Siân?"

She shook her head helplessly. This was not at all the direction Siân wanted the conversation to go. She did not want to recount all the reprimands her brother had given her since their reunion, nor discuss any of the other deficiencies she recognized in herself.

"You have a number of valuable qualities, Siân, not the least of which are your faithfulness and loyalty. Yet you seem set on underestimating yourself."

"But I've never... M-my family always...."

Kit frowned. "Families are not always best qualified to measure our worth. Each of us must do that for ourselves and by our own standards."

Chapter Thirteen

Three days after Hugh's arrival at Windermere, he got out of bed, dressed, and went in search of the young woman whose face haunted his waking hours, as well as those while he slept.

"'Tis good to see you up and about, Lord Hugh," one of the footmen said when he arrived in the great hall.

Hugh nodded to the man and asked, "Have you any idea where I might find His Grace?"

"I am not sure, my lord," the servant replied.

"What about Lady Siân?" he asked.

The footman shook his head. "I have not seen her today, my lord."

Hugh turned and made a cursory search of the main floor of the castle. No one had seen Siân, so he had to assume she was with Kit in her rooms, probably occupied with Henry.

Still feeling the effects of the fever and infection, he climbed the stairs again and headed for Kit's solar. When he finally arrived, he found Kit and Wolf, together with their children and the little king.

"Hugh!" Kit said when she looked up and saw him in the doorway.

"Hew!" Henry cried, and went running to him. "Up!"

Hugh picked up the child and walked into the room.

"You appear decidedly better, my lord," Kit said, frankly surprised at his affability and ease with the child. Hugh had always been one to keep to himself, and he'd been utterly taciturn in the last months before his departure for Clairmont. This attachment between the man and boy was wholly unexpected. "I wondered how long I'd be able to keep you down."

Hugh shrugged. "I'm looking for Siân."

"She's not here," Wolf said, "but it's high time you met my son."

Hugh had never seen Wolf looking more proud or noble. Except, perhaps, when his daughter, Eleanor Bridget, had been born.

The infant was alert, with a shock of black hair, in direct opposition to the towheaded fairness of his sister. But their eyes would be alike, Hugh thought, the bright green they'd inherited from their mother.

"Bartholomew is rather a large appellation for one so small," Hugh said as he looked back at the babe's father.

"What's this?" Wolf laughed. "Humor?"

"Don't tease, Wolf," Kit interjected, surprised by yet another change in Hugh. She turned to her husband's closest friend and said, "We call him Bart. Eleanor can't come close to pronouncing the whole thing."

"Nor can the rest of us," Wolf said, chuckling, "but Kit insisted on naming him for my father. I liked 'Bill' or 'Alf' but my lady wife wouldn't hear of it."

Hugh looked from Wolf to Kit, then back to Wolf again. He was unaccustomed to such lighthearted bantering. He supposed they'd always engaged in jesting between them, but for some reason *he* had never taken note of it.

Setting aside his puzzlement for the moment, Hugh let Henry down to go back and play with his princess, and sat with Kit and Wolf. "I have not seen Siân since we arrived three days ago," he said. "Where is she?"

"Are you saying that Lady Siân is avoiding you?"

Hugh sighed. "What else should I think?" he asked. "She has not graced me with her presence since…" Since the night when she'd sat with him, holding his hand, whispering Welsh words to him. He'd been too ill to ask her to speak English, and besides, her voice was soothing to him no matter what language she used. He'd felt strangely adrift and alone after she left him; feelings that were certainly not foreign to him, though that sense of isolation had been changing of late. "…since the night we arrived."

"Hugh, what do you know of Siân's brother settling her in a nunnery?" Kit asked.

Hugh's demeanor stiffened. "It's a ridiculous plan," he said. "There are other alternatives for her."

"What alternatives?" Kit asked. "She told me she will not marry."

"What do you mean?" Hugh asked sourly. "Siân was meant to marry, to be surrounded by children. Have you not seen the way she—"

Kit exchanged a glance with Wolf.

"What?" Hugh demanded sharply as he stood up again and began pacing in front of the fire.

"Siân feels she would not be an adequate wife," Kit explained. "I sense that she has been berated so often and so severely that she cannot believe she could ever be an asset to a husband.''

"That's ridiculous," Hugh snorted. "She is…"

"She is what?" Wolf asked, tipping his head suspiciously.

"She is…" Hugh ran one hand through his hair. "She is *not* going to become a nun!"

Wolf and Kit Colston could only stare in disbelief as he turned and stormed out of the room.

Siân sat on the steps leading to a small stone chapel in the middle of Windermere's garden. The little building, which consisted of one oblong room, was quite unusual, Siân thought, with stained-glass windows on all four sides. From where she sat, Siân could see the castle itself through the trees, but it seemed distant and remote. She was virtually alone in her own quiet world out there, with no one, not even the gardeners, to disturb her meditations.

Wrapping her cloak tightly against the breeze, which had turned chilly with the dusk, Siân got up and climbed the stairs into the chapel. She lit a few candles against the darkening gloom and sat down on one of the benches.

She felt very much at home at Windermere. Kit and her husband had welcomed her into their home to an extent that was wholly unfamiliar to Siân. She had yet to be criticized for her attire, her untamable hair, or her deportment. No one berated her lack of feminine skills or beauty. Since coming to Windermere, her confidence had grown. She was no longer the clumsy girl she'd been at Clairmont.

But could she stay here at Windermere? Could she

live out her life knowing that Wrexton still lived, still preyed on the innocent?

Could she return to Clairmont and commit murder?

Siân thought again of that morning when she'd stood over the evil earl, knife in hand, ready to plunge. And yet, she'd held back. Held back long enough for Hugh Dryden to stop her.

Hugh wouldn't be there to stay the knife next time, though. Now that she knew he was nearly recovered, Siân could bring herself to leave Windermere. She would visit his room once more while he slept, and say a last goodbye. Early in the morning, she would leave, with no one the wiser, taking what stores she'd need for the journey and leaving on the mare she'd ridden from Clairmont.

Brushing away a foolish tear, and forcing herself to think of anything *but* leaving Hugh for the last time, she considered the journey ahead of her. It would not be easy. She did not know where she would stay the first night on the road because Dryden Hall was too close to Windermere. She would need to ride a lot farther—

"Siân."

Without looking up, Siân knew the voice. She recognized the deep, rich timbre of it and knew it belonged to the one man whose presence she had wanted to elude. It had been days since she'd seen him, days of passing the hours trying not to think of him, trying to insulate her heart against the pain of the moment when they parted.

Knowing that he belonged to Marguerite, that he would soon return to that gracious lady, was more than Siân could bear. For her own sanity, she had to keep away from him. She couldn't risk becoming any more attached than she already was.

Siân arose as he stepped into the chapel and walked to the opposite side. "Hugh," she said, her voice hollow and vulnerable in spite of herself.

His stance was tense, movements controlled. He did not seem cold, though he wore no cloak, only a cordovan tunic over dark chausses. When he turned to face her, his features were cast into harsh relief by the flickering light of the candles.

"I've...not seen you...these last days," he finally said.

Siân could only nod.

He took a few steps toward her, the intensity of his gaze causing Siân to take one step back.

"You saved my life, Siân, and likely that of your little *Parry,* yet you cannot rouse enough interest in seeing for yourself how I fare?"

"I—it's not that, my lord, I—"

"What is it, then?" he asked quietly, coming dangerously close to her. So close, in fact, that Siân could feel his warm breath on her face, smell the leather of his tunic.

She swallowed hard and ignored the pounding of her heart. He was too close. She could hardly breathe without her breasts rising and coming in contact with his hard chest. If he touched her—

"Siân," he said again, his voice harsh and raw.

She could not move. When his hands cupped her face, she felt as if she'd become a boneless mass. When his lips touched hers, she was certain of it.

Seemingly without volition, and against all that she'd told herself these past days, her hands skimmed up his chest, relishing the solid feel of him. She entangled the fingers of one hand in the hair at his nape and welcomed his kiss, increasing the contact between them.

Hugh groaned and pulled her to him, running his hands up her back, sending shivers of pleasure through her. Lord, how she'd needed his touch…his strong and fierce presence. He kissed her lips, then her ear, and moved his mouth down her neck, until he reached the barrier of her gown. Siân sighed. Without further hesitation, Hugh untied her cloak and let it fall. Next were buttons and laces, of which he made quick work.

Siân trembled, though she did not feel the chilled air. She soon stood bare before him as he worshiped her with his hands, his lips, his teeth and tongue.

Because of his wound, he had some difficulty removing his own tunic, but Siân reached up to help him pull it off. Then, as she untied the laces of his chausses, his hungry kiss became desperate. Their bodies met, skin to skin, heart to heart.

"You are mine, Siân," he rasped as he lowered her to the bed of discarded clothes on the stone floor. "Never forget it."

She reveled in his touch as his hands moved over her, caressing intimately, arousing her, teaching her to please him. She ran her hands down his back, cupping the tight muscles of his hips, savoring the various textures of his body. She learned the hard muscles and planes of his body as he discovered the soft curves of hers, touching, tasting, creating a maelstrom of desire. Sensations flowed through her, foreign yet familiar, satisfying but frustrating.

She needed more.

Sensing her readiness, he moved again, shifting her, and suddenly she was over him, then part of him.

They became one with a sharp plunge that bound their souls together, along with their bodies. They moved in a rhythm born of the ages, in a cadence that propelled them toward completion, with hearts pounding, nerves roaring, and muscles flexing.

"More!" her heart demanded as she gave him all, and wrung from him every dram of passion in his soul. Liquid heat engulfed her. An animal wildness surged through her. The powerful rhythm drove her toward a culmination she could not fathom, but one she desperately sought.

When finally Hugh shifted them so that Siân lay under him, a new, more intense fire rushed through her. She met each thrust as Hugh's power and strength became her own. She felt his heart pounding against hers, the force of his muscles straining in union with her own. She heard his harsh panting breaths, his groans of fulfillment. And suddenly, in a whirlwind of sensation, something entirely untamed burst within her.

Swept outside of herself, she joined Hugh in an exquisite intensity that made them one being, heart and soul. The oneness spiraled for a seeming eternity, then exploded in a triumphant shattering expression of emotion.

Their return to earth was slow and sweet.

He ran the fingers of one hand over her wondrous features, reveling in the smoothness of her skin, the lightness of her touch. Her eyes glimmered with unreserved emotion.

"You are a dream, Siân," he said, looking into her sated eyes. "I've never…"

Hugh began to think dangerously. They were scattered, disjointed thoughts, about marriage, about Marguerite Bradley. The perfection of Marguerite's features, the care with which the lady dressed, her competency in keeping Clairmont running… None of these attributes compared to Siân's spontaneity, her generosity of spirit, her fire for him.

And Hugh had not realized until now, how important that was to him. He hadn't understood how abhorrent Marguerite's cool competence and constant aversion would be to him.

But Hugh was tied to her by his proposal, bound to uphold his offer of marriage.

Siân pulled away and sat up, gathering her clothes as she did so. Her features were soft and beautiful in the flickering candlelight and he wanted her again. Hugh knew he'd want her always.

"Don't, Siân," he said, gathering her into his arms again. "I—"

She stopped him with a few of her slender fingers pressed against his lips. "Please, Hugh," she said, "you are already promised to Lady Marguerite. I would not ask you to break your vow, and I ask you to say nothing now—"

"Siân," Hugh said, frowning as he took her hand and kissed the palm. Then he drew her to him and pressed his lips to hers. Passion flared again, but Siân wrenched herself away.

Hugh traced her jawline with his thumb and looked into her troubled eyes. She was so beautiful, so wildly passionate. She was more to him than he'd ever thought possible, but he'd had no right to do this, no right to make love to her. She was an innocent and *he* knew better. He could offer her nothing. Not even the protection of his name.

"I—I will remember this night always," Siân said, her eyes sparkling a little too brightly, her chin trembling slightly. "When...when you are back at Clairmont and—"

"Siân," he said, tracing the contour of her ear with gentle fingers, "Clairmont means nothing to me. Marguerite will never be the wife of my heart, nor does she want to be."

"How can you say such a thing?" Siân protested. A flurry of emotions crossed her face from disbelief to astonishment. "Any woman would be well pleased to have you as her husband. Lady Marguerite is no different than any—"

"Siân," he said, pressing a kiss to her mouth. "You overpraise me. Could it be that you are unaware of my flaws? My scars? Most women take one look and flee."

"That is not so, Hugh," Siân countered. "You may be scarred, but what difference does it make to the goodness of your soul? How does the possession of a few scars alter the honor in your heart?"

Hugh dropped his hand from Siân's face and looked away. He began to gather up their clothes and helped Siân to dress. "Honor is something I forfeited two years ago when I was imprisoned here at Windermere."

He saw the crease appear between her brows, as if she couldn't understand, and he felt compelled to continue.

"Many years ago, Wolf's cousin usurped his title," Hugh explained. "Wolf eventually found the evidence that would convict Philip Colston of his crimes, and I was sent from London to Windermere to keep an eye on him until the king's men could apprehend him.

"Colston...took me prisoner. I was taken down below Windermere Castle and chained to a wall in one of the tunnels."

"Oh, Hugh!" Siân cried. She stopped dressing and took his hands in hers.

"Philip had a penchant for inflicting pain," Hugh continued. "He tortured and killed his stepmother there, while I watched, unable to intervene, powerless to assist her in any way."

Siân gasped.

"Then he took his pleasure from working on me," Hugh said quietly. "He had every possible instrument of pain in that dank cellar…"

"Your eye?" Siân asked, swallowing the tears burning in the back of her throat.

Hugh gave a quick nod. "Among other things."

Siân bit her lip to keep from crying out loud.

"He was a master of exquisite pain, Siân," Hugh said. "He knew how to draw it out, how to squeeze every bit of enjoyment from it, short of causing unconsciousness…or death."

She shuddered. "Oh, my poor Hugh," she said, "how did you ever survive?"

"That is my shame, Siân," he replied, "I tried to buy my own survival with betrayal."

She didn't comprehend, and he could read that lack of understanding on her face.

"I…promised *to deliver Wolf* to Philip…" Hugh's voice was a mere shadow to her ears, "if only he would set me free."

A long silence ensued. Hugh felt there was no greater dishonor than promising to betray Wolf, his closest friend and ally, for his own pitiful life. And now Siân knew of his disgrace, as well.

"Hugh," Siân said earnestly, looking directly into his eye. "How can you hold yourself responsible for trying to bargain for time?"

"Time?" Hugh countered. "It was Wolf's *life*…he is a brother to me, and I would have handed him to his—"

"Don't you see?" Siân asked in earnest. "It was *time* that I was bargaining for, as well, when I told the earl of Wrexton that *I* was the one who stole his lambs. I was in such pain, I did not know what I was saying, only that if I kept up my story, then somehow, someone would intervene. Someone would come along and stop the horrible nightmare and everything would be all right again."

"Siân, they're two different—"

"No, Hugh," she said, "Wolf Colston is a most formidable knight! Some part of your mind knew it, remembered it! You had to know that even if you tried to give him over to Philip, Wolf would never succumb to his cousin, however powerful or devious he was."

"No. That is not how it was—"

"Oh, but it was!" Siân took his beloved, troubled face in her hands. "I know you could not have been aware of it at the time, but you *must* have realized Wolf would come up with a plan…and that Wolf would divert Philip's attention from you long enough for you—or him—to act. Hugh, you are too noble, too honorable to willingly give up the fight."

She kissed his astonished face. "Can you have so much faith in me?" he asked.

"Of course," she said. "You are nothing if not noble and kind. Chivalry is deeply bred in you, Hugh. I've seen with my own eyes that you are incapable of treachery."

"Siân—"

One crystal tear formed and spilled over Siân's cheek. Hugh brushed it away with his thumb as she spoke. "Speak no more of dishonor and betrayal," she said, her voice tight with emotion. "You did as any man would, under the circumstances. You are guilty of nothing but an attempt to delay for time."

Hugh crushed her to him, cherishing her belief in him. She was unlike anyone he'd ever known. Yet she could never belong to him. He had dishonored her, and himself, as well.

She shivered, and Hugh realized that it had become quite cold in the chapel. He released her and helped her to finish dressing, then pulled her cloak tight around her, breathing deeply of her scent, relishing the soft resilience of her skin. "Come," he said, with pain and dejection in his heart, "you've taken a chill."

They walked through the garden toward the castle, listening to the breeze rustle through the dead leaves, looking up at the moon through an overcast sky. And at the moment, Hugh could not fathom how he could possibly return to Clairmont and leave Siân here. If only he could think of some solution, some honorable way to keep Siân with him.

In the courtyard, there was a large number of horses, some sweaty and winded, some appeared to be freshly saddled. Hugh glanced around suspiciously. No large party of riders was expected at Windermere and their presence could only mean trouble.

"Go through the back kitchens and up to Kit's chambers," he said to Siân. "I'll see what's afoot."

Siân sensed urgency in Hugh's voice. She skirted around the horses and walked quickly to the back of the castle. Had Bishop Beaufort finally managed to follow them here to Windermere? Though she had no fear that Hugh and Wolf would be able to deal with the situation if it did turn out to be the bishop and his men, Siân still worried for little Henry's safety.

And she wondered what she would do about Wrexton if he had come, too.

Siân stopped to breathe deeply. She had to shake off the feelings of despair that had begun in the chapel when she and Hugh had separated.

She knew he could not belong to her, though that knowledge had no effect in stopping the tears that finally began to fall. Siân had known of Hugh's commitment to Marguerite when he'd walked into the chapel with her, when he'd kissed her and touched her so tenderly. The fact that he was not free had been perfectly clear when she'd given herself to him. But it had not mattered. For Siân, there would only be Hugh, and his marriage to Marguerite Bradley could not change that.

A sense of utter desolation and loneliness settled in her heart, but she forced herself to shake it off. These feelings were useless, she thought as she hurried around to the back entrance of the fortress. She should be accustomed to being alone. These last few days with Hugh had changed nothing. She still had decisions to make, plans to—

"*Tudor,* by God!" a harsh voice demanded as someone grabbed her and slapped one clammy hand over her mouth. Her captor put his other hand around her waist and hauled her into a darkened corner. "Didn't think I'd figure it out soon enough?"

Wrexton! Siân realized in panic. Siân tried to pull away, but it was no use.

"You're far from Pwll. Far from *Clairmont!* Imagine my surprise, the other morn at Castle Clairmont," he said with a seething anger, "to find you standing over my bed, knife in hand… I wonder what you thought to accomplish.''

Siân tried to speak, but the hand remained clamped over her mouth. She struggled to free herself, but he was too large, too strong. He had her overpowered.

''You thought to steal the king from under our noses?'' Wrexton stated more than asked. ''The council will not take kindly to the abduction of their king. The penalty is severe, Tudor wench! You will hang!''

No! she thought in a panic. She'd only done the queen's bidding. Surely she wouldn't be accused of taking Henry away unlawfully. The very thought was absurd!

Wasn't it?

She had to escape! She had to find Hugh and get him to help her before Wrexton twisted the facts as he'd done years before when he'd had her young friends killed. Siân knew little of the workings of the courts, but she was certain that Wrexton was devious enough to make it seem that she and Hugh had abducted Henry unlawfully. Owen would be of no help to her, especially if he thought Wrexton wielded some power with the ruling council.

She had to try to get away from him.

Siân tried to bite Wrexton's hand, but he crushed her face with it, punishing her for her efforts against him. She tasted her own blood and knew he was dead serious.

She tried to go limp, but it was to no avail. Not only did he hold her solidly, he let one hand go long enough to give her brutal blow to the back of her head.

It was the last thing Siân was aware of before complete blackness settled in.

Chapter Fourteen

"**Y**our visit is not altogether convenient at this time, Beaufort," Wolf said, standing at ease near the massive hearth of the great hall. Hugh could hear him from his concealed position in an alcove off the great hall. "My wife is not yet out of childbed and we have other guests due to arrive soon."

"I will baptize the infant if there is a concern..."

"My son and his mother are in good health," Wolf said. "As is Father Fowler, our chaplain." This last piece of information was unnecessary, and bordered on insulting. Who in the kingdom would not prefer to have his heir baptized by the kingdom's most prestigious cleric? But Wolf, like Hugh, had known Beaufort for years, and his aversion to the cleric was long-standing.

Beaufort frowned and sat down in front of the fire, obviously weighing the benefits of pursuing this conversation. The bishop's men gathered and warmed themselves by the fire.

"Beastly cold tonight," Beaufort finally said, then turned his beady eyes up to Wolf. "What other guests?"

"Your nephews," Wolf replied. "*Someone* summoned Bedford from France, and Gloucester is riding in with him from London.''

Hugh could feel Beaufort's anger and frustration. The presence of these two men could do nothing but thwart his plans. The bishop said nothing, just continued holding his hands out in front of him, warming them, as though he were not discomfited in the least.

Hugh was surprised to hear that Bedford and Gloucester, the brothers of Henry V, were due to arrive. He vaguely remembered Wolf saying their presence had been requested at Windermere, but he'd been too ill to think what it meant.

Between the two dukes and their uncle Beaufort, there would never be agreement. Beaufort could not force Catherine into marriage, nor would he be able to remove Henry from her custody. And the bishop could not afford to offend his two powerful nephews openly. He would lose too much sway within the council if his own play for power were too obvious.

Hugh slipped out of his alcove, satisfied that Wolf would keep the wily bishop occupied and feeling relieved that Wrexton had not come to Windermere with Beaufort. Moving quietly down a darkened gallery, he approached Kit's door and tapped lightly. Maggie, her maid, opened the door to a room lit only by a small fire in the grate and one long taper, which she held in her hand.

''Kit?'' he asked quietly.

She answered him from her bed. ''Hugh, I'm here.''

He realized that, outside of whatever was going on in her home, Kit was weary and needed to rest. It had been a mere week since she'd delivered her child and she had yet to recover her strength.

''Where is Siân?'' he asked.

Kit shrugged. "We have not seen her."

"My lord," Maggie said, "Eleanor remains here with her mother and the baby, as does little *Parry*." They had all taken to calling Henry by the Welsh name given him by Siân.

Now that she mentioned it, Hugh could see two still little forms in the bed next to Kit.

"We put them to bed in here, my lord, when we learned that Bishop Beaufort and his men had entered the town walls."

"Beaufort will have little sway at Windermere, Hugh," Kit said, stopping him from leaving. "Henry will be safe, whether or not Wolf tells the bishop he is here. Even so, don't show your presence until you know what my husband has planned."

Hugh nodded. He had already intended to wait it out until he saw what strategy Wolf intended to use.

He headed back down the gallery until he reached the room he knew was Siân's. He tapped gently and waited, but when there was no response, he let himself in. There was no fire in the grate, so the room was chilled and completely blanketed in darkness. She was not there.

Leaning against the doorjamb, Hugh frowned, considering where she might be.

It was entirely possible she'd stayed in the garden, or gone back to the chapel. If Siân discovered the horses belonged to Bishop Beaufort and his party, she very likely assumed it was necessary to stay out of sight to keep the bishop and his men from realizing that Henry was at Windermere. She could not know the kind of power he and Wolf wielded.

Wherever she was, Hugh decided, she knew enough to stay out of sight. Determined to go and find her, he was about to head down the back steps again when he heard more voices in the hall, the voices of surprise and of new arrivals.

Gloucester and Bedford had arrived.

The first thing Siân was aware of was the smell of the sea. She came to her senses slowly, only to be overcome by an overpowering nausea, and an intense throbbing at the back of her head. When she opened her eyes, she knew it was late. The moon was already down. It had to have been many hours since she and Hugh had split up, many hours since she'd run up against Wrexton in the courtyard.

Where was Hugh now? More to the point, where was *she* now?

Siân pushed herself up onto her elbows and looked around. Was Hugh nearby? He'd spoken of being imprisoned beneath Windermere Castle, but Siân knew that wherever she was, she was *not* indoors. The sky was definitely up above her, but it was thick with clouds and few stars were visible. It was too dark to see much, but she could tell she was lying on a wood-planked floor, and her back was to a wall. The smell of the sea was all around her, and very intense.

She did not know if Windermere was close to the seashore, or whether Wrexton had taken her some distance away while she was unconscious. Her body felt sore all over, but there were no clues as to where exactly she was, or how she had gotten there.

The queasiness increased and Siân felt dizzy, as well. She was shaky and ill. She lay back down on her side to quell the roiling inside her. *Where* was she?

There were odd sounds here, too, sounds she did not recognize. Creaking and strange echoing sounds...the wind causing flags to flap, only…different. Oh, if only she could think clearly, but this pounding in her head and the nausea in her belly were making it impossible!

She sensed movement, but couldn't be sure if it was the dizziness or if she was truly moving. Nor did she have time to consider it at length, because she began to retch, and then blackness took her again.

As soon as Wolf offered the information that the King of England was sleeping peacefully in an upper chamber of Windermere Castle, Hugh joined the group near the hearth. There was no point in remaining concealed any longer. It would soon come out—if Beaufort did not already know—that he and Siân had been the ones to smuggle the king away from Clairmont at the queen's request.

John, Duke of Bedford, was a handsome man, not many years older than Hugh, though the war effort in France had aged him since last Hugh saw him. His light-brown hair was now gone white at the temples and weary lines were drawn about his eyes and lips. He still had the bright beat of intelligence in his hazel-brown eyes, and the powerful voice of command.

Bedford had been well respected among King Henry's lieutenants in the French wars, and ever since Henry's death, he commanded the war effort in France. His presence in England was very potent, and he was often summoned from the continent to mediate between his headstrong younger brother, Humphrey, and his cunning uncle, Henry Beaufort.

"Dryden," Bedford said, looking Hugh over. Satisfied with what he saw, he added, "You appear fit enough."

"That I am, Your Grace," Hugh replied.

"He's Alldale now," Wolf corrected. "Your brother saw to that two years ago."

"Ah, yes...I recall now," Bedford said. "You wouldn't have any interest in returning to the front with me? I have need of men such as yourselves," he added, including Wolf in his invitation.

Wolf shook his head. "I've given France all I care to," he said. "There is more than enough to keep me occupied here, on home soil."

Gloucester muttered something unintelligible, which Bedford ignored. "What of you, Alldale? I need skilled commanders, fearless officers, men of—"

"My apologies, Your Grace," Hugh said, "I've neglected my estate too long already."

Bedford accepted their declinations and turned to his uncle. "What brings you to Windermere, Beaufort? I would have thought your diocese held more than enough to occupy your time."

Gloucester snorted and received a pointed glance from his uncle Beaufort.

"The bishop has been playing at politics again," Gloucester said sardonically. "Though this time, his game took him far from London."

"Nonsense," Beaufort said, glowering at the young man who bore a remarkable resemblance to his brother, all but the signs of age. "I merely chose to take advantage of a quiet moment in my episcopate to check on the well-being of my nephew. I do not trust that Frenchwoman who is his moth—"

"Caution, Your Eminence," Bedford said. "You are speaking of the Queen of England..."

The conversation continued in this vein as food and wine were served. Gloucester remained petulant and resentful, while the pompous Bishop Beaufort made excuses for his own actions. Bedford mediated.

Evening turned into night and still the noblemen sat and talked, their discussions bordering on petty accusations and recriminations. Hugh would have left the table to go search for Siân but for the look Wolf shot him, requesting that he stay. He let the Lancasters argue while his own thoughts drifted toward the chapel and the time he'd spent there with Siân, his hands aching to touch her, his mouth to kiss her. He'd never touched skin so soft, nor tasted lips so sweet.

How could he ever leave Windermere without her? How could he possibly have thought to wed her to Nicholas or any other man?

Life had been so simple before, when he'd passed his days in numb resignation. Siân changed all that. He was *not* indifferent. He was no longer satisfied existing in an isolated shell on the fringes of society. He needed Siân.

And, equally important, Siân needed *him*.

Hugh decided he would send a message to Clairmont immediately, to withdraw his proposal to Marguerite. It was clear that the lady did not particularly favor him—she'd been more than a little reluctant to agree to a marriage between them—and Hugh didn't doubt she'd be glad of the reprieve. There had to be another man who would be better suited as her husband, and Hugh had no doubt that Marguerite would release him from his proposal.

And he would be free to take Siân to Alldale, to wed her there, and make her his countess.

While the others talked, Hugh mulled over the things Siân said to him in the chapel and marveled at her common sense. He realized belatedly that she was right. He'd been an overproud, petulant fool not to have seen it.

Siân's experience at Wrexton's hands had given her an insight most women would never have. She understood what it was to have friends whose lives were in danger; she knew the risks of standing up for them, of trying a dangerous ploy to accomplish what needed to be done.

And he didn't doubt his fearless lady would do it again if necessary, though he fully intended to keep her safe and protected in the future. She would never again have reason to be frightened or to worry for the safety of her friends.

Hugh's hands fairly itched with the need to touch her again. Without doubt, Siân had given *him* life again. With her honesty and ready smile, she had won him a hundred times over. Carrying a babe in her arms, or kicking a ball in a courtyard, dressed like a princess or in the rough clothes of a townswoman, Siân Tudor was a treasure. A woman without equal in his heart.

He couldn't imagine what made him think he could endure a life with Marguerite Bradley. Hugh realized now that the staid and demure Marguerite would never have been able to reawaken his manhood, his pride. He'd have done his duty by her, forever believing he was less than a man, that he'd betrayed Wolf, that his only value was as the protector of Clairmont.

Hugh thanked God that he crossed Siân Tudor's path that day in the woods…that he'd been able to keep her from harm when the boar attacked.

''…it was that idiot Welshman that did it!'' Beaufort shouted as he slammed down his cup, interrupting Hugh's thoughts and nearly shaking him out of his chair.

"What of the Welshman?" Hugh asked, frowning. His thoughts had been so far from the discussion at hand that he hadn't followed a bit of it, though he had no doubts of the Welshman's identity.

"That damnable fool, Tudor, insulted Wrexton, who has no fondness for the Welsh in any case," Beaufort said. "Wrexton ran off at the mouth about Tudor and his 'high' position in the queen's household..."

Well, Hugh had no great liking for Owen Tudor, either, but Wrexton should have been more circumspect if he had any hope of winning Queen Catherine's hand. It was well known that Catherine favored Owen, and would stand for no insult to the man.

"Spouted off about Tudor's 'traitor' sister, too," Beaufort continued. "Is she here, by chance?"

"What about his sister?" Hugh asked ominously.

He made a disparaging noise. "Some cock-and-bull story about a...a..." The bishop's eyes went hazy for a moment. "By God's Cross, his tale doesn't bear repeating."

"Why did Wrexton not accompany you here?" Hugh asked, painfully aware of the tale Wrexton must have told at Clairmont.

"He did, but he left for the coast immediately," Beaufort said. Then he looked around uncomfortably at the assemblage. "He, uh..."

Hugh and everyone else knew then that Beaufort's plans had run completely aground. There would be no marriage between Wrexton and the queen, and Wrexton was, even now, running to the coast with his tail between his legs, in some haste to return to his own estates. The earl could not afford the wrath of the council, of which Wolf was a powerful member. If word got out of Wrexton's collusion with Beaufort, there could be repercussions.

"Why to the coast?" Wolf asked. "Why would Wrexton not remain at Windermere for the night?"

"His, uh, ship is harbored at Morecambe Bay," Beaufort replied. "He was anxious to return home."

"By way of Morecambe Bay?" Hugh asked, relieved that the man was nowhere near Windermere. He did not wish to risk a confrontation between Siân and the cruel nobleman. "I had the impression his estate was south...on the Welsh border."

"What do *I* know of it?" Beaufort replied, irritated by all the questions. "He fancies himself a sailor. He'll travel by sea to some port near home, then ride inland the rest of the way."

Wolf shrugged. Men of means often preferred to travel by ship when convenient. It was possible to reduce travel time, especially when traveling through craggy, mountainous regions. "Gentlemen, you must excuse me," he said as he stood. "The hour grows old and there is a newborn in my chamber. Have no doubt that I will be present to greet the dawning sun to my son's raucous tune."

Hugh stood to take his own leave as the men chuckled at Wolf's words. He went to Siân's room again and knocked, but she was not there. Rubbing the back of his neck, he went down to the rooms Kit and Wolf shared, and tapped lightly. Wolf opened the door.

"Is Siân here?" Hugh asked.

"No," Wolf said with a quick shake of his head. "And Kit's asleep."

Puzzled, Hugh headed down the back steps of the castle and went out the door into the black night. He made his way through the courtyard and garden, then reached the little chapel that was partially concealed by trees and foliage.

"Siân!"

There was no answer to his call.

Worried now, Hugh went into the chapel and lit a candle to illuminate the empty stone room. *What could have happened?* he wondered. Where would she have wandered? And as he pondered that question, an image of Wrexton came to mind, and Beaufort's information about the earl and his ship.

Even more troubled now, he returned in haste to the courtyard where he'd left her, and looked around. The horses were gone, and all was quiet. An expert tracker, Hugh studied the perimeter of the courtyard, looking for anything out of place. Branches broken, lawn crumpled... And then he found it, near the kitchen entrance of the castle.

Siân's cloak.

Hugh muttered a curse and turned back toward the main doors of the hall. He knew now that Siân had not wandered. Stupidly, he had sent her around to the back of the castle where he'd assumed it would be safe for her to enter. Obviously, that had not been the case.

Wrexton must have been there.

It was raining.

Siân felt the moisture on her face as it roused her to consciousness. A man came and roughly tied her hands, then pulled her back to a post and tied her down.

"Please!" she cried, her arms nearly wrenched out of their sockets.

"Shut yer trap, woman," the man said. "Ye'll be stayin' out here where ye won't foul the earl's cabin."

Cabin? Siân wondered at the Saxon word. It had no

meaning for her, but she had to assume it was a warm, dry haven for Wrexton.

"Where are we?" she asked weakly. "What—" A crack of thunder cut off her words and the man stood and hurried away. Suddenly the ground tipped and swayed, and the sea poured over her.

And Siân finally realized she was on a ship. She was at sea, isolated and alone. Doomed.

Lightning flashed, and there was another crash of thunder as the ship pitched wildly in the swells of the turbulent sea. Her stomach heaved again, and she was miserable, pitiful in her fear, her infirmity. She thought of Hugh, and wept knowing that he could never discover where she'd gone. She despaired at the thought that she would never see him again.

Her fingers, cold and nearly numb, tore at the bindings around her wrists. She would not lie there like a limp codfish, reeled in to await its fate. If Wrexton were to do his worst, it would be without her cooperation. She might be ill and terrified by the storm, but she would not go helplessly to her enemy.

The intensity of the storm increased, as did the shouts of the men in the distance. Siân heard cursing as well as praying, as the ship tipped and rolled, yanking her arms painfully behind her with every swell of the violent sea. She was often swamped by the briny water, and each time she retched, her throat and all her rib and abdominal muscles strained in agony. She continued to struggle with the ropes that bound her, but to no avail.

It went on so for hours, it seemed, and at dawn, when the sun should have lit the sky, there was hardly a change in the quality of light. Siân only knew it was morning because the dark seemed a bit less deep. The storm raged on, and from the angry voices of the men on deck, she gathered that they were off course.

It was either a blessing, or it was the end, Siân thought. And she wished she knew what was happening, so she could plan.

Or at least, make her last Act of Contrition.

Chapter Fifteen

By the Grace of God, she was alive.

The rain continued to fall steadily. Although the weather had calmed somewhat, Siân's stomach had not stopped churning. She was soaking wet and freezing cold, lying on the wood planking, with her hands still tied uncomfortably behind her. Every bone in her body ached, and her throat was raw from retching.

Harsh voices split the air all around her, shouting in confusion. The ship's sails were damaged, and they were far from their destination on the River Dee. The crew was frustrated and unsure what to do now.

"We're at Basingwerk now, ye tottering clotpole!" one of the hands shouted to another.

"Well, I wants to know if himself'll give us the time to repair the ship or will we be goin' on by cart."

"Damned if I know," the first one said as they hoisted the sodden canvas from the floor of the ship. "It's far and away to Chester by cart, ye know."

Basingwerk, Siân thought, letting the men's voices drift away. She was in Wales, then. Surely she could find herself a place to hide here in her homeland, though it would be better if they made it to Chester.

She'd heard of Chester town, and it was not too distant from Pwll. If she could get to Pwll…

No. By going home, she'd put the townspeople at risk. She could not do that again. She would not endanger her cousins or any other Welshman ever again. She had to figure a way to get off the ship and away from Wrexton.

But once off the ship, how would she manage to get by? She had no coin and nothing of value on her person to trade for food or shelter.

Ignoring the pain in her shoulders and arms, Siân managed to fold her legs under her and push up to a sitting position. She took a look around.

She was tied to a low railing near a stairway, but she could not see land, or any other useful thing from her position. She was helpless, and worse, she was completely at Wrexton's mercy.

There was a sudden flurry of activity and Siân watched as the men moved quickly about the ship, shouting and throwing ropes. They seemed to be pulling the vessel into a place near land. It was unclear whether they would stay until the ship was repaired, or if they would travel to Wrexton by horse cart.

Regardless of the plan, Siân was chilled and wet and she desperately wished she could change into something warm. *That* was not likely to happen, however, and once Siân saw Wrexton climbing the steps and approaching her, she knew she would be lucky if he did not just throw her overboard right there and then. His face was contorted with anger, and Siân could only hope that it was at least partially directed to the fact that the ship had ended up somewhere other than where the earl had planned.

"So. You were not swept in," he said as he walked past her.

Siân was paralyzed by the venom in his tone. She did not know what she could possibly have done to make him hate her so. Nor could she understand why he felt it necessary to punish *her* for her father's actions so long ago, during the Glendower revolt. Siân had been a mere infant during the time of the rebellion.

She gave no answer to Wrexton's words, nor did he seem to expect one. Instead, he spoke sharply to one of the men, who came around to cut Siân loose. Blood rushed to her hands, making them throb painfully, and Siân could hardly move them. When she did not get to her feet immediately, the sailor yanked her up by the back of her gown and pushed her forward.

She fell.

"Get up, y' bloody Tudor wench!" Wrexton bellowed. Siân dragged herself up onto her knees, then forced herself to her feet. "Renford! Get off and find us some horses. I don't fancy waiting for days while these incompetents repair my ship!"

"Yes, my lord," Renford replied as he quickly disembarked to do the lord's bidding.

Wrexton barked further orders to his men, then grabbed Siân by the back of her clothes, pushing and prodding her to the edge of the boat where a plank was laid across. The earl poked and shoved her all the way across the murky waters to the landing.

Wrexton surveyed the town. "Wretched little *Welsh* hellhole," he muttered. "Where the devil is the inn? Or a tavern?"

Siân said nothing, but allowed herself to be driven forward, toward a building on the quay. The rickety

building had an overhang, where she stood waiting for
Wrexton to decide what to do next.

"Scared, are you?" Wrexton sneered.

Siân held her tongue and tried to appear anything
but frightened.

Wrexton paced back and forth as he waited for Renford to return with horses. "They've missed you at
Windermere by now," he said.

Siân didn't want to think about that.

"Probably even sent a party out to search for you,"
he added. "Maybe it'll be that bastard, Alldale, who
comes for you. Wouldn't it be grand—" Wrexton
turned his malicious gaze on her "—to watch *another*
hanging, eh?"

Hugh saddled his horse and left Windermere immediately, heading south, toward Wrexton's lands. It
was late, and all of Windermere was abed, so he did
not awaken anyone to accompany him. Besides, this
was how he worked best. Alone.

He would ride all night and all the next day if necessary, to reach the Wrexton estate, to get to Siân. His
heart beat faster with the thought of her at the mercy
of the earl who seemed determined to make her life a
misery.

Hugh had never been to Wrexton, but he had no
doubt that he'd be able to find the place, and quickly.
He headed in a southwesterly direction, knowing that
he'd be able to correct his course after daybreak when
people were up and about.

He could only hope that he was not too far behind
the ship where Wrexton was holding Siân. Glancing to
the west, toward the sea where he knew Wrexton's ship

sailed, Hugh watched the progress of a violent storm, and knew that Siân was in the thick of it.

He kicked his heels into the sides of his mare and continued on, covering the miles as fast as he dared in the dark. He wanted to reach Wrexton lands before the earl did, though he knew the chances of that were slim. The quickest route had to be by ship, else Wrexton would not have taken it.

Hugh was well aware that he had no idea what he was getting himself into, what kind of fortress Wrexton had, how many knights he kept, or how heavily guarded Wrexton was. He knew only that Siân's safety was first and foremost to him.

He slowly realized, however, that he should have brought help.

Wrexton rode on ahead with two of his men, while Siân was tied again and shoved into an oxcart to be pulled along the countryside. The rain had let up, but she was still wet. She didn't think she would ever feel warm again.

Four men accompanied her, one driving the cart, the other three riding in front and alongside. Only one of the four men looked particularly dangerous, and Siân was especially leery of him. He would not think twice about bringing her to heel.

Nothing about the land looked familiar and Siân knew she was far from Pwll. She was miserable, bumping along in the cart as they traveled the rutted road. Though she was gaining new bruises with every mile, it was much better than being on board Wrexton's ship, with the waves engulfing her every minute and the rain threatening to drown her.

Siân knew they were headed for Wrexton Castle, but

she had no idea how far away it was, or how long it would take to get there. No one in her village ever traveled, and other than receiving news from the occasional monk or some other likely traveler, they rarely learned of events outside their small community. No one knew the lay of the land beyond their own fields, other than to know that London was far to the east, and that most of Wales lay to the south of them.

Siân, of course, had done a great deal of traveling since leaving Pwll at Owen's behest, but her journeys had never taken her back to Wales. She was still as ignorant of her homeland as ever, which made any plans—beyond escape—impossible.

Siân closed her eyes and lay back in the cart in an attempt to recoup some of her strength. She wondered what Hugh had done when he realized she was gone. Would he ever know that she'd been taken against her will, that she hadn't just run away?

Of course he would, she thought. Hugh knew of her history with Wrexton. The earl's arrival and quick departure along with Siân's disappearance were too coincidental. Hugh would know what had happened.

But he couldn't help her now.

An hour or so past dawn, Hugh reached a manor house near a cliff overlooking the sea. He was exhausted and the wound in his arm throbbed painfully. He could go no further.

The lord of the manor was a middle-aged, minor baron who met Hugh in the stable yard when he rode in. With a long, straight nose and ruddy complexion, he was tall and angular of build. His hair was a mixture of yellow and white, and he had thick, bushy eyebrows of the same color over clear, glass-blue eyes.

"Greetings, my lord," the baron said as Hugh dismounted. "Welcome to Northaven Manor. I am Eldred de Grant, baron of these lands."

Hugh gave a quick nod. "I am Hugh Dryden," he said. "Earl of Alldale."

"Please come in," de Grant said, motioning for one of the servants to come and attend Hugh's horse. "You have been riding long and hard, it seems," he said, leading Hugh to the house.

"I am headed for Wrexton lands," Hugh said, "but I have only a vague direction to follow."

They reached the house and de Grant gave instructions to the house servants to prepare a meal and a room for their guest. He also sent someone out to find his son.

"I cannot stay," Hugh protested.

"An hour's rest will do no harm," de Grant said. "Wrexton is quite a distance from Northaven and you look about done in."

Hugh rubbed the back of his neck. He was exhausted. The infection in his arm had drained his strength as well as his stamina. He needed to rest before he could proceed, before he could take on Wrexton, but the thought of Siân in the earl's hands made him ache with every pulse of blood in his body. While there was no guarantee that Siân had not already been harmed, Hugh *had* to believe that Wrexton would wait until he had her secured away before tormenting her. It was the only way Hugh could contain the rage and frustration inside, the only way he could stay level-headed enough to pursue her.

He nodded to de Grant, saying, "I thank you, sir," as though resigned to the delay.

"Think no more of it," de Grant said.

The baron took him to a large room where a fire
burned merrily in the grate, even though there were
signs of mourning all around. It was a prosperous
house, comfortable, well appointed, and tidy. Hugh
went over to the fire and warmed himself.

"My son and I buried my wife yestermorn," de
Grant said quietly. "If she were here, bold and forth-
right Welshwoman that she was, she'd be blunt and
ask outright what business a fine, upstanding man such
as yourself has with a pig like Wrexton."

Hugh was taken aback by de Grant's bluntness,
though he was encouraged by his derogatory reference
to Wrexton, as well as the fact that his wife was Welsh.
Edmund Sandborn was clearly no favorite here at Northaven Manor. "You speak strongly of Wrexton," he
said, intending to draw out more information from de
Grant before he spoke of Siân and her predicament.

De Grant shook his head. "Never heard of such goings-on," the man said. "Who does he think he is?
The law of England itself?"

"What goings-on?" Hugh asked.

"Well, you should know, if you're bound for the
man's territory," de Grant said. He was interrupted by
a servant who entered the room with a tray of food,
which she set on the big, oaken table.

"Young Marcus is just riding down into the dale
now, my lord," the old woman said.

"Thank you, Peg," de Grant said as he beckoned
Hugh to table.

Hugh sat down at de Grant's table, helped himself
to what he could, and encouraged the baron to talk.

"What do you know of Wrexton?"

De Grant shook his head desultorily. "Never cared

much for his father the few times I met him," the baron said, "but young Edmund… Oh, he is a rare one."

"In what way?"

De Grant tipped his chin up and squinted his eyes to look Hugh over. "Mayhap you'd like to tell me what your business is with the earl," he said, pouring himself a cup of ale, "then I'll be more at ease, telling you what I know."

Though his host had said little, his few words were not complimentary. The man would not interfere with Hugh's plans to rescue Siân, and might even be a valuable ally. "Wrexton stole a young woman from Windermere last night," he said. "She is a lady of good family, and he had no right to take her. It's my belief that he intends her harm."

De Grant said nothing, other than uttering a small "hmm" under his breath. Those heavy white brows met above his nose in a frown. "Why would Wrexton take the lady of Windermere? Even for Wrexton, this would be a feat—"

"'Twas not the lady of Windermere," Hugh quickly interjected. "Wrexton abducted a guest, a woman unrelated to the lord and lady of Windermere."

"This is most unlike Edmund Sandborn," de Grant said. "To harass a young Englishwoman who—"

"She is not English, but Welsh."

"Ah, that explains it, then."

"What do you mean?"

"Ever since the Welsh uprising, Wrexton has had an unholy hatred for the Welsh," de Grant explained. "He was a very young man at the time, but he and his younger brother fought a few skirmishes, nonetheless.

"The younger boy could only have been in his fifteenth or sixteenth year," de Grant continued. "The lad was killed one day, by a Welsh arrow. Edmund was devastated. When they brought the boy's body to the old earl, it is said that the man clutched at his heart and died on the spot.

"Edmund inherited the title and the lands, as well as the care of his young sister. Battles were waged, and Wrexton became fiercer than ever. He cared not who he cut down...even went after women and children in villages."

De Grant explained that finally a group of Welshmen, in order to gain some leverage with young Edmund, abducted his twelve-year-old sister. They hoped that, in exchange for the girl's safety, Edmund would stop his vicious raids, stop the killing.

"They treated her well, but the girl took ill. She got a fever on her lungs and died, through no particular fault of the Welshmen."

There was a long pause, during which Hugh pondered the story de Grant told him. It was not difficult to understand Wrexton's unbalanced view of the Welsh, though his practice of punishing *all* the Welsh people for the actions of a few, was absurd.

"When Marudedd Tudor went to Edmund to tell him of his sister's death—"

"Tudor?"

"Aye," de Grant replied. "'Twas Tudor himself who went to Wrexton Castle with the sad tidings. The man had ballocks of iron to go. The only reason he wasn't killed on the spot was that Edmund was so overcome with grief, he never gave the order.

"'Tis said the young earl just crumpled like a piece of wilted linen and dropped to the floor with weeping."

Hugh raked his fingers through his hair and stood. His urgency to get to Siân increased tenfold now that he understood Wrexton's position. Though Edmund's logic was faulty, he intended to exact his revenge on *Siân* for the loss of his family. Wrexton had managed to punish her in various ways through the years, but Hugh knew this would be the final episode.

Hugh was so preoccupied with thoughts of Siân that he did not at first hear the young man enter the house. It was not until Marcus de Grant greeted his father that Hugh looked up and noticed him.

The younger de Grant, a handsome, blond giant, came to stand behind his father, putting one hand on the older man's shoulder.

"Lord Hugh, my son, Marcus," de Grant said. "The earl has come from Windermere to take on Wrexton."

Marcus came around the table and sat down, showing little surprise. "Is that so?" he asked. "What has your whoreson cousin done now, da?"

They traveled all day. Siân slept at intervals in the back of the cart, but was frequently jarred awake. She could not remember the last time she'd had a drink of water, or a bite to eat—not that she wanted any now. But after all those hours on the ship, miserable with seasickness, she was weak and shaky. She would have to act soon, before she was incapable of helping herself.

The four "guards" gave little heed to Siân, and she quickly realized that they had no particular allegiance to Wrexton. They were merely men hired to do his bidding.

Their instructions had been simple: to get Siân to Wrexton as soon as possible, and without mishap. Siân could only believe that Wrexton had some new means of torture in store for her, though exactly what it would be, she did not know.

Siân did not want to alert her guards, so she refrained from sitting up and making a serious assessment of her surroundings. She merely poked her head up every now and then to take a look out the back of the cart, and made miserable moaning sounds whenever she moved. She hoped her guards would believe she was so ill she was incapacitated.

Eventually, though, Siân dozed. When she awoke with a start, it was fully dark, and she was afraid she'd missed something important. She felt moisture on her face and knew she'd been weeping in her sleep. The dream had come back. Only now, in addition to the faces of Idwal and Dafydd, she saw Hugh in chains next to the two boys, being tortured and beaten by some unknown hand.

It was agony. Siân could see his face and practically touch him as she'd slept, and her heart cried out with the injustice of it all. Could she not be left in peace, she cried inwardly, along with Dafydd, Idwal and Hugh? Why did those she loved have to be hurt so?

Siân shook her head to clear it. Her lips were dry and cracked, and when she tried to moisten them, she found that her tongue was thick and stuck to the roof of her mouth. Her head felt hazy and her vision was blurred. Her stomach turned over as the cart bounced over a particularly pitted stretch of trail.

No one was being harmed now, she realized, except for *her!*

Hugh was safe at Windermere. She knew that. And Idwal and Dafydd were beyond hurt. Siân had to do something…but what? It was all so unclear now… She could not think! Where was she? Where was she being taken?

One thing was certain. Wherever she was, Hugh could not help her now. He'd rescued her before…she could not remember exactly when, or how, but it seemed that he'd always been there for her. He was a strong and fierce warrior, but gentle and kind with her. He, and he alone, had taken care of her when she'd needed him.

But she was completely on her own now. She had only herself to rely upon—to get out of this horrible, swaying cart and away from these men.

She had to act soon. She would not go to Wrexton, trussed up like some wild game caught in a snare. She would find a place to hide, and stay there until her guards gave up looking for her. She could do this. She would succeed.

She inched her way to the back of the cart, taking care not to be noticed as they rolled along. Their speed was not great, so she doubted she'd be hurt much by the fall when she dropped out of the cart, but she would have to be careful to slip out in the right kind of terrain, someplace where she'd be able to hide. There was no point in getting out in an open field. They'd spot her quickly, she thought, even in the dark.

They reached a wooded area before Siân was in position. Even so, she slid herself to the back of the cart and prepared to roll off, hoping that she would not make so much noise that her fall would be heard over the rolling wooden wheels. With hands still tied securely behind her, Siân made herself roll off, taking the brunt of the fall with one shoulder and arm.

The cart kept going.

Siân shook off the pain of the fall as she struggled

to get herself up. It took several minutes to get to her knees—hours, it seemed to Siân, fully expecting them to notice she'd gone, and turn around and abduct her again. If she didn't quickly find an adequate hiding place, there would be hell to pay.

Finally Siân could stand, and though she was shaky and weak, she dragged herself toward the cover of the trees.

When Hugh awoke at Northaven before noon, he was ready to go on. His meager few hours of sleep had been disturbed by visions of Siân in Wrexton's clutches, and he'd tossed and turned on the bed. Somehow, however, he managed to acquire enough rest, and when he arose from the bed, he was ready and able to do what was necessary to get Siân away from Wrexton.

"We've packed food and other supplies for you, my lord," de Grant said as Hugh descended the stairs and entered the manor's great room.

"I appreciate it, de Grant," Hugh said as he headed for the door. "All I need now is some direction on how to get to Wrexton."

The baron smiled. "That won't be necessary, my lord," he said.

Hugh gave a puzzled look and began to protest.

"My son will accompany you on your quest," he said. "He has no love for Wrexton and his kind, and does not wish to see another Welsh woman hurt."

"Another—"

"My wife, Rhianwen," the baron said sadly, "Marcus's gentle mother, was hurt often by English prejudice."

Hugh went to the stable yard where he came upon Marcus de Grant, mounting his caparisoned horse. A quick intelligence marked the man's light blue eyes, but Hugh noted, with approval, that he was not given to unnecessary conversation.

Hugh was glad of the younger man's company.

Marcus de Grant made his farewell to his father, and then rode off with Hugh, heading in a southerly direction.

"What do you know of Wrexton Castle?" Hugh asked after they'd ridden several miles.

"Wrexton is a large keep that lies within a stone wall," de Grant replied. "I was only there once, as a boy, so my memories of it are vague."

"How long a ride?" Hugh asked.

"We won't arrive until well after dark," de Grant said. "With any luck, we'll get there soon after your lady."

His lady. Hugh liked the sound of that, but still he worried that he would not arrive in time to rescue Siân before she came to any harm beyond being taken captive. Wrexton had already held her prisoner her for a full night, although the storm should have kept him occupied with survival, and not with Siân. With any luck, he was traveling overland with Siân even now, to his fortress.

Because if the earl had caused Hugh's lady any harm, the retribution was going to be brutal.

Chapter Sixteen

Siân stood with her back to a tree, shaking uncontrollably with weeping. She was free. If she kept her wits about her, she would escape for good.

She worked diligently at freeing her hands from the thick rope that bound them, and finally wrenched them loose. The rope fell to the ground and Siân rubbed her hands in front of her. Her wrists were raw and bleeding, but she ignored the pain. She dried her eyes on one sleeve and made a conscious effort to compose herself.

She knew she had to pick a direction and move before the guards realized she was gone. Standing still would be a fatal mistake.

Siân looked into the darkness around her. Rather than turning around and heading back in the direction from which she'd come, Siân angled to the left, where the woods were thicker and it would be difficult, if not impossible, to drive the cart through. She hoped that by heading that way, she would at least delay the men.

She moved slowly, not only because it was dark, but also because she was so weak. The long hours of captivity and deprivation had taken their toll. Every uncovered root and loose rock tripped her up and she fell so often she lost count, scraping her knees and hands. Her vision was not reliable, nor were any of her other senses, but still she moved on, toward an unknown destination. Her thoughts began to wander again, and Siân started seeing lights in the distance.

She lost her sense of purpose as she moved. She could not remember why she was running, only that she had to keep going. She came across a small stream, where she knelt and took sips of cool, clean water. She was tempted to stay and rest, but a voice, Hugh's voice, told her to get up and move on. Siân looked around and cried out because she could not see him, but she did as she was told.

In her mind, Hugh kept telling her to walk, to put one foot in front of the other, no matter how much her muscles hurt, no matter how painful her scrapes and bruises. Then, suddenly, it was difficult to tell which voices to listen to. Siân heard horses' hooves and men whispering all around her. They were closing in and she did not know what to do.

She had to hide!

Fear gave her new impetus. She increased her pace and headed for some underbrush, with the hope of hiding in the low bushes. But the appearance of the landscape was deceiving, and after a few steps, she fell and slid down an incline into a shallow ravine, finally coming to rest at the bottom.

Too exhausted to continue, Siân lay still as consciousness left her.

"She's mightily banged up," one voice said.

"Aye, that she is," another man replied as he carefully turned her over. "Let's see if we can carry her to—by all the saints, Cai—it's Siân Tudor!"

Siân opened her eyes and looked up into the faces of two young men she'd known for many a year. Pwll men. Could she have gotten so close to her little village without even knowing it? And what about the lights, the voices she'd seen and heard in the night? Had she imagined them, or had they been real?

"Cai," she said, her tongue feeling as coarse and tough as raw leather. "Dylan."

"'Tis us, lass," Dylan said, then turned a curious frown on Siân. "But what are you doing here?"

"You're supposed to be in Londontown with that brother of yours."

Siân tried to get up, but was too weak to do so. The two men scrambled to help her.

She tried to explain what had happened, but had not the energy to give more than a brief sketch of her story. The incompleteness of her explanation did not seem to bother the two men, they just gathered her up in their arms and took turns carrying her to town.

"Your aunt Nesta will be pleased to have you home," Dylan said.

Siân had difficulty believing that. Neither of her widowed aunts had protested in the least when Siân had been summoned to London. They'd been more than happy to see her go.

"She's had to attend several births in the months you've been gone," Cai remarked.

"And tells how she misses your help," Dylan finished.

"That you were good, both with the mams and their babes."

Siân swallowed hard. Aunt Nesta had never said any such thing in all the years Siân had helped with the midwifing in Pwll. She'd been nothing but a burden to her aunts and their families.

"Your aunt Bethan's been saying she never would have managed with all *her* children had you not come to stay with each birth."

Dylan caught Siân's skeptical look. "'Tis true, lass," he said. "They've been missing you something fierce since you left."

They reached Nesta's cottage and were greeted by Siân's chestnut-haired aunt before they even had a chance to knock on the door. A range of emotions crossed the woman's careworn face before she was able to speak. Then, she became the efficient, no-nonsense, matter-of-fact midwife Siân remembered.

"Don't be standing in the lane with her, lads," Nesta said. "Bring her in. She can have Rhodri's bed."

Aunt Bethan was quickly summoned, and Siân soon found herself settled in one of her cousins' beds, where she was attended by both her aunts. Without any fuss, the two women saw that their niece was bathed and fed.

"You need your rest now, lass," Bethan said, brushing a lock of freshly washed hair from her forehead. "And when you awake, we will speak of what happened to you, and what brought you back."

For a long time, Siân slept soundly. When she finally opened her eyes, it was nearly dark, and there were people in the cottage moving quietly about. She still did not know what to think of the unexpectedly warm welcome she'd received from the aunts, but was grateful for it. She needed her family now, as much as ever, to help restore her strength, and to get over her loss of Hugh.

How long had it been since she'd seen him? Touched him? The hours did not matter. It was no effort to remember his gentle touch, or the deep timbre of his voice, whispering to her, speaking her name. Siân could almost feel his thick, dark hair slipping through her fingers, and the touch of his lips on her own.

And the rest...the wondrous experience in the chapel that had bound her to Hugh forever. She had never known such bliss could exist. Siân knew she would never forget. She would always cherish their last hour together, when she'd been given leave to love him freely.

"Ah, lass," Aunt Nesta said, "you're awake."

Siân nodded.

"And why the tears?" she asked, dabbing at Siân's cheeks with a soft cloth. "Are you not happy to be home with us?"

"I am," Siân said, her aunt's unexpected kindness causing the floodgates to open. Siân's tears came freely now, and she sobbed into her aunt's shoulder, as if the weight of the world lay upon her shoulders.

And it did. Hugh was on his way to Clairmont to wed his lady. A Windermere knight was likely en route to rescue her, but when he arrived Wrexton, he would be thrown in irons for his trouble, then hanged on some trumped-up charge. And Siân would be forced to watch, powerless to stop any of it.

Over the years she'd learned that Wrexton was the law unto himself. Parliament had little to do with the far reaches of the Saxon kingdom, and the outlying noblemen could do as they pleased on their lands. She supposed these men occasionally merited a slap on the hands for their acts, but more often than not, they were ignored.

"There, there, now," Nesta said as she rubbed Siân's back and let her cry out her sorrow. "I should have listened to Bethan, and never let you go to London."

Siân hiccuped. "Aunt Bethan didn't want me to go?"

"None of us wanted you to go, lass," Nesta said, "but Owen... Well now. What choice did we have?"

Siân was overwhelmed by Nesta's revelation. She'd been a burden to her uncles and their families. And once her uncles were gone, Siân knew that life was a struggle for their wives. They certainly did not need one more mouth to feed.

"Oh, auntie," she said, "I've felt so alone since I went away."

"Well, you're alone no longer, Siân Tudor," Bethan said as she got up from her chair and came over to the bed. "It's been dreary and dull since you left Pwll. The children have missed you."

"So have half the young men around here," Nesta added, giving Siân a surprise. She knew of no one, other than the children perhaps, who would have missed her.

"But I never—Wrexton would—"

"Would what?"

"You know how Wrexton feels about me," she said. "He exacts his revenge on my family by punishing anyone who gets close to me."

"Times change, Siân," Bethan said. "The earl has not bothered so much with Pwll these last years and you know it. Aye, times have been hard, lass, but the village has been poorer without you."

"Oh, Aunt Bethan," Siân said, her tears beginning anew, "when Wrexton learns that I'm here—"

"He will not, Siân," Bethan reassured her. "But even if he did—"

"But Wrexton was the one who stole me from Windermere," Siân cried. "He was taking me back to Wrexton Castle when I escaped!"

Nesta and Bethan exchanged a look.

"You'd better tell us what happened," Nesta said.

Marcus de Grant was as taciturn as Hugh Dryden. Knighted by King Henry V a few years before, Marcus had served in France under Henry, and then under the command of the king's brother, the Duke of Bedford. He had only recently returned to England when he'd learned of his mother's illness.

Hugh noted how well de Grant moved, in spite of his big, muscular frame, and the competent way the man handled his weaponry. He sat his horse like a soldier and rode at a wicked pace over the rough terrain toward Wrexton without a word of complaint. In a short time Hugh developed the utmost confidence in Marcus and considered himself fortunate for his company. He suspected he was going to need help in rescuing Siân.

They rode for hours, breaking only once to water the horses. It was dusk when they finally reached a hillside overlooking Wrexton Castle.

"We'll cool down the horses before we attempt the gate," Hugh said.

"What's your plan?"

Hugh shrugged. He'd been thinking about this ever since they'd left Northaven, and had not been able to come up with anything more than a basic plan of action. "We'll simply go in and see what we can learn. But not with sweating, winded horses."

De Grant cocked up one eyebrow.

"Something will come to me as we go," Hugh said. "What do you know of Wrexton Castle?"

De Grant shrugged. "I don't recall much about it, other than the keep."

Hugh assumed the keep at Wrexton would be similar to all the others he'd seen. It would be the fortress at the center of the compound, a stone building in which the great hall was located, along with a chapel, the kitchens, and sleeping quarters above.

It was entirely possible that there was also a donjon below the keep. The mere thought of a dark and dank chamber under the castle made Hugh's skin crawl. He had not allowed himself to think of Siân in such a place, but now he had to face the very real possibility that Wrexton had her imprisoned in a subterranean cavern similar to the one at Windermere, where he'd been tortured.

Hugh had to get Siân away. He could not imagine the torment she'd already endured, first with the abduction itself, then the storm while she was on board ship. For all her strength and courage, Siân had her fears, which Hugh had witnessed more than once. He hated Wrexton all the more for putting Siân in a position of having to deal with the elements while out in the open sea.

God Himself could not help Wrexton if Siân had come to any enduring harm.

Hugh looked up at the vast Wrexton holding before him. The castle wall bordered the curve of a swift-flowing river. "It appears as if the river flows under the castle wall," Hugh remarked.

"Nearly," de Grant replied. "There is a place below the wall—it's a loosely kept secret—where the water flows in. Supplies can be boated in to a small quay underneath the keep."

"Any way *we* could get in by boat?"

De Grant shook his head. "It's doubtful. When I was at Wrexton years ago, some of the other boys took me down to see the stone quay. I remember there was a portcullis that could be raised and lowered, depending on need…"

Hugh assumed the portcullis would be down, so that would not be an option. He knew of a certainty the castle gates would be watched. If he and de Grant were noticed passing through, they would be questioned. "We'll need a reason for entering the castle," Hugh said.

De Grant agreed.

"We'll gather wood," Hugh said, "haul it any way we can."

"Good thought," de Grant remarked as he started to pick up deadfall. "Mayhap when we reach the village, we can pilfer a cart and go from there."

It was the only plan they had to work with, and though it wasn't the best one he'd ever come up with, Hugh thought it was better than nothing.

He and de Grant collected as much wood as they could carry, then led their horses down toward the village along a narrow lane that ran between two fields. They came upon an abandoned wagon and dropped their loads of wood into it. After hitching the horses to the wagon, they proceeded on toward Wrexton.

Before reaching the gates, they threw their cloaks on, partially concealing their faces as well as their swords, and walked down the quiet lane. When they reached the castle gate, guards were posted, but they passed through without incident.

Hugh was accustomed to working stealthily. He knew how to blend in, how to look like and sound like a man who belonged. But this time, it was nearly impossible to practice the patience that was required to blend in. Siân was in danger, and if he did not get to her soon, he was afraid of the consequences.

He would not allow himself to begin thinking of what may have already taken place.

The two men carried their loads of wood through the bailey and beyond, until they reached the keep itself, then circled the stone fortress to the back, where they knew the kitchen would be. No one was about, but Hugh and Marcus kept their silence.

They dropped the wood onto the existing woodpile outside the door, and went to search out a place to hide their horses, which would not be an easy task. Two very large animals would be difficult to conceal—especially these horses, bred to carry knights into battle.

Eventually, they found a fairly secluded spot in the outer bailey. They tied the horses and left the wagon, then headed back to the keep, stopping only once to make a sketchy plan.

"He's probably got her locked in one of his rooms down below," Marcus said. "There is the buttery. Beneath it are storage rooms and the quay where the river flows through. Those rooms would be Wrexton's closest imitation of a donjon."

"All right," Hugh said quietly, as a cold sweat chilled him. He'd avoided closed-in spaces for the last two years. Only for Siân, would he go back into one. "Do you know how to get there?"

Marcus took the lead. Walking past the kitchen,

Hugh followed him silently till they reached the buttery, then came to a stone staircase leading down.
There was a thick, oak door at the bottom, and neither
man knew what they'd find beyond it.

Hugh gritted his teeth, and drew his sword. Marcus
did the same. They both knew they had to go down in
darkness, otherwise, they'd alert anyone guarding Siân.

Opening the door to what was sure to be a hell down
below, Hugh took the first step.

Siân sat in Nesta's small cottage and tried to pass
the time working on the unending pile of mending that
was always kept in a basket in a corner of the common
room. She gained her strength back quickly under her
aunts' care, and other than a few scrapes and bruises,
Siân was none the worse off for all the terrible hours
she'd spent as Wrexton's captive.

All that remained was for her to adjust to life back
in Pwll. A life without Hugh, for he was most certainly
en route to Clairmont even now, to claim his bride.

Siân tried to ignore the heavy feeling in the pit of
her stomach, and the aching of her heart. Hugh was
lost to her forever. He would have no reason to travel
to Wales, especially not after his marriage. Clairmont—and Marguerite—would keep him occupied;
and Siân would learn to live with the memories of the
short time they had together.

Siân let the sewing drop into her lap as she wrapped
her arms around herself, trying to ward off the dismal
chill of emptiness that came over her. She would not
give in to tears again. They served no purpose other
than to make her feel even more miserable. Facing the
rest of her life without Hugh, knowing he belonged to

Marguerite, was bad enough without weeping about it every minute.

It was midmorning already, and the sun shone brightly. Suddenly unable to deal with the damp chilliness of the cottage, Siân stood up and put the mending away. She pulled a dark, woolen shawl around her shoulders and stepped outside.

Holding her head up high, she walked through the village, meeting only a few children along the way. None of the adults were out and about, which was just as well. Siân did not think she could withstand a harsh word at the moment, and she knew she was in for some. The people of Pwll had been more than pleased to see Siân leave them to join her Saxon brother. She did not think they'd be overjoyed to have her back.

Even with the sun shining down on her, Siân was certain she'd never feel warm again. After all those hours in the cold, wearing the same torn and soaking clothes, she craved the heat of the sun. She intended to walk out to the western fields, where a few large boulders lay scattered about and she'd be able to sit in warmth and in peace. But she did not get very far. As she approached the church, she heard voices raised in dissension.

There was a gathering of people in front of the little church with the crumbling tower that had been only minimally repaired. Siân wondered what was going on, but she had the sinking feeling it was about her. She searched the crowd, and finally saw the faces of her aunts and several of her older cousins.

"We hide her, that's what!" cousin Rhodri cried, and Siân knew he was talking about hiding *her*.

She could not tell if the villagers were in agreement

or not, but there was a loud murmur of reaction to his statement.

"No one has to admit to seeing her," Nesta said with an urgency in her voice. "Just because he lost her does not mean she would come here to Pwll!"

"But where else would she go?" one skeptical man demanded.

"It does not matter," Bethan replied. "Wrexton does not know *where* they lost her. She could have gotten away miles and miles from here."

"My sons have already gone out to the woods and seen to it that Wrexton's men will not find any trail leading back to Pwll," Nesta said, surprising Siân, who had no idea that the boys had done any such thing.

"We all keep quiet about her, and Wrexton will be none the wiser," Rhodri said.

"Besides, she's one of us!" another one of the villagers called. "Like it or not, we must take care of our own!"

"We cannot abandon the lass," the squire of Pwll said, "not when her father was one of the leaders of the great rebellion."

There were rumbles of discussion again, and Siân could not tell whether the consensus was for or against her staying among them. She hadn't known she would cause such a stir by returning home. Tears burned the backs of her eyes when she realized she was still not wanted. Even if her aunts and cousins and the squire managed to convince the people to remain silent about her return, her presence was just as dangerous as it had always been. She could not stay.

Too overcome to speak to the crowd, to tell them she would leave Pwll, Siân backed away. She felt like a child again, with nowhere to go, no one to turn to.

She was alone again, but this time she was forced to flee in order to avoid bringing disaster again to the people of Pwll.

"Whoa, there!" called a gray-bearded man from his perch high upon his swaybacked nag. He was directly behind Siân, and she nearly ran into him and his horse. "You're in a terrible hurry, lass."

Siân still could not speak. She gave the old man an apologetic look and started to back away, but her desire for escape was thwarted by the crowd of people who were interested in the stranger in their midst.

"Ho, peddler," Squire Powicke called as the villagers began to gather around.

"Greetings to you fine people of...Pwll, is it?" the old man said as he dismounted. He turned to loose his packs and pull them off the horse. "I bring you fine herbs and potions from my travels abroad...."

Siân did not care to stay and listen. Dejected as she was, she tried to make her way through the crowd, but was stopped in her tracks by the peddler's words. "I bring comfrey from York, dittany grown in Llanfair, lavender of the Cumbrian hills, and fresh, precious foxglove from Castle Wrexton. Who of you has the dropsy...?"

Siân pushed her way back to the peddler. "What news from Castle Wrexton?" she asked the man.

The old fellow grinned. "Oh...now that's a pretty story," he said.

"Tell us!" the people cried, always hungry for news from abroad.

"It can be told from yon public house," the peddler said as he shouldered his packs and started walking toward the alehouse. A large number of people followed him, crowding around when he got himself situated comfortably on a short, wooden stool.

"The earl's got two men imprisoned, both," the peddler said after a pint was poured, "mighty knights of England."

"Who are they?" Siân asked, dismayed over the possibilities. If Windermere had sent knights to rescue her, and they'd been caught...

"Never heard any names, but they say the earl was expecting these villains."

"Villains!" some of the voices exclaimed excitedly. Talk of villains was a good portent of a lively story ahead.

"Of a certainty," the peddler reiterated. "The two came in disguised. *Disguised!* As wood peddlers, of all things, when all they were after was the earl's gold."

Siân breathed a sigh of relief. Clearly, no knight of Windermere would go thieving across the countryside. It was no one of consequence to her, and she turned to make her way out of the room when the peddler continued.

"They stole through the castle gates, but the guards had their eyes peeled for just such blackguards," the peddler said. "You see, the earl had a notion that they were to be invaded, and set the guard to watching for a man with a black eye patch."

Siân stopped cold. The room swayed and she closed her eyes.

"Wrexton had them bound and taken to the courtyard, where they were whipped and beaten," the visitor continued, "and he plans to hang 'em on the morrow."

Siân put trembling fingers to her lips. "Dear *Jésu*..." she whispered, then turned and pushed her way out of the crowded public room. She did not stop running until she reached Aunt Nesta's cottage.

"Dear God in Heaven," Siân said, raising her teary eyes to Nesta, who had followed her home after hearing all that the peddler had to say. "It's *Hugh*. Oh, why did *he* have to come for me? He should have been safely on his way to Clairmont...."

But Hugh Dryden was an honorable man and a chivalrous knight. Of course he had come for her.

Siân suddenly stood. "Madoc," she said to one of her young cousins as she wiped the tears from her eyes. "I'll need to borrow some of your clothes."

"What are you going to do, Siân *verch* Marudedd?" Nesta asked, lines of worry crossing her face.

"I must go to Wrexton," she replied, following Madoc to his box of spare clothes. "I have to help Hugh."

"But you cannot go alone," Nesta said, "Wrexton will—"

"—never even know I'm there."

"Oh, Siân, how can you—"

"I'll dress as Madoc," she said. "No one will know I'm female, and they will certainly never know I am Siân Tudor."

Nesta shook her head and Siân hugged her aunt. "This is something I *must* do," Siân said earnestly. "Don't you see, Auntie? When I tried to kill Wrexton for what he did to Dafydd and Idwal, I wasn't able to carry it out. I'd have been as evil and twisted as *he* is. But I can save another two men from him.

"I won't let Hugh and his companion hang for me."

Chapter Seventeen

Siân thought it through, and decided that she could not allow anyone from Pwll to go to Wrexton with her. She would not endanger any more lives than necessary, and Hugh's was already on the line.

She dressed in her young cousin's clothes, pinned up her hair and put on a cap, effectively obliterating all femininity from her appearance. For good measure, she rubbed a thin layer of dirt across her nose and cheekbones before setting off for the hills to the east.

She took the higher ground because she could see farther, and the choice of paths soon turned to Siân's advantage. As she hiked east, toward Wrexton, a company of knights rode past on the lower road. None of them glanced her way, and luckily, there were enough trees for cover, so she was not readily obvious to them.

From her vantage point on the wooded bluff, she turned and watched Wrexton's knights ride west. There was no doubt in Siân's mind that they were headed toward her village. No matter where her "guards" had lost her, it was reasonable for them to assume she had somehow gotten back to her old home.

Siân vacillated between going back to Pwll to try

and keep her village from trouble, and continuing on to Wrexton. Finally concluding that the villagers would remain silent about her return—after all, that's what her family had already proposed—Siân decided she had no choice but to continue on her way.

Returning to Pwll would serve no purpose, anyway, other than to get her captured again, and taken to Wrexton under the watchful eye of a new guard. She could not help Hugh that way. But if all went well in Pwll, the knights might be set to scouring the countryside in search for her—keeping them away from Wrexton and her attempt to get Hugh away from the unscrupulous earl.

It was several miles to Castle Wrexton, and Siân followed the instructions given her by her cousin, Rhodri, who'd once journeyed there. However, she walked quite a bit off course at one point, and did not realize her mistake until she reached a promontory that overlooked the entire valley. And that's when she spotted the majestic castle, nestled on the banks of a small river, in the distance to the north. It looked as if the river flowed *under* the castle wall, but Siân could not be sure from this distance.

Correcting her course again, she headed due north for Wrexton.

She did not know exactly what she would do once she reached the castle, only that she had to find where Hugh was being held and somehow free him. It broke her heart to think of him going through anything even remotely similar to his imprisonment at Windermere. For all she knew, he was jailed in some donjon beneath Wrexton castle, subjected to some of the same horrors he'd experienced two years before.

Siân would not stand for it. Somehow, she was going to free him.

When she reached the castle, there was plenty of commerce going back and forth on the bridge over the river, but she was worried. If Wrexton had anticipated Hugh's arrival at the castle, would he not have warned his men to watch for *her* as well?

Ambling like a young boy around the town at the foot of the castle wall, Siân occasionally glanced up at the guards within. Somehow, she had to get in without alerting them to her presence. But how?

She tried to move as if she had somewhere to go, some other children to find, so as not to attract attention to herself. But still, she had no idea how she would manage to gain entrance to Wrexton's keep.

And then she saw it. Lying on the ground, among the high reeds that grew alongside the river, was the one thing that was going to make her task at Wrexton child's play.

It was a nice, round leather camp-ball.

Siân looked around. There were plenty of children about—children who could easily be drawn into a game, if only it looked interesting enough. She pulled the ball out of the reeds with one foot, clasped her hands behind her back and started kicking the ball, tipping it back and forth between her own two feet. This was a version of camp-ball that was particularly popular in Pwll, so Siân was quite proficient at it.

She continued maneuvering the ball around her feet as she crossed the drawbridge and moved along to the outer bailey. She showed considerable skill as she kicked the ball around, attracting a small audience of young faces.

One young boy joined her, and they volleyed the ball

back and forth, sizing up each other's abilities. Then another two came along, and soon there were enough to make a game. They moved to the upper bailey, where there was more open space. Goals were determined and teams quickly chosen. Siân, who was presumed to be an older boy, started the game in the center of the "field," kicking the ball toward the haywagon goal. Someone from the opposing team intercepted, and the game was on.

She was in!

Siân scored the game-winning point of a spirited game, making her a favorite among her new young friends. The boys were in awe over her skilled footwork in this game of camp-ball that required the use of feet only to move the ball toward the goal. She'd played fairly, passing the ball and making sure to include all of the others, even the smaller boys who had little experience and even less ability at the game.

Children were gullible. Siân knew it and had counted on that fact when she gave her explanation of who she was, and where she'd come from. Not for one minute did they doubt that she was an orphaned Welsh boy named Madoc, who'd left home to come to Wrexton to serve the earl. They saw it as a great adventure.

Luckily, several of the young boys also saw it as their chance to show their new acquaintance around. Siân was able to explore every nook and cranny within the walls of Wrexton Castle, and listen to their talk of the two prisoners who were being held in the tower, at the top of the keep.

Siân was relieved to hear that Hugh was not chained in a dark dungeon, but wondered how she would ever be able to get him out of the high tower. It was likely to be filled with Wrexton's guards and Siân could not imagine how she would ever get past them. She shaded her eyes with one hand as she gazed up at Hugh's prison.

Somehow, she would have to gain entrance to the place, disable the guards and free Hugh, without getting herself caught in Wrexton's web.

It was impossible, she thought, completely discouraged now that she'd seen the place. How would she ever get up there, let alone get Hugh out?

Refusing to give in to despair, she forced herself to assess the stronghold as well as she could, notice every possible entrance, evaluate every weakness. Unfortunately, there were few.

The boys stopped at the well for drinks of water, and one boy, Robby, offered to go filch a bite for them all to eat from his mother, Wrexton's cook.

"Might I come along?" Siân asked abruptly, handing the ladle to the boy next to her.

"Suit yerself," the lad replied as he ambled off toward one of the doors that faced the rear of the bailey. "She's liable only to have a bit of bread, but the lads will like it. She's a good cook, my mum."

Siân didn't care how good a cook the boy's mother was, only that this was a way to gain entrance to the keep, and perhaps manage to take a look around. She did not think she'd be able to slip away to wander freely about the stone fortress, but it was worth a try, as long as she remained cautious.

The kitchen was hot. But it smelled heavenly to Siân, who had not had a bite to eat since leaving Pwll. "Where is that jackanapes, Raulf?" one of the women demanded.

A huge joint of meat cooked on a spit over an open

flame in the center of the kitchen. A burly-armed woman turned it, and Siân's mouth fairly watered with the savory smells of the cooking meat. There was a lot of activity in the kitchen, with the comings and goings of servants preparing to serve the evening meal, and Siân blended right in with Robby.

"Raulf's gone, Mum," Siân's companion said as he slipped an apple to her. Siân shoved it into her pocket. "Have ye any wafers for the lads?"

"Go away, Robby, I've my own work to do," the mother said as she put a flask of water and two crusts of bread on a tray, "and now Raulf's work, to boot."

"We can help you, Mum," Robby said. "Just tell us what you need."

Robby's mother handed him a bucket and told him to fill it with water. She directed Siân to the buttery for ale.

When the two "boys" returned, Robby's mother was still as flustered and overworked as before. She blew a strand of hair from her face as she picked up the tray that was now ready. Handing it to her son, the woman spoke quietly to him with one hand partially covering her mouth. Robby took the tray and headed toward the hall. Then he stopped and winked conspiratorially at Siân. "Come on!" he said quietly.

Siân did not wait to be invited again. They went to the far end of the hall, then exited the keep and walked around the corner of the buttery, where the stone building was built low over the river. She could hear the water rushing underneath, and wondered where they were headed. "Where are we going?" she whispered as she followed him around to an outside stairway leading down.

Robby admonished her to keep quiet and started down the long flight of stone steps.

Hugh sat on the cold, damp stone floor and watched Marcus sleep. Their little prison was a small storage room, closed in by a thick wooden door with a stout iron lock. It was a stuffy little room with no windows, and a sweet-sour smell permeated the place, like over-aged ale. Hugh was grateful it did not smell like the dank and rotting cavern where he'd been held prisoner at Windermere.

Hugh stood and paced the small chamber, thankful that at least there was one torch to burn. He knew he would not have been able to endure complete darkness. It was all he could do to bear this confinement—the stone walls around him and the low ceiling above him.

Worse, though, was not knowing what had happened to Siân. He had not seen her since their arrival at the castle, nor had Wrexton said anything about her. The earl seemed particularly gleeful, however, to have captured Siân Tudor's two champions, and Hugh had a sinking suspicion that history was about to repeat itself. A fool like Wrexton would know only one trick, which he was likely to repeat at any opportunity.

From everything Siân had said about Wrexton, Hugh should have foreseen the trap at the castle gates. Obviously, Wrexton had surmised that someone would come after Siân, even going so far as to anticipate that it would be Hugh himself. He'd had his guards looking out for any strangers, especially a man with an eye patch. Now, he and de Grant were locked up in an impregnable little room where they could not help themselves, much less Siân.

Where was she now? Did Wrexton have her locked

up, only to bring her out when he was ready to execute her would-be rescuers? What was Wrexton waiting for?

Hugh knew he had to get de Grant and himself out before Wrexton had a chance to repeat his vicious stunt for Siân's benefit.

But how would he manage it?

One of Marcus's eyes was bruised and swollen shut, and the other was damaged almost as badly. He'd taken a lot of vicious blows to the midsection and Hugh suspected the young man had some cracked ribs, although he was a strong, well-conditioned knight. He would recover. The question was—how soon?

Hugh's back and shoulder wounds were painful, as well. The stitches in his upper arm had torn out, but that was the least of his problems. He did not know whether he'd be able to wield a sword, even if he could get his hands on one.

They were a pitiful pair.

Muffled noises were audible outside. "Marcus," Hugh said as he crouched down next to his companion, touching his shoulder gingerly.

De Grant tried to open his eyes, with only partial success. He groaned and pulled himself painfully to a sitting position, leaning his back against one of the large wooden casks that lined the walls of their cell.

"Someone's coming," Hugh said. "Do you think you can—"

All too quickly, there was a key in the lock, and the door slammed open. They'd missed their chance to act.

"Stay back, now!" the turnkey demanded harshly as a young boy entered the chamber, carrying a tray laden with coarse, brown bread and drink. An archer stood just behind, with his bow at the ready, an arrow knocked and ready to fly.

Hugh stood still, keeping his eye on the archer, knowing that one untimely move could get either himself or Marcus killed. A small cough from the doorway distracted Hugh momentarily, and he glanced at the second boy who'd come to look at the prisoners.

Then he glanced again. Siân!

Sweet *Jésu* in Heaven! Hugh was not high in the tower, but here! Down *below* the keep! And still, there was nothing Siân could do! She could not overpower the burly turnkey as well as the archer. She'd managed to push her way through with Robby, and gotten Hugh's attention, but what now? At least Hugh could rest at ease somewhat, knowing she was not in Wrexton's clutches.

But *he* still was!

Her eyes drank their fill of him, taking in all the new injuries, the new damage to his arm. He was battered and filthy, a few days' growth of beard shaded his jaw, and his eye patch was gone, so the scar was fully visible. But the sight of him had never been more appealing. She could not have loved him more.

Siân would have to get him out. Somehow, she would figure a way to return to free Hugh and the man imprisoned with him. Catching his eye again, she silently mouthed the words, "Soon. Be ready!"

With no idea whether or not he understood her message, Siân took the tray from Robby as the jailer shoved her back. She turned of her own accord and went back through the passageway with the boy and the two guards. Discreetly studying her surroundings, she realized that this would be her only chance to get a good look around, to come up with a plan for getting Hugh out.

Beyond the room where Hugh was being held was another short flight of steps that led down to the water, and with the waning sunlight streaming into the tunnel below, Siân could see that there was a small boat tied there.

This would be the only way to get back in, she thought dismally, though she needed more information. Where did that tunnel lead? Would she have to swim to get back here again? Somehow, she had to get a better look at the jetty where the boat was tied.

Knowing this would be her only chance, she pretended to trip on a step, and dropped the wooden tray she carried, letting it go flying down to the stone jetty. Turning quickly, she said, "Sorry, I'll get it!"

Seeming to skip casually down the steps, Siân took a good look around as she picked up the tray, then ran back up, ignoring the nasty words that the jailer directed at her for her clumsiness.

"Go *on*," Robby said in a rasping whisper, landing a punch on Siân's shoulder. "I'd a never 'ave brought you if I'd a known you were gonna be so clumsy."

"Sorry," Siân said simply as they reached the upper door where the turnkey unlocked the door and let them out into the late afternoon sunshine. "Didn't mean to," she mumbled petulantly, hoping she sounded like one of the boy's peers.

It was getting late, and would be dark soon. When would Wrexton act? Tomorrow, as the herb peddler had said? Or tonight? Siân had a feeling that time was of the essence. She had to get Hugh and his companion out of there, and quickly.

Hugh was in terrible condition. Siân didn't know how she'd managed to keep from crying out at the sight of his new wounds, or throwing herself into his arms in spite of the guards's presence. Somehow, by sheer force of will, she'd maintained her composure.

The other prisoner was in even worse shape than Hugh. Siân did not know if he would be able to walk, or how she would get him out of the little prison.

Siân chewed her lip and considered the problems she faced. It was obvious that neither Hugh nor the other man would get far on foot. Even if they were able to walk or run, it was miles to Pwll. And Pwll was the first place Wrexton would look for them. Once Siân freed Hugh and his companion, they would have to travel in any direction but west.

She was going to need horses and weapons, too, but where would she find them and how would she steal them? The obstacles seemed insurmountable, but Siân refused to be foiled. She would need all of her wits, and every ounce of courage she could muster. Hugh's life depended on it.

Siân nudged Robby and said, "Let's get some of the other lads and go throw stones in the river."

She spent the time examining the fortress as she asked questions of her guileless young companions and discovered the location of the tunnel's entrance. There was no way to get to it without swimming, and that would be a challenge. She was an excellent swimmer, but the current was strong and the water icy cold. She would be lucky not to freeze to death crossing the wide, watery expanse.

Once she reached the tunnel, Siân would have to disable the guards, and hope there would not be more than the two who were there earlier. Then, she could get Hugh and the other man down the steps and into the boat, where they would float to safety beyond the portcullis Robby mentioned, then on outside the castle walls, and across the river to the far bank.

An hour later Siân was alone in the stable, looking over the horses. She recognized Hugh's warhorse, as well as several other huge destriers, but could not figure how to take his mare or any other horses out of their stalls and get them past the stableman.

"Go on with ye now!" that man said sharply, shooing her out of the long, low building that housed the horses.

She scooted away from the man before he could swat her, then ran around to the side of the building. Sliding down the wall to sit on the rough ground, Siân buried her face against her knees and tried to stop shaking.

Her pathetic tears would not help the situation, she thought, sniffling. What was she going to do? The first part of her plan was in place, but it would be no good if she couldn't get the two men away from Wrexton once they crossed the river. There had to be a way to get some horses over to the far bank. Reaching into her pocket to move the uncomfortable bulk of an apple Robby had purloined from the pantry, she rubbed it absently on her tunic. She had to settle herself down and *think!*

Absently, Siân took a bite of the apple, and gathered her thoughts. Hugh and the other knight needed mounts. They would not be able to stay in the little boat and float down the river because it flowed right past the gatehouse. They would be discovered before they had half a chance to get away.

She was stuck. She was right back where she started, with Hugh and his companion locked in that room, and her only access to the little prison was by way of the

river. And even that passage might be blocked if the
portcullis was down.

Siân sighed heavily. She finished her apple and stood
up, brushing off her bottom, then stepped over to a
workhorse waiting to be unhitched from his cart. She
palmed the apple core and fed it to him.

And a new plan suddenly came to her. Siân realized
she'd need a diversion to be successful. Glancing
around the bailey, Siân looked to see which of the lads
were still hanging about, who could possibly become
interested in another game of camp-ball before it became fully dark.

It was all Hugh could do to keep from leveling the
jailer who'd laid his grimy hands on Siân to push her
back. Only the lethal point of the arrow trained on his
heart had kept him from grabbing her and hugging her
close.

She'd told him to be ready. Hugh did not know for
what, but he had no intention of being caught unprepared again. Though there was not much he could do,
locked in this small room, there might be one thing.

He started moving barrels away from the wall to
make a barrier just inside the doorway. The barrels
were full, and most were heavy, but Hugh managed to
roll or slide them into place.

"Marcus," Hugh said, waking the man again,
"you've got to move back here."

De Grant looked up and saw what Hugh was doing,
and hauled himself painfully to a standing position. "I
can help," he panted.

"I doubt that," Hugh said, "but you're welcome to
try."

Together, they formed a wall of barrels in front of

the door. When the guards came in again, Hugh and Marcus would be somewhat shielded, and might possibly be able to overpower the guards.

With high hopes, Hugh began to pound on the door and shout for the jailer to come.

"Look," Marcus said from his position behind the barrels. Hugh came around and noticed a mound of white sand flowing from a crack in one of the barrels. He smelled it, then tasted it.

"Salt."

"Won't feel very good...in the eyes," Marcus said as he gathered two handfuls of the common spice.

Hugh almost smiled as he went back to the door and began pounding again. He shouted everything he could think of that would get the guards to come, while Marcus flattened himself up against the wall next to the door.

The noise and distraction behind Hugh's prison door was all Siân needed to pull herself up out of the water without notice. Thankfully, the portcullis had been up, and the little boat was still there. There was precious little light to work in—only just barely enough from the torches of the guards far above. She sat for a moment on the little jetty and caught her breath, fully aware that there was little time.

Soaked and shivering with the cold, Siân got up and quickly loosened the heavy knots that kept the boat tied to an iron loop on the quay. Then she retied it loosely, so she'd be able to pull away quickly once she had Hugh and the other fellow on board.

She took one of the paddles from inside the boat, and moved across the jetty to the stone steps that led to Hugh's jail room, where someone inside was still making an awful racket.

"Quit yer caterwaulin', ye shard-borne maggot feed!" the turnkey growled as he lumbered down the steps toward Hugh's door. The archer walked behind, just as he had earlier, just as Siân hoped he would.

The jailer shoved the big key into the iron lock, turned it, then slammed the door wide open. At the same time, Siân ran quickly and silently up the steps, carrying an oar.

Confusion broke out. The burly jailer suddenly staggered backward. Siân took the opportunity to raise the paddle and strike the archer with it, hitting him square across the back of his shoulders, then jumping back as the man fell down the stone steps.

Hugh disabled the turnkey, and relieved him of his sword, while the other prisoner, wincing in pain, picked up the fallen torch and came out to look around. "Siân Tudor?" he asked as the slightest curve of a smile lit up his battered face.

Siân nodded, glad of the poor lighting in the passage. She'd left her tunic and hose on the on the other side of the river before swimming across, and wore only Madoc's long, linen shirt. She felt naked. "We've got to hurry. Can you walk?"

"Out of here? Absolutely," he said gravely. "I'm Marcus de Grant. Your timing could not have been better."

Then Hugh stepped out. "Siân!"

With one breath, she was in his arms, and nothing else was important, not his ragged clothes, nor the coarse, dark stubble of beard. Only the beat of his heart mattered as it pressed against hers, the tingle of his breath near her ear, the strength of his arms around her, and the very real possibility that they were all going to escape.

"We've got to go," Siân said reluctantly, looking up at Hugh, into the face of the man she loved. "Quickly."

Hugh rubbed away the tears Siân did not know she'd shed, then drew her back and kissed her forehead. He put his hands on her waist and said, "Lead the way."

And as he spoke, a pounding at the top of the outside stairway erupted, clearly illustrating that their time was limited.

Chapter Eighteen

They flew down the steps as fast as their various injuries permitted, and Marcus climbed into the boat behind Siân. Hugh asked no questions, but tossed his stolen sword into the bottom of the small craft. Then he pulled the mooring rope free and eased himself into the boat with the others.

"When we get past the portcullis, you'll have to put out the torch," Siân said urgently to Marcus as she knelt up and manned one of the paddles. "We'll be visible to anyone on the parapet or in the towers."

"If they break through that door up there," Hugh said, "then douse it sooner."

Wrexton men would soon be upon them. They had to row hard and fast because there would be no doubt about where the prisoners had gone. It was obvious that the only passage out was by way of the river. "The current will take us past the gatehouse," Siân said quietly, holding her body low in the little wooden boat. "We have to paddle against it, to get to the north side."

"Marcus, keep down," Hugh said. He took up the spare paddle and alternated strokes with Siân, letting her steer, since she was the only one who knew where they were going.

They heard voices as they reached the outer edge of the tunnel, and Marcus disposed of the torch. They were abruptly drenched in darkness. "Just keep going straight," Siân whispered. The boat was in the center of the channel, and there was no possibility of hitting a wall. Siân and Hugh continued to paddle, keeping the boat on course, while Marcus stretched out as well as he could, in the back.

Within seconds they were on the open river, with the curtain of Wrexton Castle rising high above them. Siân shivered not only with cold, but with the dread of capture. She had been lucky so far. *Too lucky.*

The alarm sounded.

In desperation, Siân increased her rowing speed, and Hugh followed her lead. She threw a glance back at the wall, terrified that archers would be able to see them in the open water.

"Just keep going, sweetheart," Hugh said, though it took all his energy to keep moving. "They won't see us in time."

The current was strong, and they were drawn downstream. Siân had hoped they'd be able to control the boat better, but it was not possible. She had no experience with such things, and Hugh's wounds prevented him from rowing with much strength. Every stroke was a struggle, and she heard him straining with the exertion. She wished she could tell him to sit back and rest, but that would spell certain disaster. As long as he was able, he had no choice but to row.

"Give me a go at it," Marcus said from behind.

"No," Hugh grunted. "We're nearly out of arrow range. Can't waste any time."

Siân realized he was correct. Though the powers who commanded Wrexton still hadn't put archers in place, they had to know the prisoners were headed for shore. Even if no one shot at them from the wall, there was certain to be a troop of soldiers out scouring the countryside for them.

They had to hurry.

When the little boat finally made it to the riverbank, Siân quickly climbed out and held it close to shore so that Hugh and Marcus could crawl out.

"Siân," Hugh rasped as he lay supine on the grassy bank, "does the boat figure anywhere in the rest of your plans?"

"No," she replied as she looked up and tried to get her bearings. She was exhausted and wished she could afford the time to lie down on the ground along with the two men. Unfortunately, that was not possible. "I have a horse and cart somewhere nearby."

"Then shove the boat out, as far as you need to, so the current will catch it."

"Good idea," said Marcus, who was trying to garner enough strength for the next step of their escape.

Siân did what Hugh said, hoping that the Wrexton men would find the boat and assume they'd drowned. And if not, at least there would be no clear evidence of where they'd alighted on shore.

When Siân returned from setting the boat adrift into the current, Marcus was either asleep or unconscious, his breathing shallow.

Hugh was awake. Siân fell to her knees next to him, afraid to touch him, to hurt him any further, but desperate to be near him, if only for the moment, before they continued on.

"Sweet Siân," he said as he raised his arm and

pulled her head down, desperate to taste her, in spite of his weakened condition.

Their lips met in a kiss that melted her resolve not to touch him. He pulled her closer, and Siân cupped his face, the only part of him that did not appear to be injured. She whimpered as he deepened the kiss, even though she knew they had to stop. They had to get away from there.

"I thought I'd lost you," Hugh said, his voice husky and tight.

Siân would not dwell on the fact that she had already lost *him*. To Marguerite. "I—I thought I was lost, too," she finally said, between fevered kisses. "On the ship…the storm…and later… But I got away…" If only they could crawl away somewhere together, she thought, away from life's realities, away from Wrexton. But that was not to be, and Siân was well aware of it. *"Hugh!"*

"I know, love," he said as he dragged himself to a sitting position, "we have to move."

"Will you see to Sir Marcus while I find the horse and cart?"

He nodded, then kissed her again before going over to de Grant. Siân stood and wrapped her arms around herself to ward off the cold. Turning away from the river, she looked for the landmarks that would help her find where she'd left their only means of transportation.

Siân had planned as carefully as possible before making the swim to the castle. She'd taken off her outer clothes, knowing she would need a dry tunic and shoes if they got this far. Then, well aware that the men would not be capable of walking any distance, she'd left the cart downstream, knowing the river

would draw them that way in the little boat when they
made their escape.

After securing the horse and cart in a secluded part
of the woods, she'd walked quite a distance to start her
swim from a point upstream so that she would not have
to battle the current, letting it carry her downriver to
the inlet under the castle wall.

So far, so good. But it was fully dark now, and difficult to see the stand of oaks where she'd tethered the
horse. She turned and looked across the river at the
castle and tried to get her bearings. Soon realizing that
she would find the horse and cart a little ways upstream, Siân started to trot eastward.

And prayed she was not mistaken.

Her feet were raw by the time she came upon the
little oak forest. Her teeth were chattering, and she was
shivering nearly out of control. Her exhaustion had not
abated, but Siân managed to continue on by the force
of sheer nerves. She found the horse, sleeping right
where she left him. Quickly, she discarded the wet linens she'd worn for her swim, and pulled on the dry
tunic, hose and shoes. Instantly, she felt better.

She untied the horse, then got up onto the cart and
rode back to get Hugh and Marcus.

As Siân climbed down from her perch to help them
into the cart, she realized that Hugh was smiling. And
so was Marcus.

It could not be, she thought. Their situation was too
precarious for humor, and she was certain Hugh would
not see anything funny in their predicament. Then she
heard a mirthful snort.

''It pains me when I laugh,'' Marcus said, grinning
wryly.

"There's nothing to laugh at!" Siân cried. "We have little time, as well you know it!"

"It's the irony, Siân," Hugh explained as he climbed up behind her. "This wagon is the very same one we stole to get *into* Wrexton."

"And now it will carry us out!" Marcus said weakly, but with enthusiasm.

Their laughter was Siân's undoing. Torn between laughing and crying, she began to weep in earnest.

Hugh pulled himself up next to her on the seat and took her in his arms. "Hush, love," he said, tucking her head possessively between his neck and shoulder. "You've done so much, worked so hard for us. No other woman in the kingdom could have done what you have. All will be well now...."

Siân sniffled and pulled away. "We m-must go now," she said, embarrassed to have broken down at this juncture. She had been strong so far. Now was not the time to fall apart.

"Your turn to rest now, sweetheart," Hugh said, taking the reins. "Lean on me, and I'll try to get us out of here."

He wrapped one arm around her and drove the horse slowly through the dark woods, trusting that the old workhorse would not step into a foxhole or run them into a tree.

Hugh could not fathom what Siân had gone through to get to him, other than the fact that she must have swum across the river to get to the little prison under the keep.

She was truly amazing.

"I never planned beyond this," she said. "I didn't know where we would go once I got you here—I just concentrated on getting the wagon over here, and then getting *you*."

"It's all right, Siân," Hugh said, hugging her fiercely to him. "At least now we have a chance. We'll head north and look for shelter," he said.

"You know this area?" Siân asked.

"Only what de Grant and I saw when we arrived," he said. "Which was not much. We were anxious to get inside the castle to find you."

"Oh, Hugh…I was never there!" she repined. "After Wrexton's ship landed, I was tied up and put into the back of a wagon… We traveled for hours, but I managed to get away. In the dark. I heard…"

"What did you hear?"

"I—I heard *you!*" she said, fully aware of how fanciful she sounded. "You told me to keep going, keep running."

Hugh gave a shake of his head. "Mayhap it *was* me you heard… For I never stopped thinking of you, Siân." Then he kissed her lightly.

"I fell," she said, "and that was the last thing I remembered until some Pwll men found me in the morning." Siân described her homecoming to Hugh and how she'd learned that he was held captive at Wrexton. "I knew I had to come. I had to do what I could to get you out."

"Siân," Hugh said quietly, abruptly interrupting the flow of her narration. "Do you know how far this forest extends? Does it go on for miles or is it a shallow copse?"

"I d-don't know, Hugh," she said, quickly turning around to see what had Hugh concerned.

"There are patrols coming, love," he said. "Wrexton had to know there were only two directions available to us—along the riverbank, which would have left us in plain sight, or through the woods.''

''Abandon the wagon,'' Marcus said from the rear. ''Unhitch the horse and let him wander,'' he added, ''and we'll have a better chance losing ourselves in the underbrush.''

''You may be right,'' Hugh remarked as he jumped down to the ground. He turned to help Siân down, then freed the horse. Marcus managed to climb out without help, and he handed the stolen sword to Hugh.

''Which way?'' Siân asked.

''Over here,'' Hugh said, his voice an urgent hiss.

He led them deeper into the woods, helping Marcus as they walked. Siân took Marcus's other side and gave what support he needed.

''Is that a ridge above us, to the east?'' Hugh asked.

''I think so,'' Siân replied, her vision being slightly better than Hugh's. ''Do you think we can climb up there?'' she asked, fully realizing the advantage of getting above their pursuers. Wrexton's knights were still quite a distance behind them. There was time.

''Let's try,'' Hugh said. ''Marcus, can you do it?''

Breathless, Marcus did not waste his breath on speech, but he nodded.

''Let's go, then.''

The climb was difficult. The grade of the hillside was fairly steep and laden with loose rock and soil. Many times they lost their footing or tripped over loose vines. Marcus fell once and Siân did not think he'd be able to get up and go on. She did not know how *she* was able to keep going, either. The muscles in her legs were shaky and burning. Her mouth was dry and her feet were in agony. But somehow, they made it to the summit.

And when they finally climbed over the top of the ridge, they were met with a silent row of lethal, steel points belonging to a battalion of swordsmen.

Chapter Nineteen

Siân felt that she would faint. She was at the end of her endurance. After an entire day fraught with challenge and danger, she had reached the top of the ledge, only to have a sword thrust in her face. And then she heard Hugh's incredulous voice.

"Douglas Henley?" he asked in astonishment. "Alfred Dunning?"

"Aye," one of the men replied. "We're here to help ye, lad. Claude Montrose is here, as are Ranulf Bele and Egbert Gunne and a whole host of Windermere knights."

This time, Siân thought she might faint with the reprieve. She recognized those names. She had heard about Hugh's exploits with Wolf Colston and these knights. She might have realized that they would show up here, as a fighting unit. Naturally, these men would not allow Hugh to face Wrexton alone.

Hugh helped Siân up over the edge of the ridge, then got a couple of the Windermere men to help with Marcus. "He seems badly hurt, Hugh," Ranulf said, frowning. "How did you manage to get him all the way up here?"

"The climb looks worse than it is," he replied glibly.

"The climb is *much worse* than it looks!" Siân contradicted, nearly giddy with relief.

"Oh!" the men exclaimed, taken aback at the sound of a woman's voice. "M'lady!" Her appearance was anything but that of a lady, and they'd mistaken her for the boy she'd been all day.

"You rescued her!" Claude exclaimed.

Hugh laughed out loud, causing a stir among the men who hadn't seen even a smile from their old cohort since he'd lost his eye. "Not exactly," he said with humor, and a full measure of pride in his lady's ingenuity. "'Twas *Lady Siân* who got *us* out of Wrexton."

"God's Cross!" Henley muttered, astonished. "It'll be a tale for later, if you've a mind."

"Douglas, how did you manage to—"

"Now, ye know better than to ask that, Dryden," Henley said. "We were just ponderin' whether to storm the castle or wait for an opening."

"When we saw patrols come out of the gates," Alfred said, "we knew something was amiss. We held our position until we could determine what mischief you'd caused."

"Now you've got Wrexton's knights right on your tail," Claude remarked quietly as he walked to the ridge and looked down at the shadows of the mounted knights below. "And a fine lot they are, all rested and ready for a skirmish."

"Wolf will surely be sorry to have missed this," Henley muttered as he drew his sword again. "They'll be comin' over the ridge in a few minutes."

"Hugh," Claude said, "you'd better take your lady and head for cover."

Marcus had already limped out of the way, anticipating the battle that was to come, and knowing full well he would be more a hindrance than a help to the Windermere swordsmen. Hugh and Siân withdrew as the Windermere knights arranged themselves in a formation that would allow them to take the offensive as soon as the Wrexton men came over the precipice.

Wrexton's knights reached the precipice only to be met by a surprise attack. Hugh's hands itched to get involved in the fray, but he would not leave Siân's side for any reason. Nor did he wish to test his endurance any further. Though he felt better now than he had hours ago, the beating he'd sustained, and the wounds it had caused, gave him pause. He had no wish to die now that he had Siân by his side.

So far, the only action was at the precipice of the bluff they'd just climbed, where the knights were engaged in fierce battle. Hugh felt secure for the moment, away from the fighting.

Siân felt ready to collapse. If she'd had any right to do so, she'd have thrown herself into Hugh's arms and begged him to take her away somewhere. Someplace where she would not have to worry about the earl of Wrexton and his loathsome soldiers. A place where she could indulge in Hugh's strength, and not worry about having to swim, or steal a boat, or overpower any guards.

She only wanted to be free to love him now, while there was still time.

She and Hugh were essentially alone, with soldiers fighting on the westernmost edge of the ridge, and Marcus lying on the ground at the edge of the forest. When

Hugh turned to face her, all rational thought fled her mind. It was too dark to see clearly, but she sensed an intensity in him that had nothing to do with the battle being waged nearby. He closed the space between them and took hold of her upper arms, then drew her close to him.

"Siân," he said, "It's been forever since I touched you like this…" And then his lips were on hers, searing her with his heat, drawing her into him, making her part of him.

Her lips parted and he invaded her mouth with an intimate caress that promised more. His hands left her arms, only to traverse the length of her back, pulling her body into close contact with his own. Trembling, Siân moved against him, torturing herself with wanting what she could not have.

Her eyes drifted open as Hugh pressed smoldering kisses to her jaw, and her neck, and she saw a threat looming behind him.

"Hugh!" Siân cried. "Behind you!"

Hugh pushed her away as he turned and pulled the sword from his belt. He stood firm against the earl of Wrexton, a coward who would attack from behind.

"Alldale," Wrexton said menacingly. His own sword was drawn, and if it annoyed him to be discovered before he could get in the first blow, he did not show it.

Siân could see that Wrexton was in better form than Hugh, having been well fed and rested these last few days, while Hugh had not. Her alarm increasing with every moment that passed she knew the fight would be grossly unfair.

"You would sacrifice your *life*," Wrexton said,

punctuating the last word with the first strike of his sword, ''for this bit of Welsh offal?''

Hugh met Wrexton's thrust with surprising strength and struck back, ignoring the inflammatory jab at Siân's worth.

One glance toward the hardwood forest told Siân that Marcus was unconscious, incapacitated, and of no help to Hugh. The soldiers were heavily engaged in fighting near the ridge. Siân stood away from Hugh, her body fraught with tension, but as she watched the two earls battle it out, Siân realized that Hugh was holding his own against Wrexton. She took heart as she watched him parry and thrust with the skill of a master swordsman, in spite of his wounds and weakened condition.

She should have known! Wrexton was not nearly the seasoned soldier that Hugh was, but he seemed to have counted on Hugh's wounds inhibiting him.

It was not to be. Hugh defeated Wrexton conclusively, and when he had disarmed the winded and wounded earl, Hugh pushed him toward his men, who were still fighting desperately. ''Tell them to halt,'' Hugh ordered Wrexton.

''Nay, Alldale,'' Wrexton replied. ''You will have to kill me first.''

''Do not doubt that I will kill you, Wrexton,'' Hugh said, ''and our men will destroy yours. But you might spare some of their lives if you order them to halt.''

''I will not.''

Hugh shoved him to the edge of the battlefield. ''Your last chance, Wrexton,'' Hugh said. ''Say it—''

But before the earl made his response to Hugh's demand, one of Wrexton's knights turned and charged, his deadly sword pointed directly at Hugh's unprotected chest.

Siân screamed, but Hugh saw it coming and lunged aside, at the same time shoving Wrexton into the arc of the lethal sword. The blade ran him through, and Wrexton fell heavily to the ground.

Silence and stillness swept over the men on the ridge until it reached the soldiers engaged at the farthest edge. None spoke as swords were resheathed and men split apart to walk away. The knight who killed Wrexton stood motionless over his lord, in shock over his misdeed.

Shaken by what had just transpired, Siân went to Hugh's side and linked her fingers with his.

"We'll raise camp here," Douglas Henley said, directing men to set up tents high on the escarpment overlooking the river in the distance. "You'll have your own, m'lady," he added.

Though she was beyond exhaustion, Siân did not want her own tent. She did not care to spend the remainder of the night alone. Not this night. In the morning, she would return to Pwll, and Hugh would begin his journey back to Clairmont.

This would be their last night together, Siân thought, girding herself against the moment she would be compelled to part with the man who held her heart.

She looked around the camp. Hugh had been taken away to have his wounds tended, as had Marcus, and Siân had not seen either man since then. She had wandered aimlessly around the camp, dazed and exhausted, wondering what to do, when finally she found herself retreating into her tent to clean herself up. After the ordeals of the day—especially after that final climb up the escarpment—she was grimy with dirt and sweat.

Siân was able to stand inside the tent, but the space just barely accommodated her meager height. A mat of furs covered the ground, and a coarse, woolen blanket was folded at one end of it. One lonely bowl of wax with a lighted wick flickered, warding off total darkness. A bowl of water, along with several clean cloths lay on the ground in one corner.

Siân wasted no time as she removed her clothes and washed. Someone had heated the water, so it helped to combat the chill that had sunk into her bones.

"Siân."

She whirled instinctively at the deep, masculine voice that spoke her name, and tried, inadequately, to cover her nakedness with her hands. "Hugh…" she whispered, her eyes glistening.

He ducked and took the two steps necessary to close the distance between them. "You are so beautiful," he said, taking a lock of her hair and letting it run through his fingers. Her hands fell to her sides and he gazed hungrily at her in the glowing candlelight.

Against all reason, she spoke her wish. "Kiss me, Hugh."

His mouth descended on hers and all the days and hours spent apart fell away. They were one again, and Siân intended to savor every moment. She ran her hands through his hair, teased the overlong mane at his nape with her fingers, pressed her bare body against his fully clothed one.

Hugh groaned and lowered her to the fur-covered ground. His touch was untamed and possessive, and there was nothing reminiscent of the gentle lover who'd taken such care with her in the quiet, secluded chapel at Windermere. His mouth ravaged hers as his hands crushed her to him. She arched against him, her response eager, willing, and just as turbulent as his own.

He filled his hands with her breasts, then moved his head down to lavish desperate attention on them with his lips, his tongue. Siân reveled in the scrape of his whiskers against her sensitive skin, writhed against his strong, hard body, flexed with tension. A knot of savage pleasure unfurled deep within her, and Siân responded with all the passion and vigor of her being.

Hugh's wounds did not impede him. He moved over her, using hands and mouth, teeth and tongue, to brand her as his own. Small fires erupted all through Siân as Hugh made love to her, fires that he stoked with every movement, every intimate touch, brought her ever closer to the pinnacle of sensation.

He tore away his clothes and met her naked, skin to skin, claiming her with his first deep thrust. Braced above her, she saw fierce possession in his expression, and she cherished it, knowing that for this moment, they belonged only to each other.

"Yes!" was her whisper.

"Mmm," was his moan. "Siân!"

"Again," she demanded.

They were one as she gave him everything, and took all he could give. He moved with an urgency that grew with every second, every nuance of touch, every whispered word. They melded their bodies and souls together, and suddenly flared with impossible heat, until they caught fire and burned wildly over the precipice of ultimate sensation.

She had never experienced anything so fierce, so profound.

Hugh pulled her body close to his under the blanket. He wrapped himself around her, his chest and thighs to her back and buttocks, his warm breath stirring the hair near her ear. "Come to Alldale with me," he said quietly, his voice thick and harsh.

Siân did not answer. She had already decided to return to Pwll. There could only be heartache for Siân if she went to Alldale with him. She knew she could not bear to be near him after he made Marguerite his wife.

"Do you hesitate, Siân?" Hugh asked.

She swallowed loud enough for him to hear.

"What's this?" he asked. "Tears?"

"W-when you wed Marguerite and—"

"Cease right there, Siân," he said, turning her so that she faced him. "I will wed no woman but you."

"M-me?" she sniffled. "But you and Mar—"

"You thought I would take you to Alldale as my leman?"

She gave a slight nod. "You are betrothed, Hugh," she said quietly. "It will not be easy to—"

He hugged her to him and kissed her forehead. "Siân, I am *not* betrothed. The question was merely put to Marguerite, and she was none too anxious to accept. Before I left Windermere to come after you, I sent a missive to Clairmont, withdrawing my proposal. Siân, my love...no banns were to be posted until my return. Nothing's been done that's irreversible."

Siân still had difficulty accepting that what he said was true. The laws of betrothal were very clear, but yet...if he were not truly pledged...if he *were* free... Faint inklings of hope began to rise in Siân's breast.

"I care deeply for you, Siân," Hugh said, his mien serious, intense. "No other woman could touch my

heart as you have. Come with me to Alldale and be
my countess. Bear my children and comfort my soul.''

"Oh, Hugh!" Siân said, throwing her arms around
him. "I've loved you for so very long. My heart ached
to think of you with Marguerite. Yes, I'll go to Alldale
with you. I'll be your wife.''

After returning to Pwll, Hugh's wounds healed
quickly under Nesta's competent care. Marcus's took
longer, as his injuries were deeper and more severe. He
was tended with great care by Nesta and Siân, and as
his condition improved, it was learned that Marcus's
father, Eldred, was Wrexton's only living relative. The
elder de Grant was now the earl of Wrexton, and Marcus, his heir.

The Parliamentary Council was notified of the earl
of Wrexton's death, so that the earldom could be of-
ficially and legally conferred to Eldred de Grant. The
Wrexton knights who chose to stay would be compelled to swear fealty to Eldred, their new lord. Douglas Henley and some of his knights remained in Pwll
to await Marcus's father, and assist him with the trans-
fer of power to the de Grant family.

Hugh and Siân were wed by the village priest in
Pwll, nearly two weeks after their victory over Wrexton. Siân had been surprised that the reading of the
banns had been waived, but did not question the
bishop's decree. She was all too anxious to become
Hugh's wife, to share his life, as well as his bed again,
which, of course, had not been possible in her small
village.

The newlywed couple took many days to ride lei-
surely to Alldale, treasuring this time alone together.

Hugh came to learn everything that could make Siân sigh with pleasure, and Siân discovered the things that could make him laugh. And what a wondrous sound it was. Siân wanted nothing more than to fall asleep and awaken to the sound of his happiness and contentment every day.

She could only hope she would be able to live up to his expectations when they reached Alldale. After all, though she was of gentle birth, she had no experience as a noblewoman. She could never be the grand lady that Marguerite Bradley was. She wanted to be a good wife to Hugh, and make him proud of his countess, but her life in Pwll had never required skills beyond basic housekeeping, tending sheep, and helping her aunt midwife the women in the village. How would she ever learn to become the wife Hugh Dryden needed?

Siân worked hard to suppress her worries, trying to remember some of the things Kit Colston had said to her, things about her spirit, about…perfection. Though she could not be the same kind of countess that Marguerite Bradley was, Siân hoped that her own talents would surface and she would somehow become an adequate chatelaine of Hugh's estate.

Their week-long journey to Alldale was uneventful, and it was a brilliant, golden afternoon when they reached the distant promontory that overlooked their new home. Castle Alldale rose majestically over the low hills that surrounded it, its stone edifice gleaming bright white in the late sunlight as Hugh and Siân approached. They dismounted and stood together, gazing at the beautiful, imposing palace in the distance.

"Oh, Hugh," Siân said guardedly, her worries resurfacing. "It's…magnificent!"

Hugh nodded once. It *was* magnificent. King Henry had rewarded him generously. Castle Alldale was much more than Hugh had ever expected from life, but not nearly as significant as the other prize he'd recently won.

He looked at Siân, his beautiful lady, and his heart was full as it had never been before. The woman he loved had given him back his life, in every way, and he would cherish her forever.

"I...I had no idea that Alldale was anything quite so grand, my lord," she said haltingly.

"Siân," he said menacingly as he took her in his arms, "this is no time to turn respectful on me now."

"But this—"

"Is nothing but stone and mortar," Hugh interrupted. "*You* are my life, Siân."

"But I—I can never be as—"

"As what, Siân?" he asked. "As perfectly controlled and prepared as some other lofty ladies might be?"

She nodded lamely.

"I love you, Siân," Hugh said, enfolding her in his arms. "I love your wild unpredictability, your big, open heart and your loyalty. I love your honesty and generosity. You are my wife, Siân, and my love. We'll meet Alldale's challenges together. Never doubt it."

29 November, 1423

Catherine, by the Grace of the Almighty Father, Queen of England, to her dear friends, by the power of God, Hugh, Earl of Alldale and Siân, his lady wife:

Greetings and tokens of sincere affection.

I pray my belated missive finds you in good health and in God's care.

How gratified I was to learn of your marriage, Alldale. I wish you every happiness and a long and fruitful life together. My dear Siân is a most charming and talented lady. I have no doubt that she will make you very happy, and provide you with many delightful and blessed children in the years to come.

I must give both of you my deepest, heartfelt thanks for taking care of *mon petit Henri,* and transporting him to the safety of Windermere. Without your assistance, I fear I would have been placed in an untenable situation, but that is now past, for the moment. Owen and I will return with Henri to London in time for the Christmas celebrations, so we will soon leave Clairmont, before the weather turns any colder.

It is my pleasure to inform you, Alldale, that Lady Marguerite received the withdrawal of your proposal calmly and without acerbity. Since you saw her last, she has chosen a husband, a man who has captured her heart and her passions. She and Lord Nicholas Becker were wed one week ago, and are remarkably happy. Suffice it to say that when I recently happened upon them in the garden in an outrageous state of dishabille, I knew that Marguerite's choice was perfect for her. Only our dashing Nicholas could bring out *"la petite sauvage"* in my dear friend. With great fondness, I say that she deserves such passion in her life.

If, at any time, you find yourselves in London, I beg you to attend on us, for Henri pines for his own dear Siân, and does not understand why he sees her no more.

I keep you both in my prayers and ask that you do the same for me and *petit Henri,* as well as Siân's brother, Owen.

Yours in Christ,
Catherine, Reine

* * * * *

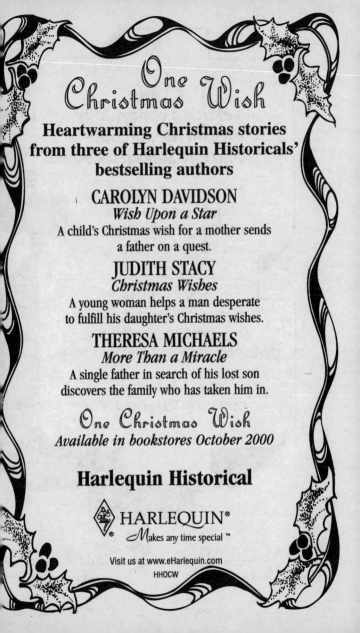

**Don't miss
an exciting opportunity
to save on the purchase of
Harlequin and Silhouette books!**

Buy any two Harlequin or
Silhouette books and save
$10.00 off future Harlequin
and Silhouette purchases

OR

buy any three
Harlequin or Silhouette books
and save **$20.00 off** future
Harlequin and Silhouette purchases.

*Watch for details
coming in October 2000!*

PHQ400

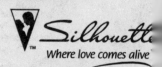

HARLEQUIN
Duets™

HEAR YE! HEAR YE!

Harlequin Historicals does hereby invite
one and all to partake in five adventurous
stories of Merrie Olde Englande!

In September 2000 look for

HALLOWEEN KNIGHT
by **Tori Phillips**
(England, 1542)

THE DUKE'S DESIRE
by **Margaret Moore**
(England, 1800s)

DRYDEN'S BRIDE
by **Margo Maguire**
(England, 1423)

In October 2000 look for

A SCANDALOUS PROPOSAL
by **Julia Justiss**
(England, 1812)

MY LORD DE BURGH
by **Deborah Simmons**
(England, 1280)

Harlequin Historicals
The way the past *should* have been!

Makes any time special ™